MW01118399

To D&

Girls Who Dare – Book 1

By Emma V. Leech

****

Published by Emma V. Leech.

Copyright (c) Emma V. Leech 2019

Cover Art: Victoria Cooper

ASIN No.: B07MC5QQ2S

ISBN No.: 978-1091388345

Table of Contents

Members of the Peculiar Ladies' Book Club

Prunella Chuffington-Smythe – first Peculiar Lady and secretly Miss Terry, author of The Dark History of a Damned Duke.

Alice Dowding - too shy to speak to anyone in public and often too small to be noticed.

Lucia de Feria - a beauty. A foreigner.

Ruth Stone - heiress and daughter of a wealthy merchant.

Matilda Hunt –blonde and lovely, and ruined in a scandal that was none of her making.

Bonnie Campbell - too outspoken and forever in a scrape.

Jemima Fernside - pretty and penniless.

Kitty Connolly - quiet and watchful, until she isn't.

Harriet Stanhope – serious, studious, intelligent. Prim. Wearer of spectacles.

Chapter 1

My dear Alice,

The fateful day of departure is approaching like a dark cloud on the horizon, blowing lace and frills and inanity in our direction. Are you as miserable as I at the prospect? Oh, Lord, how will I tolerate it? Thank heavens for you and the girls. We <u>will</u> endure and survive another season. The ton will not crush us. We will overcome! Together.

—Excerpt of a letter from Miss Prunella Chuffington-Smythe to Miss Alice Dowding.

***

1st April. Otford, Kent. 1814

The duke crossed the ballroom, tall and handsome, dark, wicked eyes flashing fury as everyone around held their breath...

Prue stared down at her inky fingers, her brow furrowing. There was something lacking, something…. She tapped the end of her quill against her chin, her lips pursed.

Ah, yes.

The duke ~~crossed~~ prowled the ballroom, tall and handsome, dark, wicked eyes flashing fury as everyone around held their breath...

She smiled, pleased by the addition. A depraved, cold-hearted man like her duke would certainly prowl. It recalled night creatures stalking their prey, teeth bared for the kill. The frisson that ran over her at the idea was pleasing, her readers would surely agree.

Prue jolted as a sharp rapping upon her bedroom door forced the wicked duke from her mind and dragged her back to reality.

"Prue! Mama wants to know if you're getting ready." Her cousin Minerva's sharp tone concealed none of her irritation at being sent to fetch Prue. No doubt she'd been preparing for this evening since the moment she got out of bed this morning.

Damnation.

"Er… yes," Prue replied, lying through her teeth. She glanced up, realising with a sinking heart that the skies had darkened into evening and she'd not even noticed.

"Well, you'd better be. We leave in fifteen minutes."

Prue cursed a bit more and hurried to put her writing away. A loose floorboard in her room had proven a useful hidey-hole for things she needed to keep private and away from Minerva's prying eyes. The young woman did not enjoy Prunella's company and found a good deal of enjoyment in causing her aggravation. Prue endured Minerva's presence with the fortitude of one who had no option, but did not hold her tongue as often as she ought. In her less prudent moments, the two of them fought like cat and dog.

With a great deal of haste and very little skill, Prue dragged a comb through her hair and pinned it up in a style more haphazard than fashionable, before attempting to wrestle herself into her dress. She looked around as their maid of all works hurried through the door and rolled her eyes.

"I knew it," the woman muttered, tsking and setting herself to fastening the back of the dress.

Prue sighed and gave the woman a fond smile over her shoulder. "Thank you, Sally. I don't know what I'd do without you."

"You'd cop a deal more nagging from Mrs Butler than you already do, as if you ain't got enough to be going on with," Sally replied tartly as she shook her head over the state of Prue's coiffure. "She'll not like that, I can tell you."

"Oh, what does it matter?" Prue replied with a shrug. "The worse I look, the more her lovely Minerva can shine."

Sally pulled a face. Prue snorted before leaning in to give the older lady a fond kiss on the cheek. She was a ruddy faced woman, of generous proportions and an equally warm heart, and she had quickly become Prue's saviour. Sally was an ally in the battle for her sanity.

Prue looked around the room for her gloves and cursed under her breath. She seemed to have a problem with gloves; they were never where she thought she'd left them. The maid sighed.

"I found them on the path by the front gate; lucky for you I washed them. They're downstairs in the hallway."

Prue bit her lip and tried to look contrite for her sins. She knew she failed. "You're an angel. You know that, don't you?"

With a roll of her eyes, Sally ushered her out the door.

"Have a nice quiet evening without us, Sally," Prue said as she headed for the stairs, adding in an undertone: "You have no idea how much I envy you."

"Oh, aye? You can polish the silver then, miss. I'll leave it out for you."

Prue gave a snort of laughter, knowing Sally wouldn't believe her if she protested it was better than the evening ahead of her, even if Prue really thought it was.

At least the rout party was being held by Charles Adolphus, Baron Fitzwalter, who lived at the 'big house' and held a position of authority and respect. The old man was a good sort and not like the stuffy busybodies that seemed to populate the rest of their tiny village. So, it was possible there would be some interesting conversation, if she could wrest him away from the other guests. For reasons best known to himself, the baron seemed fond of her despite her awkwardness in social situations and her utter disinterest in improving said awkwardness, as her aunt constantly pleaded for her to do.

The sooner Aunt Phyllis gave up on the idea she would marry and stop being a burden to them all, the better. Not that Prue *was* a burden. Her contribution to their household made a significant difference to her widowed aunt and Phyllis' only daughter Minerva, who both lived perilously close to the edge of shabby genteel respectability. Aunt Phyllis was not in fact her aunt at all, but her deceased mother's cousin, though *Aunt* Phyllis always seemed easier than explaining the ins and outs of their relationship to others.

Prue had every intention of getting out from under Aunt Phyllis' roof as soon as she could, but marrying to do it was not a feature in her plans. Far from it. Prue had every intention of being an independent female, and she was well on her way to being just that. If her aunt had the slightest suspicion of her scandalous plans, and—even worse—how she intended to do it, she'd likely suffer an apoplexy.

"Oh, there you are," the woman herself said, emerging from the parlour amidst an aggressive cloud of violet perfume. "Honestly, Prunella. Is it too much to ask that you are ready to leave at the appointed hour? I chaperone you to these events out of the goodness of my heart, when I have my own daughter's future to think of. A more ungrateful creature would be hard to find."

As that was entirely true, Prue opened her mouth to say something to soothe her relation's ruffled feathers and instead gave a violent sneeze.

Phyllis' mouth compressed into a thin line and her faded blue eyes widened in despair as Prue's hand rose to cover her mouth and nose.

"Look at the state of your hands!" she exclaimed. "What have you been doing, and where are your gloves?"

Prue blanched and hurried to cover up her inky fingers.

"I'm not even going to comment on the state of your hair," Aunt Phyllis said with a disapproving sniff, though she then contradicted this statement by doing just that for the next several minutes, and in detail, as they walked to the grandest house in the village.

It was a handsome red brick building, as solid and impressive as the baron himself, who was also a touch on the florid side. He was still a large man, despite his advancing years, and he greeted her aunt and Minerva with gracious attentiveness, though Prue was aware he couldn't stand them. Her aunt's ingratiating ways irked him, and he believed Minerva was no better than she ought to be.

It was one reason they got on so well.

"Ah, and Miss Chuffington-Smythe," the baron said, turning to Prue with a wide grin. "How are you? Recovered from your recent bout of ill-health, I hope?"

The old man's eyes twinkled with conspiratorial glee, as if he'd guessed that she had been telling fibs. She sent him a look, half glare, half amusement that he'd figured her out. It was true: Prue had sworn off a recent dinner party, claiming to be laid low with a dreadful megrim. Prue had never suffered a megrim in all her life, but they were a handy excuse when the next social event on the calendar struck her as being unendurable, or the next chapter in her novel could not wait.

"Quite recovered, thank you," she said, giving him a sweet smile.

"And how is your nephew, *the duke*, my lord?" her aunt demanded, with such a proprietary air that any casual observer might suppose she was well acquainted with the man himself. The baron, perfectly used to such tactics, replied with little more than a twitch of his lips, unnoticed by any but Prue.

6

"His grace is in fine fettle, last I heard, Madam. I thank you for the gracious enquiry." He turned back to Prue, holding out his arm. "Miss Chuffington-Smythe, I wonder if I might borrow you? I have recently acquired a wonderful copy of Claudius Aelianus' *Variae Historiae*. It's an intriguing collection of excerpts and anecdotes of a moralising nature, and I should like your opinion. I know what a love of books you have and feel certain you will appreciate the quality of the binding."

Prue stared at him, attempting to keep a straight face.

"Indeed, my lord," she said, her tone even lest her amusement become apparent. "I should be pleased to see it."

"I'm not sure it's at all the thing for a young lady to take an interest in dusty old books, my lord," Aunt Phyllis said, before the baron could usher Prue away to the library which had been set up as a card room for the evening's entertainments. "I mean, my Minerva has never read a book in her life and look at her."

Prue choked as Baron Fitzwalter eyed the pretty blonde at her aunt's side. Minerva looked up at him with what Prue guessed was supposed to be a sweetly shy expression from under her lashes. To Prue's eye she looked like her shoes were pinching her, but then she knew Minerva too well to be fooled.

"Er, yes… indeed," said the baron, a noncommittal answer that Aunt Phyllis seemed to take as one of approval.

"There, you see, Prunella? Even his lordship does not approve."

Prue fashioned her expression somewhere between a smile and a grimace and decided it best to keep her mouth shut. Occasionally she thought before she spoke. Rarely enough, but still.

"If you would excuse us, Mrs Butler, Miss Butler."

She gave a sigh of relief as the baron bore her away.

"Claudius Aelianus?" she queried, looking up at her companion.

He gave an unrepentant shrug. "It was all I could think of. My dear, how do you stand it? It's beyond anything. You know we really must get you suitably married."

Prue gave an impatient tut and shook her head. "Please, my lord, do not begin on this hopeless path once again. My aunt is really very kind, and her vulgarity stems only from a desire to see myself and Minerva well established. As for marriage, you know very well I have neither fortune nor beauty, nor any talent for housekeeping, added to which I have no interest whatsoever in becoming any man's chattel." She laughed at the heavy sigh the baron gave at that comment and turned to him with an impatient tone, as they'd discussed this many times before. "Being added to a list of belongings, my person subsumed by the rights of my husband? No, I thank you. I shall guard the keys to my destiny like Cerberus guards the gates of hell."

The baron looked down at her with an indulgent eye. "A rather violent metaphor, don't you think?"

For a moment Prue allowed her thoughts to drift back to her childhood, and the spectre of a man who ought to have been her and her mother's protector. "Yes, it is. I think it rather apt."

She felt the old man's gaze upon her and avoided it.

"Now then, what's the gossip?" Prue asked, turning the subject and forcing away the ghosts of the past, preparing instead to enjoy a comfortable chat with her most favourite source of news and intrigue.

Once they had turned over every aspect of life in the village and beyond to their satisfaction, the baron wandered off to mingle with his guests. Prue found a book she had not read—the baron had given her free run of his library some time ago—and settled down in a quiet corner. She had barely read the first line when a voice hailed her.

"Prunella?"

Prue looked up, startled to have been called with such obvious enthusiasm.

"Oh, it *is* you!"

A young woman hurried towards her. A slender and delicate redhead, she was as fragile and petite as a porcelain shepherdess.

"Alice!" Prue exclaimed, and jumped to her feet in such a hurry her book almost tumbled to the floor. She caught it before it hit the rug at her feet and then straightened to find Alice laughing at her.

"I might have known I'd find you skulking in the corner with a book in hand," she said, grinning with such affection it was clear there was no criticism in her words.

"I was *not* skulking," Prue retorted with a sniff. "I was just...."

She trailed off as Alice arched one elegant red-gold eyebrow. "Oh, well, yes. I was skulking, but honestly Alice, what else is there to do?"

"Avoid my mother?" the young woman suggested with a twinkle in her eyes.

Prue snorted and took her friend's arm. "Oh, that goes without saying, but tell me, why are you here? I didn't know you were coming."

"Nor did I," Alice replied as Prue put the book down and they set off on a walk about the grand house. "My uncle lives at Dunton Green and his wife has taken ill. Mama brought me to help her with the children for a few days until she's feeling better. It was all very last minute, so I didn't have time to write and tell you."

"But, if that's the case, why are you here tonight?"

Alice rolled her eyes, giving a despairing shake of her head. "My mother has made such a song and dance to my uncle about the difficulty of getting me suitably married that he took pity on her. I'm here with friends of the family. They have a son...." She grimaced.

"Oh, lord," Prue said, with heartfelt sympathy. "Is he ghastly?"

"Buck teeth, bad breath, *and* a stutter," Alice said on a sigh. "I mean, really, I do try not to be too fussy but—"

"But?"

"But there's something about him, Prue," Alice said, lowering her voice. "He ... he's very attentive but he makes me feel—" Alice shuddered, and Prue grasped her hand.

"What?"

"He frightens me a little."

"Good heavens, Alice," Prue exclaimed, turning to stare at her in horror. "There's fussy and there's ..." It was her turn to run out of words, at a loss for what could possibly induce her friend to even consider the idea for a moment. The idea of lovely Alice married to a man who might be even a little like Prue's father. She closed her eyes. "You can't be considering such a match, Alice, truly. You cannot marry a man who frightens you. It's not as if you're penniless or at risk of destitution. Surely, you're not so desperate to get out from under your mother's clutches?"

"Not *so* desperate," Alice agreed, sounding thoroughly desperate.

Prue sighed. "Oh, well. The season is almost upon us, and you can husband hunt to your heart's content."

Alice cut her a look. "Oh, yes, because I was so successful last season."

"It was your first year," Prue said with a huff. "You've got some town bronze now; you know what's in store, so it won't come as such a shock."

Their eyes met and both gave a heavy sigh. Yes. They did indeed know what was in store, and Prue well knew that Alice dreaded it every bit as much as she did.

Chapter 2

Dear Prunella,

Oh heavens. Not only buck teeth, bad breath and a stutter. He thinks women ought not to read lest it give them opinions. I had the most appalling row with mama about it, who quite agrees with him. Sadly, he is quite obscenely wealthy and is the youngest son of an earl, which is naturally the only thing she cares about. I won't do it though, Prue. I won't. There is a season to come yet. I shan't give in. Not yet.

—Excerpt of a letter from Miss Alice Dowding to Miss Prunella Chuffington-Smythe.

***

5th April. Otford. Kent. 1814

Prue reached for another sausage and ignored Minerva's grimace of disgust. Her cousin had spent the last ten minutes nibbling at a piece of toast like a dainty mouse. Well, if she wanted to starve herself to look fragile and waif like, it was entirely her own affair. Prue couldn't think on an empty stomach and, as she often forgot to eat lunch when the words were flowing well, a hearty breakfast was a necessity.

"Oh, do look at this one," her aunt exclaimed, turning the latest copy of *The Lady's Weekly Review* to show Minerva one of the fashion prints. "Isn't it lovely?"

Minerva dropped her toast with a little squeal of excitement and Prue rolled her eyes.

"There's a small fortune in the lace alone," Prue observed, aware of her aunt's slender finances and her penchant for frittering it away on frivolous items they could ill afford.

"I wasn't asking you," her aunt snapped, glaring from under an extravagant lace cap that she'd bought the day before, and which rather proved Prue's point.

Still, her aunt was quite correct. It was not her affair. Once she had enough money put aside, and hopefully a commission to write another novel, she would be free to leave. If she was careful, she had calculated she would be safe to do so by the end of this year. Fond imaginings of a dear little cottage filled her mind's eye, somewhere close to friends, where she could see them often. Why, they might even come and stay with her.

That idea was more than a little problematic, as a woman living alone would be a scandalous creature. Prue had hoped to convince one or more of her friends to join her, for their mutual benefit and to ease the costs, but she knew it was a lot to ask. There were few women who would countenance such a situation. She, however, was one. Anything for her freedom, her independence. The idea made her smile, though she suppressed it at once as Minerva caught sight of her.

"What are you looking so pleased with yourself for?" her cousin snapped. "I know you think I'm stupid, but I need new dresses for the season, you know I do. I shan't let you stop us buying them. Not this time."

Prue pursed her lips and bit back the retort that was brewing there. It would only cause a row which would make her late getting upstairs and back to the Duke of Bedsin. If Phyllis was such a pea-brain as to get them both into debt, why should she care? Yet despite her impatience with the two frivolous creatures, her aunt had taken her in when no one else had. Prue owed her a good deal for that. She was grateful and tried to help where she could.

"I don't do it to spoil your fun, Minerva," she said, wishing she was better at sounding reasonable instead of merely irritated. "Only to ensure you have enough to pay your rent and put food on the table. We all have limited funds and you must see that a gown like that would use every penny your mother has saved, and more besides. It isn't feasible."

Minerva's temper erupted with a flash of fury and she stood, her chair toppling over backwards with a crash. "You're just jealous, that's all! I might not be as clever as you, but I will catch a duke, you miserly old Prune," she said, using the childish nickname she'd saddled Prue with years ago. "So, it doesn't matter how much we spend. When I've hooked him, he'll pay for everything. He'll beg to do it."

Prue stared at her and then turned to her aunt, waiting for her to suppress her daughter's idiotic flights of fancy, but Phyllis only gave a nervous little laugh.

"Oh, Min, dear. We said we'd not talk of this to anyone, did we not?"

Minerva gave a snort of disgust. "It's only Prune, it's not like *she's* anyone. Not anyone that counts. Besides, she'll see soon enough."

Prue blinked, wondering what manner of madness had possessed them. She'd always known Phyllis had hopes of her lovely daughter catching a title, and she *was* lovely—and penniless and without connections—but a *duke*?

An unpleasant shiver of foreboding crawled down her spine and she turned back to face Minerva.

"Which duke?" she demanded.

Minerva righted her chair and made a show of smoothing out her skirts and sitting down again, a prim little smile settling over her bow shaped mouth.

"The Duke of Bedwin."

Prue gasped and looked to Phyllis, who had the grace to colour a little and would not meet Prue's eye.

"If you hadn't spent all night sitting in a corner with your nose in a book, you'd have heard the news," Minerva continued, turning Prue's attention back, her voice sweet but laced with arsenic. "His grace is on the lookout for a new duchess."

The idea was horrifying enough to make Prue gape in astonishment. Her gaze flew once more to her aunt.

"You can't be serious! You would want Minerva married to… to such a man?"

Aunt Phyllis put her chin up. "He's a duke."

As if that was all the answer required.

"Aunt Phyllis," Prue continued, her heart thudding in her chest. "You know the rumours as well as I do. He's a libertine, depraved! My God, they say he murdered his first wife!"

Phyllis made a waving motion with her hand, brushing the argument aside. "For heaven's sake, Prunella, even you said you set no store by such scurrilous stories. You did say that," she added, wagging a finger.

Prue nodded, unable to deny it. For all the stories that had circulated about his grace, she had not believed the one about his wife's untimely demise. That he was a rake and blackguard however, the *ton* had circulated those stories widely enough and they were such common knowledge there had to be some truth in them. Indeed, anyone getting a glimpse of the man would be hard pressed not to conclude it without even ever having heard the stories.

Prue swallowed down a sigh as she remembered the last time she'd caught a glimpse of him. He'd looked like sin on a moonless night, dark and forbidding and full of unseen pleasures.

"Nonetheless, Aunt, he could ruin Minerva and even if he does seek a wife, surely he'd choose—"

"I told you she was jealous," Minerva said to her mother, before Prue could finish the sentence. "You're jealous, Prue, because you're plain and dull and boring, and no man will ever want you."

Prue's breath caught at the spite of her words, which was foolish. She ought to be used to such outbursts from her cousin by now, and besides, she knew it was true enough. Plain might have been a little harsh, but she really could not deny it, and whilst she didn't believe herself dull or boring, she could not pretend to find enjoyment in the things most young ladies seemed to go into transports over, either.

"Now, now, Minerva, that will do," Phyllis said, frowning a little. "That was rather uncalled for."

"No," Prue said. Her smile felt a little too tight, but there was no point in pretending otherwise about things that were true. "Minerva is correct, which is why I have no intention of marrying."

Both women gaped at her.

"Well, you need not think you'll be living off my charity till the end of your days," Phyllis snapped, looking affronted.

"I don't live off it now," Prue pointed out dryly. "I pay you for my room and board, and have never asked you for a penny towards my upkeep."

Aunt Phyllis' face darkened, and Prue sighed. "I have no say in how you spend your money, or what plans you make for the future. It is entirely your affair and none of mine. If Bedwin is what you want, then I wish you every success with him."

Minerva returned a dazzling and somewhat unnerving smile. "Oh, don't fret, Prune. I'll be a duchess before the year is out, and I'll make sure his grace finds you a little cottage somewhere. You could keep cats," she added, and though she kept the smirk from her mouth, Prue could hear it loud and clear.

"Yes, that sounds ideal," Prue replied, amused that Minerva thought it such an appalling fate. The young woman's expression faltered, a look of curiosity in her eyes as Prue got to her feet. "If you'll excuse me."

***

"Hell and damnation!"

Robert Adolphus, the Duke of Bedwin, flung aside the latest copy of *The Lady's Weekly Review* in fury. His sister, Helena just smiled and gave a little shrug as she piled marmalade onto her toast.

"I know it's awful," she said, her voice full of sympathy. "But it is awfully good, too."

Robert turned to glare at her and she blushed, giving him a rueful grin. "Well, it is, you know. I mean, if one must be thought a villain, then best to be the kind that makes women swoon and long to be debauched—"

"Helena!"

How his eighteen-year-old sister even knew such a word… good god, he'd been a terrible brother. The dreadful creature gave an unrepentant gurgle of laughter. "Well, really, Robert. You've done very little to disabuse people of the notion. Quite the contrary. I can't help but think you rather enjoy your dreadful reputation."

Robert sent her a dark look that suggested she close her mouth. As terrifying as his reputation might be among the *ton*, however, his baby sister was not in the least bit impressed.

"Oh, pooh. Glare all you like, it's at least partly your own fault and well you know it."

He folded his arms, seething even though he knew there was truth in her words. She reached out and patted his arm to soothe his prickly temper.

"I know Lavinia made a horrible mess for you, dearest, and I know it haunts you, but sooner or later you must start over. It's time, don't you think? The rumours already fly you're in search of a wife. Why not make them true?"

Robert said nothing. His sister was far too mature for her years, mostly because of his idiotic actions as a young man. He knew she had suffered from his behaviour, not that she'd ever complained. That she was the one giving him good advice now though, was bad enough. He ought to have protected her, and yet all he'd done was make everything as black as bloody pitch.

Damn it.

The day had got off to a bad start. He was in a wretched temper and unwilling to be reasonable about anything now. If he didn't loathe wasting a day, he'd go back to bed and be done with it. Yet that would be unproductive and it was, at least, a glorious spring morning. He'd just have to find something to take his mind off things.

"I'll write to them," he said, perking up at the notion. "Tell them I'll sue if they don't withdraw the story."

Helena gave an impatient huff. "Honestly, Robert, you may as well admit that the Duke of Bedsin is you and hold your hands up for murder. It's what they'll all think."

"So, I'm supposed to let this anonymous lunatic author destroy my character and write such… such ludicrous nonsense?"

His sister shrugged and took another bite of toast, chewing with the air of someone with something to say. "If you don't want things to get worse, yes," she said once she could, and reached for her tea. "It will only last so long, and then there will be someone else in the spotlight and you'll be forgotten. Unless you make a huge scandal of it, then it will take years to die down and everyone will believe you've really something to hide."

"Everyone thinks that now!" he raged, frustrated by his inability to act.

Helena smiled, her green eyes—the same shade as his own, the same as their mother's had been—warm with affection. "No, they don't. Not everyone. Not the people that matter. If anything good came of the whole disastrous affair, at least we discovered who our friends were."

Robert snorted. "Oh, yes, that was marvellous," he said, dry as dust. He snatched up the paper again, waving it in his sister's face. "I wouldn't mind so much if it wasn't so preposterous. Listen to this…."

He cleared his throat and turned to the offending page.

"*Lydia trembled in the darkness as she realised, she'd been tricked. She ought never to have come, ought never to have slipped away from the ball and the lights, and sought the shadows. She ought never have been tempted by the velvet night, soft and warm with promise, but now there was no going back. He was there before her, full of wickedness and dark pleasure. Her breath caught.*" Robert gave his sister an *I ask you* look but found nothing but rapt concentration in her eyes. "Oh, for God's sake. What utter rubbish!"

Helena gave a heavy sigh, smiling a little.

"I think it's romantic."

"Romantic?" Robert spluttered, staring at her in horror. "The bloody man is set on ruining an innocent girl, and no doubt murdering her too if they follow the story to its logical conclusion. In what perverse world could you believe that romantic? And," he added, thoroughly unsettled, "you're never being let out of this house again! Heaven alone knows what I'll find you about. Romantic, indeed."

Helena returned a scathing look. "I'd like to see you enforce that."

"And," Robert continued, too irritated to stop now, "that's supposed to be about me. I'm your brother, for God's sake!"

"More's the pity," Helena muttered before giving a huff of annoyance as he glared at her. "Oh, for heaven's sake, Robert. The *ton* might think it's you, but I know it isn't. I can assure you my villain doesn't look a bit like you," she added with a dreamy smile.

"How terribly reassuring."

She grinned at him and Robert sighed, reaching for her hand.

"Sorry," he muttered, feeling like an arse. Helena was his staunchest ally and she'd not had an easy time. His first wife, Lavinia, had tainted her reputation just as she had his own, and Helena was entirely innocent in a way he was not. To cap it all her come out had been delayed by their mother's death, whose kind and loving presence they both missed sorely.

At least she had put off those dreadful blacks now for half-mourning, and the pale lavender she wore today looked charming.

"Idiot," she said, giving him a sweet smile even as her eyes twinkled with mirth. She enjoyed insulting him. He snorted and went to withdraw his hand but, to his surprise, she kept hold. "Seriously, though, Robert. It's time we put the past to rest. Start over. You need to go back into society, let them see you're not the monster they have painted you."

Robert hesitated. "And what if I am?"

Helena squeezed his hand tighter. "That, I will never believe. You... You allowed the darkness of life to swallow you up for a while, that's all, but you've promised me that part of your life is over, and I believe you."

He frowned, staring down at the table, unwilling to meet her eyes. God, he was a bastard for having put her through this.

"You must go back out there, Robert, and you must meet people and make friends and... fall in love."

Robert jolted and snatched his hand away. "This is what comes of reading such twaddle," he said, revolted by the notion. "As if I would, after the mess I made the first time around?"

His sister sighed, her expression too full of pity for comfort. "I know you're afraid, but—"

"Afraid?" he barked. "No, Helena. Not afraid. I've been educated, schooled by the very best teacher I could have had. It's just as Father told me, and I was a bloody fool not to heed him. Love is not for the likes of us. What's more, I don't want it!"

"That's a lie, Robert," she said, her voice soft and so full of sorrow for him that he wanted to hit something. "We all want to be loved."

"Not me," he said firmly, his expression hard and implacable. "It's the last thing in the bloody world I want. I'll not have it. Not at any price."

Silence rang between them for a long moment, but his sister was nothing if not persistent. "And what of the title?"

He turned and gave her a measured look, forcing his temper down, knowing she of all people did not deserve to receive the scalding blast of his fury and frustration. "I will ensure the title. Just as father wanted, as is expected of me."

"Then you must marry," she said, smiling a little.

"Yes," he agreed. "I must. I've already said I will find a wife, haven't I?"

She held his gaze, unblinking. He let her look, wishing she could see the extent of the damage wrought by one he'd thought he'd loved. If Helena could only see, then she would never say such things to him again.

"And will you not care for her, Robert? Will she not share in your life?"

"Did Father and Mother share each other's lives?" he said, his tone scathing.

"They were fond of each other, at least," she said, though she did not meet his eye now.

She was no fool. Surely she knew love was a fairy story, a lie told to fool people into doing foolish things. Yet, if it had been real, if it had been something attainable, he would want her to find it. Of all people, she deserved it, and was worthy of it.

"Well, then. Perhaps I will find someone to be fond of, too."

Helena frowned, the expression sitting ill on a face that was too ready to laugh, too open and honest for its own good. "Will that be enough? Will that make you happy?"

Robert snorted and shook his head. "Stop trying to mend what's been broken, love. It's beyond repair, the damage done. I don't aim for happiness, but I'll be content enough, and so will my duchess, I promise you. She'll have everything she could possibly desire."

His sister's gaze was unwavering, unnerving.

"Except for you," she said.

Robert got to his feet, unwilling to explore this conversation any further. What was done was done; there was no undoing it, no going back. Helena was right about one thing. It was time to move forward, and that was exactly what he would do.

Chapter 3

And so, it begins …
Courage, dearest.

—Excerpt from a letter from Miss Prunella
Chuffington-Smythe to Miss Alice Dowding.

***

9th April. Otford. Kent. 1814

Robert grinned at the shock on his uncle's face as a deferential butler showed him into his office.

"Robert!"

"Hello, Uncle Charles," he said, moving to shake his uncle's hand. "You're looking well."

The man snorted and returned a dark look. "If by well, you mean old and fat, yes, nephew, I would have to agree."

"Nonsense," Robert replied. "You're a fine figure of a man still. I hope I look half so good at your age."

"What flummery," Charles replied, laughing, though he looked pleased enough by the words. "Well, and what brings you to this neck of the woods? There's naught amiss, I hope?" he asked, growing serious at once and sitting a little straighter.

"No, no, sir, nothing of the sort," Robert said, smiling. "I have come for some advice."

"Really?" Charles frowned, his expression so sceptical that Robert couldn't help but laugh.

"Is that so hard to believe?"

His uncle returned a look that would have put him in a quake as a young man. As it was, it still made him feel as if he was eight years old and had just been caught stealing jam tarts from the kitchens.

"Well, it's true," he said, a trifle defensive, knowing he'd never listened to his uncle's advice before now. More fool him.

His uncle beamed at him, however, and it was impossible to feel irritated with him. Robert felt a rush of fondness. His own father had been a decent enough sort, if a little remote, but his uncle had been the one who'd spoilt him and made a fuss. Charles had taught him to ride and to shoot, and had taken pride in his achievements where his father had simply accepted them as his due. To his sire, Robert was the heir to a dukedom, and anything less than excellence was failure. Yet he'd never been beaten or ill-treated, and occasionally his father had been moved to tell him he was proud of him. Compared to many of his ilk, he'd been lucky.

"Well, I'm flattered," Charles said, folding his arms and regarding Robert with affection. "So, what is it that's so delicate you felt obliged to see me in person?"

Robert drew in a breath, suddenly reluctant to say it aloud but… well, there was no escaping it.

"I intend to marry."

For a moment his uncle stared at him in surprise, and then he let out a breath and smiled. "I'm so happy to hear that. I'd heard the rumours of late, of course, but I must admit, I had feared…. But never mind that," he added, brushing past whatever he might have said. "How delightful! We must celebrate."

He got up and bustled over to the decanter, pouring them both a generous measure.

"Now then, young man," he said, beaming at Robert as he handed him a glass. "Who's the lucky lady?"

Robert cleared his throat, a little uncomfortable as he returned a rueful smile. "I… er, I don't actually know yet. I was rather hoping you'd help me choose someone."

Charles gaped at him, the glass suspended halfway to his mouth.

"Look," Robert said, deciding he'd best be blunt. "There's little point in denying I made a bloody mess of it first time around, and we all paid the price for it. I didn't listen to you, or Father, or… or anybody," he said, wishing the heat of humiliation would die away as time passed, and feeling certain it never would.

"You were in love," Charles said, giving him a sad smile.

Robert gave a snort of disgust. "That's one word for it," he said darkly. "In any case, I have no intention of making the same mistake twice. I need a duchess, a sensible young woman with no romantic notions about our union. I need an heir. Further than that, she will be free to live her own life. All I want is someone who will stay out of the spotlight, someone who would enjoy a quiet life in the countryside with any children we might have. A woman who does not long for excitement and notoriety, or society on a grand scale. I will keep our name from being dragged through the mud this time, Uncle."

He watched as his uncle frowned and stared down into his drink, swirling the amber liquid about the glass.

"Well?" Robert prompted as the man showed no signs of responding. "It's not so much to ask, is it? I'm not asking for a beauty, in fact I'd be very pleased if she wasn't. Just an ordinary young woman of good breeding who would be willing to be my wife, and mother to the future duke, without causing a scandal every time she set foot outside the house."

Charles chewed on his lip, his expression thoughtful and Robert sat forward in his chair.

"You have someone in mind?"

"Perhaps," his uncle admitted, though his expression was serious. "In truth, I think…." He turned and looked at Robert, a slight smile tugging at the corner of his mouth. "Yes. I think she would suit you admirably."

"Oh?" Robert queried. Something in his uncle's tone unnerved him a little. "You're sure?"

Charles smiled then and gave a decisive nod. "I think she's perfect," he said, sounding so certain that Robert felt a weight fall from his shoulders.

"Excellent. Is she local? Can we call on her tomorrow? I'd prefer to get things wrapped up as soon as possible."

Charles stared at him aghast. "Good lord, you can't expect to meet her one day and propose the next?"

Robert shrugged. He'd expected to meet her and propose as quickly as was decent, if not sooner. What did it matter? He just needed it over and done with.

"No, no," his uncle said, his expression disapproving. "Besides, it's not that easy."

"Why ever not?" Robert asked. Charles sighed and raised one eyebrow.

"For starters, duke or no, your reputation would give any sensible girl pause."

Robert flushed, unable to deny that. Any sensible girl would run a mile in the opposite direction. "I know that," he said, terse. "Which is why I came to you. I thought, if you knew the girl, if she trusted your opinion you could… speak to her. Explain."

"Well, of course, I'll speak to her," Charles replied, impatient now. "If I gave her the truth of your character, I think she'll believe me, even though it's my word against years of rumour and speculation, but I don't believe that's the biggest issue."

"Well, what is?" Robert demanded, feeling a little prickly now. By God, he knew he was not offering a love affair, or anything in the least romantic, but he *was* a duke for heaven's sake, surely that counted for something?

"Only that the girl has professed a desire to never marry at all. She intends to keep her independence and has no intention of being any man's chattel."

Robert blinked. "What?"

"She does not want to be yours or any man's property, Robert."

Robert threw up his hands. "Well, she'll be my duchess, for heaven's sake. I've just said she can live independently from me. Indeed, it would be a non-negotiable part of the deal."

Charles nodded, his expression serious, though there was something in his eyes that Robert couldn't read. "Quite so. In which case, you ought to make an irresistible argument for your future, er... *companionship.*"

"Hmm," Robert said, wishing he could put his finger on whatever it was he was missing.

"Good," Charles said, grinning at him.

"Good," he agreed, hoping that it was. Still, his uncle couldn't make a bigger mess of it than he had himself first time around. He must have faith. "So, we'll call on her tomorrow?"

To his frustration, Charles shook his head. "They left this morning for London."

Robert groaned. He'd been hoping to have everything nicely tied up so he could avoid the social scene altogether.

"Now, now, Robert. It's time you showed your face in society again. Got to stare down the gossips and show them they're all barking up the wrong tree, eh?"

He repressed the urge to snort. They may have been barking up the wrong tree once upon a time, but he'd long since decided he may as well be hung for a sheep as a lamb and live up to his black reputation. His uncle regarded his less than enthusiastic response with a sardonic expression.

"It wasn't a suggestion, Robert. If you want my help in this matter, then you'll listen to my advice. Otherwise I shall wash my hands of the entire affair. It's time you returned to society and stopped behaving like the black sheep. You're Bedwin, for heaven's sake. That ought to mean something."

Robert blew out a breath, glowering but knowing he had little choice unless he wanted to spend the next weeks searching a prospective bride. The idea filled him with horror.

"Very well. I'll send word to have the house made ready."

Charles rubbed his hands together, looking well pleased with himself. "Excellent, excellent. I take it Helena will be making her come out later this year?"

Robert nodded. "Indeed. She'll be out of mourning the week after next, so she'll be in town later this month, though Aunt Agatha is taking her in hand. I'm not exactly a suitable escort. In fact, I had hoped to keep a low profile to distance my reputation from hers."

His uncle gave a snort, indicating that a distance rather larger than was possible across England, Scotland, and Wales would be required for such an endeavour. As depressing as it was to acknowledge, Robert could hardly refute it.

Charles got to his feet and bustled back to him, bearing the decanter to top up their glasses. "A little toast then, eh, Robert? To getting you and your sister both successfully leg shackled."

Robert glowered at his glass, trying to find some enthusiasm for the idea.

"As you say, Uncle," he said, forcing his lips to curve upwards instead of into a grimace. "As you say."

***

12th April. London 1814. The Earl and Countess March's Ball.

Prue shifted in her chair, trying to find a more accommodating position on the hard wood. As this row of seating in an unobtrusive corner of the ballroom was given over to the wallflowers, she thought the organiser might have given them something a little more comfortable. After all, they were likely to sit unmoving for the better part of the evening, which was torture enough; there was no need to rub it in.

"You can't see him, can you?"

Prue craned her neck, scanning the crowd for a certain buck-toothed, stuttering son of an earl. "No," she said, turning back to smile at Alice. "I think you're safe for the moment."

Alice sighed, but didn't look much happier. Bonnie Campbell, sitting on Prue's left, leaned forward and grinned at Alice.

"Do point him out," she said to Alice, her eyes alight with amusement. "We can see if he's more repulsive than my cousin Gordon."

Both girls turned to stare at Bonnie. She was a ward of the Earl of Morven, a bad-tempered Scot who wanted rid of his youngest dependent as soon as possible. He had threatened to marry her to her cousin Gordon Anderson if she didn't make a match. Each year, Bonnie's descriptions of Gordon became ever more unflattering.

"Is he so awful?" Alice asked, wrinkling her nose.

Bonnie nodded, her expression growing dark. "Worse," she muttered, kicking the leg of her chair. "And bloody Morven has told me this is my last chance. Either I make a match this year, or I'm to marry Gordon bloody Anderson and my life will be over."

Prue and Alice stared at her, both impressed and slightly appalled by the ease with which she cursed.

"Well, you never know, you might make a match this year. The season is only just begun."

All three girls turned to look at the lady who'd spoken.

At first glance, Matilda Hunt did not appear to fit among the wallflowers. Indeed, the description could not have been less appropriate. Matilda was a white-blonde beauty, likely the most perfectly lovely woman in the room, but she was tainted by scandal, dubbed *The Huntress,* and had therefore found her place among the unwanted and unmarriageable. She had adapted to the role with surprisingly good grace.

At first, the rest of their little coterie had looked upon her with awe and no little suspicion, but they had soon discovered that, beauty or no, she was a sweet-natured girl and a good friend.

"Never mind that." Bonnie waved away the conversation, a conspiratorial light gleaming in her eyes. "Who has been reading *The Dark History of a Damned Duke?*"

Squeals of delight accompanied this question, and suddenly chairs were being pulled closer as many more of the wallflowers crowded together, all of them eager to share in the conversation.

"Did you read last week's?" Alice asked, reaching across Prue to clutch at Bonnie's arm.

Bonnie nodded and closed her eyes. "*He was there, before her, full of wickedness and dark pleasure.*" She breathed rather than spoke the words, the Scottish accent she suppressed ruthlessly creeping into her voice and softening the line, making it somehow more seductive.

A collective sigh murmured through the air and Prue bit her lip against the desire to crow with delight. No one knew she was the author of the scandalous piece. She'd never dared share her secret, but not because she didn't trust these girls. She did. They were her closest friends, her allies, but the knowledge would be a burden to them. What she did was dangerous. The Duke of Bedwin was a powerful man, and every bit as dark as her thinly disguised character. If he knew who was responsible for the salacious tale, he'd punish them.

It was a risk Prue would take on her own behalf, but she would involve no one else in her mad schemes.

The next instalment came out in three days.

Prue had received her break by sending a short story to *The Lady's Weekly Review*. It had been a risk, as the magazine was often publicly scathing of the submissions it rejected. Prue had at least had the presence of mind to publish under a pseudonym, but the rejection would still have been crushing. Yet, publish they had.

Emboldened, she'd sent another, and another, each greeted with more enthusiasm than the last until the proprietor of the magazine had written to her personally, commissioning a full story to be published weekly over eight weeks. It had been a tremendous success, with readers clamouring for more, and had led to *The Dark History of a Damned Duke,* her longest and most ambitious piece to date.

Prue had sent a synopsis and the first three chapters. They had published the first chapter before they'd even replied to her letter, agreeing to all her terms in full. The public loved her, or at least they loved Miss Terry: the rather foolish, mock mysterious name she had created for herself.

Miss Terry was the talk of the *ton.*

The only problem with this one was that she had not completed the story before publication, due to the magazine's eagerness to please its public. So, she was only two weeks ahead of the publication date. It had given her some sleepless nights already and would only get worse now that the season was upon them. Her writing time would be seriously curtailed. Still, she would manage.

Smiling to herself, Prue returned her attention to the conversation, which was growing animated. She loved this, she realised, and not only the fact that they were discussing her own work with such enthusiasm. This gathering of her friends was the only good part about the season. If only they could do it without sitting on the edges of every lavish event, feeling foolish. If only they could do it just for the fun of it, for the conversation, the camaraderie, the friendship.

"We should begin a book club," she said impulsively. "Then we could discuss such things without...." Prue waved a hand at their grand surroundings and wrinkled her nose.

"A book club is a terrific idea," Miss Jemima Fernside said, bouncing in her chair with delight.

"I agree," said Matilda, her lovely blue eyes wide with enthusiasm. "But only if we discuss *The Damned Duke* first."

This proviso was met with a chorus of approval until a hesitant and rather grave voice added:

"Should we be concentrating on such a frivolous title? I mean, perhaps something more improving? Shakespeare, maybe? I always thought *The Taming of*—"

Everyone turned to glare at Harriet Stanhope, who shrank back into her chair with a crimson blush at her cheeks.

"You can come to my house if you'd like to. Papa won't mind," piped up another excited voice

Now, everyone looked towards Miss Stone.

Among the *ton*, her father was that most reprehensible creature: a Cit. A man of the merchant class who had gained vast wealth from his work, propelling him and his family into society via the backdoor. Too wealthy to ignore, too low born to belong. Gentlemen did *not* work, and Miss Stone's family had none of the breeding to match their wealth. They were neither fish nor fowl. Ruth Stone was a wealthy heiress and, whilst not a beauty, pleasant enough in appearance and manner. Yet, only the desperately poor of the *ton* would touch her, and only if no other option presented itself. She was new to their ranks this year and Prue had only spoken to her briefly, but she seemed a cheerful sort of girl.

"That would be wonderful, Miss Stone, thank you," Prue said, rushing to fill the silence whilst everyone else wondered what to say. She didn't doubt some among their number would have difficulty getting permission to visit the family, but those who wanted to badly enough would find a way.

The young woman smiled, looking thrilled to have her invitation accepted. "Oh! Lovely. Shall we say the day after tomorrow?"

This date was deemed acceptable, and the rendezvous was made.

Chapter 4

I know he's supposed to be the wicked villain, but there's something about Bedsin that makes my heart flutter. If only he could be redeemed.

—Extract from a letter from Miss Bonnie Campbell to Miss Alice Dowding.

***

12th April. London 1814. The Earl and Countess March's Ball.

Robert gritted his teeth as the streets of London scrolled past the window. It had been some time since he'd shown his face at polite affairs such as the one that awaited him. A prickle of unease ran down his spine. Damn them. Damn them all. He'd do this, find the girl, and get it over with.

His uncle looked over at him and tutted as their carriage drew up outside the impressive London residence of the Earl and Countess March.

"If you go in looking like that, you'll send any young lady with an ounce of sense running away screaming."

Robert snorted. "And so they ought," he muttered.

If only a fraction of the rumours about him were true, they'd be mad to be anywhere near him. Yet a dukedom was apparently carrot enough to overlook many indiscretions.

Cruelty, violence, adultery….

Even murder.

Before Lavinia had come into his life, no one would have believed such scurrilous gossip about him. Not for a moment. But

Lavinia had tangled him into her web and driven him as close to madness as any sane man had a right to go... if, indeed, he could even be considered sane anymore. He'd looked into the darkness and seen himself there, and it had destroyed him.

Lavinia might not have died at his hands, but that didn't absolve him of one appalling truth: he'd come damn close to wishing she had.

"Robert," his uncle said, his name spoken with stern accents. "Miss Chuffington-Smythe is a gently bred young lady. She's neither a flirt nor a flighty sort, nor prone to nerves and fits of the vapours. However, that does not mean she will take to meeting the *Damned Duke* without a little misgiving, no matter my approval."

Robert flinched at the name the gossips and tattle mongers had given him, but Charles hadn't finished.

"You'll find some of that legendary charm, do you hear me? Dredge it up from whatever dark pit it's been languishing in and put it to good use."

"Yes, Uncle." Robert glowered out of the window, reflecting that his uncle had never been the least bit impressed by his lofty title and still spoke to him like he was a gap-toothed, grubby boy begging for a puppy. He released a little breath of laughter at the idea. Well, thank God for that.

As they entered the ballroom a ripple of shock moved over the gathering, eyes widening, fans flapping with increasing vigour as ladies ducked their heads behind them to whisper.

"Courage, Robert, and smile, damn you," Charles growled, an urgent whisper in his ear.

For a moment, Robert made a concerted effort with the idea, wondering how he could ease his rigid features into something approximating such an expression. Then he heard the first whispering of *The Damned Duke*, followed by giggles and *The Duke of Bedsin*, his bloody alter ego in that wretched story.

God damn it.

They traversed the room, the *ton* parting before them like silk against a razorblade.

"Is she here?" Robert demanded. The sooner his ordeal was over, the happier he'd be.

He watched as his uncle scanned the crowd a smile of remarkable affection curving over his mouth as his gaze settled at the corner of the room, among the wallflowers. Well, that was a good sign, at least. Lavinia would have rather died than go anywhere near a wallflower.

"She is," Charles replied, tilting his head a little.

Each chair at the far end of the ballroom was occupied by a girl. Girls with spectacles, girls with spots, chubby girls, girls with squints, bad reputations, appalling families, stutters, or an inability to speak to a man without turning crimson.

"Between Morven's ward and Miss Dowding, the fragile-looking redhead," his uncle directed.

Robert scanned the row, finding the earl's dark-haired, troublesome ward, and then the tiny redhead who looked as though she might snap in a strong gust of wind. Between them was Miss Prunella Chuffington-Smythe, his future duchess.

She was not quite blonde, her hair an unremarkable shade between that lighter gold colour and a mid-brown. It appeared she had the correct number of arms, legs, eyes, etcetera, and a perfectly straight nose set in a face that was all angles. Very high cheekbones sculpted a rather severe countenance, which gave Robert a moment's pause.

"Are you quite sure?" he asked Charles. "She looks a little… stern."

"Serious," Charles corrected, turning to look at him. "Which I believe is what you wished for? Though that's not to say she doesn't have a sense of humour, far from it. I think her a delightful companion, though I admit she's somewhat… *unusual*. She's intelligent, witty, and forthright, but loyal to a fault."

Loyal to a fault.

The words rang through him, easing a jagged edge of tension that had been ever present since he'd decided he must marry again.

There was nothing more he needed to know.

"Will you present me, then, Uncle?"

Charles grinned and gave his arm a squeeze. "With pleasure, my boy. With pleasure."

They moved closer to the women and Robert knew the moment the wallflowers saw him. One by one their postures changed, rigid with alarm and the desire to flee. Eyes widened, and mouths fell open in shock as cheeks blanched white. All except the woman who was to be his wife. She was deep in conversation with the Morven chit.

Then she looked up.

Even compared to the other girl's horror, her reaction was a little surprising. Her already pale skin became so white he thought perhaps she'd swoon, and then two spots of colour, burned high on her cheeks. Her lips parted, her chest heaving, and she gripped the edge of her chair as if forcing herself to keep still. She looked a little as if she might vomit.

Robert stilled.

"Uncle…." But Charles was already closing the distance between them.

"There you are," he said, ever cheerful as he held out his hands to her in greeting. "My favourite young lady."

The girl forced her terrified gaze from him to Charles, and Robert could see the effort she made to find a smile.

"L-Lord Fitzwalter," she stammered, standing and taking his uncle's hands as Charles greeted her with as much warmth as if she were his beloved granddaughter. "I had no idea you were in town, you never said—"

"I know, I know," Charles said, skilfully moving her a little away from the wallflowers, who were all agog. "But my nephew desired my company, and it's so long since we had any time together. Oh, but where are my manners? Bedwin, please may I present, Miss Chuffington-Smythe."

For a moment, Robert wondered if she might do as he'd feared and vomit. God, that would give the gossips something to talk about. He could visualise the headline already.

Damned Duke terrifies wallflower into casting up her accounts.

There was a long stretch of silence in which the girl stared at him in mute dismay, and then she gathered herself with a visible straightening of her spine that he could only admire. She curtseyed. A rather ungainly affair to be sure, but better than throwing up on his boots.

"Your grace," she said, avoiding his eyes.

"Miss Chuffington-Smythe," he said, doing his best not to look like a villain who ate wallflowers for breakfast. From the glint of panic in her eyes he thought he'd best try harder. "A pleasure to meet you."

"Well, now, if you young people would excuse me. I see an old crony I must catch up with. Have to hurry. At my age, friends drop like flies," Charles added with a cheery grin.

Both he and his bewildered duchess-to-be looked at Charles with wild-eyed panic, which the baron blithely ignored. Before he left, however, he leant into the girl's side and whispered something in her ear that Robert didn't catch. Whatever it was made her eyes widen further, so far that Robert feared they might pop from her head. Good god, what a disaster this was going to be.

And then they were alone under the scrutinising gaze of the *ton*.

***

Prue couldn't breathe.

God in heaven. She was exposed. Ruined. *The Damned Duke* himself was striding towards her, those cold green eyes she had written of so many times entirely focused on her.

Her heart was thundering, her hands clammy as they clutched at the seat beneath her. Well, she'd known this was the risk, she… she'd just have to face it.

The urge to run away was so strong she had to grip the chair harder and harder to keep herself still.

Courage, Prunella, she murmured to herself.

"My goodness, Prue, he's staring straight at you," hissed Bonnie, as Prue wondered if she might be sick. It seemed a distinct possibility.

Yet, there was Baron Fitzwalter, ahead of the duke, and looking pleased as punch to greet her. She knew, of course, that he was Bedwin's uncle, though he rarely spoke of his nephew and she'd been too polite to ask, despite her curiosity. She'd always assumed his reticence stemmed from shame for his relation's dark deeds, but he seemed to own the relationship fully enough in this moment. What the devil was going on?

"There you are," said the baron, his cheerful booming voice heard clearly over the sound of the orchestra. "My favourite young lady."

Prue stammered something in reply, she wasn't entirely sure what, too focused on the glowering figure standing a few paces behind the baron.

Looming.

Well, naturally he loomed. That's what villains did. The only question was, why was he looming at her? Her stomach twisted.

"My nephew desired my company," said the baron, forcing her to turn her attention from the looming duke and back to him. "And it's so long since we had any time together. Oh, but where are my manners? Bedwin, please may I present, Miss Chuffington-Smythe."

Oh, good heavens. He was introducing them!

Prue froze. It was one thing writing about a villain, a despicable man you'd never met and felt no desire to meet. Quite another to stare him in the face. Her breath was coming hard and fast now, and she felt a little light-headed. Belatedly, she realised she was staring. *Pull yourself together*, she commanded herself.

She'd done this. She'd known the risks and she'd taken them. This duke had made his own decisions too, and here they both stood.

Prue doubted he was as black as he was painted, but he'd never tried to refute the gossip, so she could only assume he enjoyed his notoriety. Well, he might not be entirely black, and she might not be entirely white. That seemed fair. Stiffening her spine, Prue ducked an awkward curtsey. At least she hadn't fainted.

"Your grace."

He murmured a polite, if unenthusiastic greeting, and Prue wondered once more what on earth was going on. Then the baron began making his excuses to leave them alone and Prue was thrown into a panic. Going on the undisguised horror in the duke's eyes, he was of the same mind.

Before Prue could figure a way of making the man stay, he'd leaned in and whispered in her ear.

"Give him a chance, my dear. For an old man's sake."

Prue stared at the baron, thinking she must have misheard him, but there was nothing she could do or say to protest. She was alone with the *Damned Duke*, and she had to make the best of it.

The two of them stared at each other, and she knew he was just as aware as she was of the hundreds of eyes upon them, glassy with fascination, watching to see what happened next.

The duke's jaw tightened, his severe features growing harder. He hated this, she realised. That was a surprise; she'd always believed he revelled in his infamy.

Wait.

This was a stroke of luck. If he'd meant to expose her, he would have done so, which meant he didn't know.

He didn't know!

Prue's heart skipped a little as she wondered if she were brave enough, but… what better way to get into the head of her own *Damned Duke,* to understand him, to draw his character, flesh out his motivations, than via the man himself?

It was a golden opportunity.

She could explore the character of this dark, complex man. This was first-hand research of the kind that did not come along every day. She would not waste the chance by being too shy to converse with him.

"I hope you didn't make a mistake?" she ventured, daring to speak to the glowering figure opposite her.

"A mistake?" he repeated, his frown deepening as his angular, dark brows drew together.

Lord, but he looked sinister when he did that. Prue suppressed an odd prickling shiver which was not entirely fear.

"Well, I can't help supposing it was my cousin to whom you wished for an introduction. She's the beauty in the family."

Those green eyes watched her, and she felt a little like a specimen in a jar. Prue cleared her throat.

"Miss Minerva Butler," she ploughed on, gesturing to the other side of the room, where Minerva was dancing with a besotted looking young man and staring daggers at Prue.

The duke's gaze followed her direction, settling on the vivacious blonde, whose expression instantly settled into something shy and appealing, which was somehow subtly flirtatious at the same time. Goodness, Minerva was good at that. Prue couldn't have pulled off such a look if she practised it in the mirror daily for a decade.

She turned back to look at Bedwin, who gave an almost imperceptible shudder and turned away. Prue blinked in astonishment.

"There's no mistake," he said, his voice firm. In a determined movement—in the manner of a man forced to deal with a large spider—he held out his hand to her. "May I have the honour of this dance, Miss Chuffington-Smythe?"

Prue gaped.

"You're not serious?"

The words were out before she could think better of them, but really…. You couldn't spend three seasons as a wallflower and then have a duke ask you to dance without thinking something underhanded was at work.

"Is that a refusal?" he asked, quite obviously offended.

"Er… no," she said, forcing herself to remember that this was *research*. "No, it isn't, but you can't expect me not to wonder why."

"Can't I?" he asked, an undertone of frustration behind the enquiry. "Most women would trample their friends for the opportunity to dance with a duke."

Prue considered this. "Most women, with *most* dukes," she allowed.

Something lit in his eyes and she quailed a little, unsure if it was anger or not. "But I am not *most* dukes."

Prue shrugged. "And I am not *most* women."

They stared at each other for a long, uncomfortable moment.

"Well," she said, a little exasperated. "It's not as if we don't both know it."

The duke stared at her for a moment longer. "If I promise I won't murder you before the music ends, will you dance with me?"

There was something that might have been amusement in his question, though his tone was too impatient and rather too sinister for her to be certain. Sadly, Prue had always admitted to a warped sense of humour, and found the corners of her mouth turning up.

"I never did believe that one, you know," she said, putting her hand in his.

He tilted his head a little, considering her but not giving her any indication of whether she was correct.

"My uncle was right," he said, frowning a little. "You are unusual."

"I'm not entirely sure that's a compliment, but I shall take it as one," Prue replied.

Unusual might not be a good thing to be under the judging eyes of the *ton*, but as a writer… yes, she'd be happy with that.

"You are an unusual duke, also, your grace." He looked down at her in surprise and her lips quirked. "Well, I thought I ought to return the compliment."

"*If* it was a compliment," he murmured, the words a dry rumble.

Prue snorted, for which her aunt would have scolded her soundly. The duke just raised an eyebrow. "Well, if it wasn't, I've returned your insult. It seems fair, doesn't it?"

She thought perhaps his lips twitched just a little.

"Eminently," he replied, drawing her towards him as Prue realised with a jolt of alarm that the next dance was a waltz.

Her eyes flew to his as the music began, and his hand settled upon her waist.

Good heavens.

He'd been daunting enough to stand opposite. It had taken all her self-possession to speak with him, refusing to let him intimidate her. Yet he was intimidating, so tall and broad, powerful, with heavy-lidded green eyes, that arrogant cold look assessing her. Still, she'd held her own. One hand at her waist and her own disappearing into the firm, warm grasp of his other, however, and all at once she was in danger of becoming a quivering wreck again.

To think, some women might even envy her.

They were mad.

Stop this. You are a sensible woman, Prunella. This is research. Nothing more. It will all be over in a few minutes, don't waste it. Now, what do you need to know about the Damned Duke?

Concentrating on the question allowed her to move through the first few turns of the dance without stepping on his toes. He was a very good dancer, she thought, a little distracted by the warmth of his palm at her waist as it radiated through the muslin of her gown.

Concentrate.

"If you were to choose a lair, where would it be?"

The words escaped her before she'd thought them through. For a moment it had been as though her own *Damned Duke* were before her, and she was simply asking him his preference on the matter so she could write it as he desired. Bedwin stared at her, outraged.

"I beg your pardon?"

Oh dear.

Prue cleared her throat. "Well, everyone believes you a villain, don't they, and villains have lairs? I was curious. If you were to have a lair, where would you choose?"

He stared down at her, green eyes unblinking, and for a moment she didn't know if he would walk away from her in fury, or say something cutting before doing so. He was silent for such a long time she wished he'd just get on with it, get it over with. She was on the verge of apologising for her insolence when he spoke.

"What are the options?"

There was something that might have been curiosity in his gaze, and relief coursed through her.

"I don't know, you're the villain. A cave? A dungeon? A remote castle on a moor?"

He snorted, shaking his head. "A cave and a dungeon would be damp, cold, and uncomfortable, ditto a remote castle on the moor, I should think. It would not make for a very enjoyable night of debauchery."

"Oh," Prue said, her eyebrows lifting. "I suppose that's true. But I might also suppose that such minor irritations would not put a true villain off. Are you always so hen-hearted?"

He made a choking sound, and she wasn't sure if this was further outrage or laughter.

Perhaps both?

"Perhaps I'm not a true villain," he offered, his eyes dancing as she realised it *was* laughter.

"No, perhaps, not," she mused, feeling all at once a little uncomfortable, and then his grasp on her shifted, pulling her closer, tighter, as he leaned down. His mouth was so close to her ear that his warm breath touched her, making her shiver.

"True villains like to tempt the innocent into giving freely what they know they ought not give at all, forcing them into wanting what they should not desire. It is not about the brute force of a larger body over a weaker one, but seduction, and seduction is far harder to achieve in the cold and damp."

Prue felt her breath catch and she looked up at him, getting caught in that cool green gaze, heart pounding, and then she laughed. Her grin was wide and irrepressible.

"I say, that was terrific," she exclaimed, wishing she had a notebook to hand. She wanted to write it all down, every nuance. Her fingers twitched to write about the dark, thrilling tone of his voice, the shiver of something that was not quite fear, but desperately tantalising. His words had been a heated flutter against her neck as they moved over her skin and made her knees quaver as if they'd buckle. "I felt almost breathless. You're really an excellent villain, aren't you?"

Too late, she realised he was staring at her in consternation, as though she'd said something extraordinarily odd. Sadly, it was an expression with which she was quite familiar. She shrugged and returned a rueful smile.

"Would you like to swap unusual for peculiar?" she suggested, referring to his earlier estimation of her.

The duke stared at her a moment longer, and then let out a surprised huff of laughter.

Chapter 5

I can't believe you danced with the Duke of Bedwin! What was it like? Were you terrified? What did he say to you? What did you say to him? Everyone is talking about it, Prue. I was so frustrated not to get to speak to you afterwards. I'm practically bursting with impatience.

<u>*Tell me everything*</u>*!*

—Excerpt of a letter from Miss Alice Dowding to Miss Prunella Chuffington-Smythe.

***

Still, 12th April. London 1814. The Earl and Countess March's Ball.

Once the dance had ended, Bedwin guided her from the floor where they were immediately pounced upon by Minerva and Aunt Phyllis. Mortified, Prue had little option but to introduce them to the duke. He did not appear thrilled with this, though he was scrupulously polite.

Prue watched, fascinated as Minerva fluttered and smiled and toyed with her hair. She really was a beautiful girl; it was hard to believe any man could resist her. Yet as Prue turned her attention back to the duke, it was plain to her that he was unmoved by her lovely cousin. In fact, beneath the polite smile he wore, she was almost certain he was bored. Bored and irritated. How peculiar.

She smiled a little, realising she had upgraded him from unusual to peculiar, just as she had suggested he do with her.

"Oh, another waltz," Minerva exclaimed, one slender hand settling over her heart. "I do so love to waltz." As she said the words, she turned her bright blue eyes upon the duke. "Don't you, your grace?" This was pronounced in a breathless tone, almost a whisper, quiet and intimate.

If asked in that moment, Prue would have laid money on the next word out of the duke's mouth being a resounding *no*. She hadn't counted on her Aunt Phyllis.

"Oh, do indulge a young lady, your grace," her aunt said, giggling like a schoolgirl.

Prue stared at her in horror. She had practically asked the duke to dance with Minerva, and in such a way it would be impossible for a gentleman to refuse. She wanted to curl up and die from the impropriety of her aunt's manoeuvring. What must the man think of them? No doubt she'd now been upgraded to that significantly worse title—*climber*.

She held her breath, wondering what he would do. With chagrin she found herself torn between praying he would dance with Minerva, because she'd be crushed if he didn't, and hoping he'd say no, as he'd been about to. Prue didn't like to consider why it was she hoped he'd refuse, but... it was likely only to protect Minerva, who did not understand what she'd be getting herself into.

He didn't do either. Silently, he held out his hand to Minerva, who flushed with pleasure and triumph and allowed him to lead her onto the floor.

***

15th April. Upper Wimpole Street. London.

"And he said I was a superb dancer," Minerva said, sighing over her teacup.

Prue repressed a remark which would have done nothing but ruffle Minerva's feathers and cause an almighty row. It was harder to do than she liked to admit. Three days later, however, and Minerva and Aunt Phyllis were still discussing every minute detail of the dance with *her* duke.

Prue wouldn't put it past her to have already begun a guest list for the engagement party. In Minerva's mind—and, to be fair, Aunt Phyllis did not seem to contradict her—the duke was as good as won.

In her less charitable moments, now being one of them, Prue might have pointed out she had watched their dance with interest, and the duke hadn't once opened his mouth to speak with Minerva. Yet, in Minerva's version of events, the man had talked nineteen to the dozen.

To escape the incessant chatter, Prue retreated behind a newspaper, a treat bestowed on her by Baron Fitzwalter. Once he'd read the paper himself, he had it sent around to her. It was an indulgence she thoroughly enjoyed. For a moment she considered starting a conversation about the abdication of Napoleon. Surely a moment of such historical import could stop the flow of conversation about the blasted Duke of Bedwin. For several minutes she tried to find a break in the conversation.

"Did you see *The Sorrows of Boney*?" She reached for the paper and turned it to show them the cartoon by John Wallis, showing the emperor Napoleon perched on a rock in the middle of the ocean with crows and bats flying around his head whilst he wept copious tears. "The alternate title is *Meditations on the Island of Elba*," Prue added with a grin. "Doesn't he look pathetic?"

She tilted the cartoon to admire it but, by the time she looked back at Aunt Phyllis, the conversation had returned to the duke.

Prue sighed and returned her attention to *The Lady's Weekly Review*. She had already checked the next instalment of her story had been published correctly and with no errors. This one should please the girls, she thought with a smile.

As she turned the page, an article among the *on-dits*—which were nothing less than salacious gossip—took her attention.

We noted the return of a certain notorious figure at the lavish ball given by the Earl and Countess of March. Two waltzes danced, though his dance partners had little in common they do share a family connection. A little bird tells us that this enigmatic figure hunts a wife…. Surely not from this quarter?

Prue scowled at the print. The allusion to their own less than ideal circumstances didn't bother her—it was nothing she didn't know—though Minerva would be furious if she saw it. Using the phrase *hunts a wife*, however, was deliberate and cruel. She had learned only a few days ago from Alice that the duke's wife had actually died in a hunting accident. There had been so many versions of her demise that it had been impossible to tell fact from fiction. This more than anything had told Prue it was all a fabrication.

Alice's father however, had got the truth from the Earl of St Clair's younger brother. The Earl had been there. There had been other witnesses that day. Witnesses who had sworn Bedwin was not to blame, but the two men—the Earl of St Clair and Viscount Cavendish—had been his closest friends. It appeared that even this was not enough to absolve him.

Of course they'd say that, whispered the *ton*.

For the first time since she had begun her story about the Duke of Bedsin, Prue experienced a pang of guilt. She could hardly complain about the author of this piece when her own work had destroyed his character so much more comprehensively. What she had written was far more devastating than that spiteful comment, though she hadn't known of the exact circumstances of his wife's death when she'd done it.

For a moment she closed her eyes, reliving those words he'd breathed in her ear, his voice low and sinful.

It is not about the brute force of a larger body over a weaker one, but seduction.

Despite herself, she shivered. It wasn't entirely unpleasant. The duke, she decided, was a far more complicated man than the one she had presented so far. She should have realised he would be. A successful rake would have to have more about him than a pretty face and a glib tongue. The duke certainly possessed both, but he could laugh and be amused, and amusing too. Clever and interesting. Intriguing, in fact. He could also be surprised. A little smile curved over her mouth as she realised she knew a deal more about the man than she had, and her character deserved fleshing out accordingly.

A warning bell sounded in her mind as she appreciated that the man had piqued her interest. *He's dangerous,* she reminded herself. A man like that could make a woman sigh and believe he loved her alone, and then gamble her fortune away, spending it on light-skirts and opera singers, and giving his beloved a slap if she dared to challenge him for it.

Prue knew that. She knew men like that. Her father had been just such a man. The duke had a dark side that was well documented, and she'd do well to remember it.

Still, their conversation turned in her mind, beguiling her into wanting to know more about him.

The Damned Duke was more than just a villain; he had hopes and dreams, surely? There were things he feared, perhaps even people he cared for? What had made him a villain in the first place, and was there anything that might redeem him?

With a surge of excitement, Prue got to her feet and hurried from the table without another word. She had a chapter to write.

***

16ᵗʰ April. Upper Wimpole Street. London.

Prue had been pleased to discover that Miss Ruth Stone was a near neighbour, living further along Upper Wimpole Street, where her aunt had rented their own house. The street itself—on the fringes of that exclusive quarter of Mayfair inhabited by the *haut ton*—was not one of the finest addresses, not that some of the houses weren't lavish.

The small, simply furnished and, honestly, frayed around the edges lodgings that Aunt Phyllis had bespoken were the best they could afford. Miss Stone, however, daughter of a wealthy merchant, could afford to rub shoulders with dukes and earls, if only they would let her. The finest houses on Upper Wimpole Street were grand and quite fine enough to satisfy the *ton*, yet they reeked of new money, and that was an unforgiveable sin.

Prue stared around at the opulent magnificence of Miss Stone's home as an immaculate butler showed her in.

"Oh, Miss Chuffington-Smythe," Miss Stone exclaimed, beaming as she hurried towards her. "You came!"

"Of course I came," Prue replied, returning her smile as she handed her pelisse, hat, and gloves to a footman. "I've been looking forward to it."

"I'm so glad," the young woman replied, her wide brown eyes earnest. "I was afraid no one would."

"Is there no one else here yet?" Prue asked, a little surprised. She'd felt sure some of her friends would have made the effort.

Miss Stone shook her head, flushing a little.

"Well, don't lose heart yet," Prue said, hoping they were on their way. "It's early still, and do please call me Prue," she all but begged. "Chuffington-Smythe is such a ridiculous mouthful. The only thing that could ever induce me to marry would be the relief at losing such an appalling name."

The young woman stared at her, wide-eyed. "Prue, then," she said, a little hesitant, clearly taken aback by Prue's forthright words. "And you must call me Ruth, but… you really don't wish to marry?"

Prue grinned at her and linked their arms together. "Ruth, you may as well know now. I'm peculiar. There's no getting away from it."

With a laugh of delight, Ruth guided her towards the parlour. "In that case, I am extremely pleased to meet you. I adore anything peculiar."

"Then we shall get on like a house on fire," Prue replied, pausing as she walked into a quite spectacular parlour. Everything was the best money could buy. Her slippered feet sunk into a luxurious carpet, and the furnishings had been chosen with exquisite care, every inch of the room decorated with skill and finesse.

Yet it wasn't just the room that held her attention.

A young woman stood as they entered. She was petite, with jet black hair and such stunning dark eyes that Prue could not help but stare. Her rich golden skin glowed with vitality against a dress of deep amber. She was glorious.

"Prue," Ruth said, moving between them. "This is Senorita Lucia de Feria. Lucia, may I present Miss Prunella Chuffington-Smythe."

"I'm pleased to meet you," the woman said, surprising Prue for the second time that day as she had expected to hear a thick Spanish accent. Yet her voice was the low and cultured tone of a proper English lady. "I was raised among an English family," she explained with a smile before Prue could comment, apparently used to such reactions.

"My word, but you're lovely," Prue said. As ever, the words slipped out before she could consider them.

The young woman opened her mouth, a little taken aback. Ruth gave a merry laugh at Prue's honesty and then sighed.

"Isn't she, though? It's most disheartening, I assure you, to come down every morning and face such devastating perfection."

"Oh, but—" The beauty opened her mouth, about to protest the comparison but Prue held up a hand, silencing her.

"Please, don't make excuses for us, or for yourself. You're a goddess and we mere mortals are happy to be in your presence."

Senorita de Feria laughed, and it was not the dainty, tinkling laugh one might have expected from such a delicate and lovely creature, but more of a chortle. "That's the most ridiculous thing I've ever heard," she sputtered.

"Oh, well, you should stay," Prue said, grinning at her. "There's far more nonsense where that came from."

Muffled voices from the entrance hall had Ruth clutching at Prue's arm with excitement.

"More people!" she squeaked with delight, before hurrying off to greet them.

***

The first meeting of the *Peculiar Ladies Book Club*, as named by Prue, Ruth and Lucia, and voted upon by the new members, began with tea and cake. Though, to Prue's mind, cake was a poor descriptor of all the lavish treats and delicacies which were paraded before them.

"I vote this as being the Peculiar Ladies' headquarters," Prue spoke to the room at large whilst deliberating over a choice of mouth-watering delicacies. Whichever she chose would be her fourth.

"Mmm," Alice mumbled, nodding her agreement and licking cream from her fingers.

"Well, it's all well and good for you skinny beans to make such arrangements," Bonnie replied as she sighed with longing over a selection of cream cakes. "Some of us only have to look at a cake to have our gowns straining fit to burst."

"Oh, come now, Bonnie," Alice replied, staring at her friend with chagrin. "You know as well as I do, I'd swap my skin and bones for a few of your curves."

Bonnie snorted and snatched up a cream cake with a defiant glint in her eyes. "Aye, well, I've curves enough to spare."

The group of women chuckled though their laughter was cut short as Harriet Stanhope spoke up.

"Shall we get started?"

And thus began the *Peculiar Ladies Book Club*. Prue looked around at the members with a smile. There were nine of them in all, each of them forced to the fringes of society for a variety of reasons.

For the first fifteen minutes, conversation was a little reserved, a touch stilted, and then they spoke about *The Dark History of a Damned Duke.*

"Oh my," said Matilda, the beautiful blonde closing her eyes with a sigh. "When he threatened to attack the earl for having insulted her, I swear I thought I would swoon, and I was sitting down," she added with a dry tone, causing all the women to burst out laughing.

Harriet scowled, pushing her spectacles a little further up her nose. "Oh, but he only did it to get Lydia to trust him," she said, her voice grave and disapproving.

"But don't you think maybe he could be redeemed?" Bonnie asked.

Various cries sounded from all quarters. "Oh, no! He's far too wicked."

"I'd like to try."

"And besides, Lord Worthington is the hero."

"I'd rather have Bedsin."

A heavy sigh fluttered about the room.

Prue sat and enjoyed the back and forth of the conversation, the happy bickering and giggling. She had done this, created a story that had them all captivated, that had them wondering, discussing, disagreeing, teasing, and laughing. It was a wonderful feeling, and then her thoughts strayed to the man who had inspired her story, the man with a dark past, full of secrets, and rumours of violence and betrayal.

What would he do if he discovered she was Miss Terry?

Unbidden, his voice whispered in her ear again, deliciously wicked. Despite herself she smiled. Perhaps this was a dangerous game, perhaps she was playing with fire, for a man like that was not one you crossed without reprisals. Yet, she was committed. Her future hung on the success of this story, on the publishing deal that would surely follow.

She couldn't stop now, but perhaps she could do a better job at giving the duke his day, shining a light upon him so that he was neither black nor white, but the many shades of grey that made any normal person what they were.

Prue remembered his cool green gaze, and the flicker of amusement that had tugged at his mouth.

Yes, she could do that.

***

17th April. Mrs Banbury's Ball. London. 1814

Prue was regretting that she'd dressed in such haste, again, and had hurried out the door without picking up a fan. Whilst she hadn't the slightest interest in using the dratted thing to flirt with, it would have been nice to stir the air in the soup-like atmosphere of Mrs Banbury's party.

The place was a crush, which was no doubt the mark of a successful soiree, but nonetheless uncomfortable for those forced to endure it. Mrs Banbury had emptied almost every stick of furniture from the house to create room enough for the event, which meant sneaking away and finding a quiet corner to read in was not a possibility. The only seating remaining was in the card room, and Prue had no love of gaming.

Across the sea of silks, tailored coats, and ostrich feathers, Prue glimpsed Matilda, who offered her a jaunty wave and then rolled her eyes. Prue chuckled, wondering if she might endeavour to find her way through the crowds to speak with her friend, but a moment later Matilda had disappeared into the melee. She sighed. There were far too many people for comfort, and she was hot and sweaty. The longing to remove her gloves was almost irresistible, and possibly even worth the scolding she'd get if Aunt Phyllis noticed her inky fingers were on view.

Prue was just toying with the advantages of finding herself a glass of lemonade, versus the effort required to make it to the refreshment room, when she noticed the atmosphere change. The room quietened, voices dipping to murmurs, and as though a path had been cleared by an invisible force, the Duke of Bedwin appeared before her.

Prue's heart did an odd little flutter in her chest; odd because she'd described such a thing in her writing, yet she'd never experienced it. Scrutinising the sensation before it dissipated, she discovered it to be a mixture, of shock, anxiety, and excitement.

How intriguing.

To her astonishment, the duke was moving forward, his sights set on her, of all people. For the life of her, she could not imagine why. Their conversation at the Marches' ball had entertained her immensely, but the suggestion a man like the duke had given her a second thought, let alone sought her out… it was preposterous.

Yet, there he was, moving towards her with single-minded purpose.

Prue swallowed, wondering if it might be sensible to make a run for it in the circumstances, but Baron Fitzwalter's voice rang in her ears.

"Give him a chance, my dear. For an old man's sake."

"Good evening, Miss Chuffington-Smythe."

Prue took a moment to look the man over. He was splendid. The most marvellous looking villain a woman could ever wish for. Thick dark hair that curled in unruly waves, eyebrows that were simply made for glowering, and those cool, green eyes. His expression was aloof, the curve of his mouth a little cruel, and yet she felt certain there was amusement in his voice, just the slightest twitch of humour at his lips.

"Good evening, your grace," she said, endeavouring to curtsey in the crowd without treading on anyone's toes. "Were you in the market for some more odd conversation?" she demanded with a smile.

He stared down at her, his expression unreadable. "Well, it was either that or kick my heels in my lair all evening," he replied with the utmost seriousness.

Prue gave a delighted bark of laughter. The duke smiled, for the first time a proper smile that lit up his face… and all the breath left her lungs in a rush.

Good lord.

The smile transformed him, chasing away any suggestion of villainy and leaving in its place something boyish and rather charming. In a moment it had vanished, his expression returning to its usual appearance of cool disinterest, but Prue had seen it and felt her world would never be quite the same again.

Well, what a ridiculous thing to say, she thought, trying to laugh at her own whimsy, but finding herself unconvinced. A villain with the smile of an angel.

Possibly the most dangerous creature on earth.

"Aha. So, you admit you have one," Prue said, a teasing note to her voice. Why on earth the man was speaking to her at all she couldn't fathom, let alone why he allowed her to speak to him in such an insolent manner, but if he didn't complain, she wasn't about to stop. It was too tempting an opportunity to pass up.

"I never said otherwise," he pointed out. "I only suggested that dungeons, caves, and remote castles were not to my taste."

Prue bit back a grin and schooled her expression into something thoughtful, tapping her chin with a fingertip. "Ah, yes. I remember, a villain with a taste for the finer things in life."

"I *am* a duke," he said, all seriousness.

"And have you tempted many innocent victims into the dark recesses of this secret place?" she asked, the laughter apparent in her voice.

Prue faltered, for a moment wondering if she'd gone too far, if he wouldn't answer. There had been a flicker of something in his eyes that might have been hurt but then he spoke, his tone mocking.

"Perhaps it was I who was tempted in, did you ever consider that? Perhaps I await rescue?"

Prue raised her eyebrows, staring at him in surprise. She opened her mouth, to say what she wasn't sure, but wanting to know what he meant by the comment, when a familiar voice sounded beside them.

"Your grace! How lovely to see you, no doubt you've been looking for Minerva. So good of Prunella to keep you company. Run along and fetch us a glass of lemonade, there's a dear. Such a nice girl, an orphan you know. I took her in when her father died...."

And like that Prue was dismissed. She seethed a little but found she didn't have the effrontery to refuse her aunt, even though the slight of being sent off in such a manner stung. Like she was a servant or a poor relation. The latter of which, of course, she was. Just because Minerva and Phyllis were equally poor would not change people's perception.

She glanced around once she was halfway across the room to see if she could catch another glimpse of the duke, but he'd gone. Minerva and Aunt Phyllis were still there, heads bent in conversation, but he was nowhere to be seen.

Chapter 6

He's fascinated with you Prue, darling. There's no other explanation for seeking you out. Surely you can see that? He spoke to no one else that night, he practically cut your aunt dead and left immediately after he'd spoken to you. I think you've made a conquest!

—Excerpt from a letter from Miss Matilda Hunt to Miss Prunella Chuffington-Smythe.

***

18th April. Beverwyck. London. 1814

"Damnation!"

Robert flung *The Lady's Weekly Review* across the breakfast table. He hadn't read the last issue until now and had promised himself that he would not. What was the point? He didn't care what people thought, he never had. Not for years now. Except it seemed part of him still did. If only Helena hadn't left the blasted thing lying about, he wouldn't have been tempted to read it, and he might be in a rather better mood than he was now.

In fact, this morning he'd felt almost optimistic. His uncle had been correct about Miss Chuffington-Smythe. She wasn't beautiful, rather plain really, but neither was she unattractive; just an ordinary girl who wouldn't get a second glance if you passed her on the street. The lady was not hungry for fame or notoriety as far as he could tell, and as Charles had known her for some years, he felt satisfied in his estimation of her character as serious and loyal.

Loyal.

That word rang through him like a bell, a welcoming sound he wanted to grab hold of. She was not a woman who would take a lover within days of marrying, not the kind to lure his friends one by one into her bed and laugh in his face when he discovered it.

Not that she was perfect. She had her oddities. Her conversation, for example, was surprising. It had been a long time since anyone had surprised Robert, and that was not unappealing. Her fascination with his apparent villainy was a little disconcerting, but at least she was honest. She faced his reputation head on and confronted him with it, albeit amusingly. Insolent, but certainly amusing. His mouth curved into a smile as he remembered her *"Aha!"* of triumph when he'd admitted to having a lair. Not that he had, though he rather thought he should get one, so she'd not be disappointed in him.

He snorted at that.

She'd never believed that he'd murdered Lavinia.

Robert let out a breath. It hadn't occurred to him that there was anyone among the *ton* who believed him innocent. The whispering and the gossip had been so incessant in those months after her death that he'd felt the entire world was judging him, condemning him. It wasn't true, of course; there were a few loyal friends who had stood beside him, defended him. Those that had not succumbed to his wife's bed.

The chattering and the scrutiny had been too much to bear, however, and he'd gone to ground, disappearing from polite society and finding solace in a darker world. A world of gambling halls and rough men, of women who were openly sluts instead of playing the doting wife in company and then working their way through every man he'd ever been friends with.

His marriage had dissolved into a war of attrition, with silk stockings and heated gazes as her weapon of choice, leaving him isolated, jealous, and sick with remorse for marrying a woman he'd believed he'd loved but not known, not understood.

Though he'd understood well enough in the end, he'd just been too blindly in love to believe it at first. What he'd believed had been love at the time, anyway. Too late, he'd realised his error. Infatuation was not love. From the moment she'd tricked him into marriage—a set-up where her father walked in on them at the crucial moment—he'd known it had been the title she wanted, not him. She'd even admitted it. Yet he'd forgiven her for that, he'd been so thoroughly besotted he'd still hoped they could make it work, make a life together....

What a goddamn fool.

Well, that was done. Lavinia was dead through her own recklessness, he was free, and this time he'd not take a chance. There would be no emotion clouding his choice, no desire clawing at his skin, or a desperate need to touch so intense that he'd believed he might die of it. There would be no desire at all.

Decision made.

Prunella Chuffington-Smythe was available. She was from a decent if impoverished family, free of scandal, and thoroughly vetted by one of the few people in the world whose opinion mattered to him.

She would be his wife.

That decision reached there was little point in beating about the bush. There was no point in courting the girl when he hadn't the slightest desire for her to fall in love with him, and he certainly had no intention of falling for her. He hoped they could be amicable; indeed, he hoped they could be friends. That was as much as a man in his position could hope for. His father had told him that once, and he'd failed to listen. Not this time.

Robert got to his feet and called for his carriage. He would propose to Miss Chuffington-Smythe and make her his wife without delay.

***

Prue sighed with relief as the sound of the front door closing resounded through the house. Thank heavens.

Minerva and Aunt Phyllis were off shopping—shopping they could ill afford. There was no way in hell Prue had been about to point that out, though. Not after a morning listening to Minerva prattle on about what it might be like to be Duchess of Bedwin. Prue had always believed she was the one blessed with a vivid imagination, but if the poor girl believed her fantasy, she was deluded.

There was about as much chance of the duke proposing to Minerva as there was of him proposing to—

She stopped as a sharp rap sounded at the door.

Who the devil was that? Prue waited for the sound of Sally's footsteps hurrying to the door, the low sound of voices, moving in her direction. With a muttered exclamation of annoyance, she stood, smoothing out her dress and wishing she'd put on something a little less drab. Why did people always call when you least wanted them to? Prue had hoped to have a lovely quiet afternoon in which to write the next chapter. Some intriguing thoughts had occurred to her about *The Damned Duke,* and she was eager to put pen to paper and explore them.

Footsteps moved towards the parlour door and Sally walked in, her eyes on stalks. She bobbed a curtsey.

"His grace, the Duke of Bedwin to see you, Miss."

Prue was so startled she had to reach out and grab the back of the chair she'd been sitting on just a moment earlier. With horror, she realised she'd left her writing on the desk, and her heart pounded, a flush of heat creeping over her skin.

The duke entered the parlour, taking up all the space and all the air, as Prue felt anything she'd been breathing rushed from the room the moment he'd come in. Her lungs locked down.

What was he doing here?

Had he figured it out at last?

After several moments dumbstruck with shock, she curtseyed, still clutching the chair back for support. She glanced at the half-filled sheet of paper left upon her desk with a sickening sense of foreboding.

"Your grace?" she said, lacking anything more intelligent and hoping he'd get to the point with haste before she suffered a nervous collapse.

"Miss Chuffington-Smythe," he said, and then turned to look at Sally who was dithering in the doorway, uncertain of what to do next.

"You may leave us, Sally," Prue said, aware that was grossly improper but not wanting Sally to be a witness to the coming scene if she were about to face ruination.

Sally's eyes grew wide and she gave an almost imperceptible shake of her head.

"You may leave the door ajar," the duke said, giving orders as though it were his home. "I'll not be here above a moment. Miss Chuffington-Smythe will be safe, I assure you."

Prue watched the battle on Sally's face, the desire to keep Prue from harm or scandal warring with the likelihood of a mere servant defying the will of a duke... and not just any duke, at that.

"It's all right, Sally," Prue said again, her voice soothing. "I'll be fine."

Sally gave Bedwin a direct look, almost a glare, and Prue felt a swell of affection for the woman that she would risk that much.

"I'll not be far away, Miss," she said, keeping her eyes on the duke, the words firm as she left them alone, leaving the door open a good six inches.

Silence filled the room, the only sound Prue's heart beating in her ears. She wondered if he could hear it too.

"Miss Chuffington-Smythe," the duke said, turning to face her. His expression was unreadable; he did not appear to be angry, but those dark eyebrows and darker eyes were so intimidating it was hard to be certain. "I'll come straight to the point."

Prue's stomach lurched as if the room had pitched sideways and she grasped the chair back a little tighter.

"I would like to ask you if you would do me the honour of becoming my wife?"

Prue blinked. She'd misheard obviously; the shock and the expectation of imminent doom had addled her brain. He couldn't possibly…. She hadn't just heard him say—

What had he said?

His *wife?*

Good lord!

The silence that had reigned after Sally had retreated, crept into the room once more as Prue stared at him, too shocked to react. She didn't know how to react. Hysterical laughter or fainting seemed a distinct possibility.

"Did you hear what I said?" the duke asked, studying her with curiosity. Those dark eyebrows pulled together. "I asked you to marry me." There was a distinct thread of irritation in the repetition of his question.

"I-I," she stammered, before swallowing and trying again. "You asked me to marry you?" she said, posing it as a question despite having heard it twice now, just to be on the safe side.

"I did," he said, his expression grave. He was staring at her, his piercing gaze unnerving. "And I await an answer."

She almost did laugh then. What on earth did he expect her to say?

"No."

His eyebrows hit his hairline and, in that moment, she realised he'd not even considered the possibility she would refuse him. She put her chin up, wondering if she ought to have softened her refusal and grasping the fact, she may have been just a tad ungracious.

"That is to say, your grace, I am very flattered by your offer, of course, and—"

"Is it my reputation?" he demanded, for the first time appearing unsure of himself. "Because if so, I can promise you—"

"No," she said, shaking her head. "Your reputation is not one that recommends you as a husband, that is without question, but as that is not the reason for my refusal it is neither here nor there."

"Then what the devil do you mean by saying no? If you were afraid of me, afraid the rumours have truth to them, that I can understand, and I would endeavour to put your mind at ease. However, there is no other earthly reason you should refuse such an offer."

He sounded so outraged that her desire to save hurting his feelings evaporated.

"I mean only what I said. No. Thank you. I will not marry you," she repeated, sounding remarkably calm when her heart was performing an agitated tattoo in her chest.

For heaven's sake, she was standing in front of the next chapter of *The Damned Duke* and the inspiration for her devilish villain had just proposed to her! It was beyond any plot even she could have come up with.

"Am I not good enough?" he asked, the words mild though there was annoyance flashing in his eyes.

Prue gave a huff of impatience and folded her arms, her nerves dissipating as her irritation grew. "I have never had ambitions to marry a title, *your grace*," she said, exaggerating the address a little. "If, however, you are so anxious to marry into my family, I assure you that my cousin Minerva would be more than pleased to assist you."

That was likely the understatement of the century. She made a mental note to never, ever, mention this to Minerva. She'd make Prue's life unbearable if she knew.

The duke snorted at that, looking revolted at the suggestion. "Of that I have little doubt," he said, folding his arms and mirroring her stance. "And I have no intention of marrying a social climber, I thank you. Quite the opposite."

She stared at him, considering. "Is that why you chose me?" she asked, finally making some sense of it. "For I can think of no other reason. We barely know each other, and I have no money, nor connections, nothing that could bring anything to the relationship. It certainly isn't a love match," she added, laughing a little at the idea.

"Is that why you refuse me?" he demanded, narrowing his eyes with suspicion now. "Because I've not taken the trouble to court you?"

Prue rolled her eyes at him. "No."

He stood staring at her, looking as if she was a puzzle for which he had the final piece and couldn't understand why it wouldn't fit. She bit back a laugh at his consternation. He'd probably chosen the one woman in the whole of England who would refuse him.

"Do you not think you at least owe me an explanation?" He folded his arms, looking imperious and cross and for some reason not the least bit intimidating any more.

She shrugged. "Not really."

He looked quite appalled now, and she almost felt sorry for him.

"So, I am to believe you would rather continue to live in penury, dependent on the charity of your vulgar aunt, than become the Duchess of Bedwin, with power and wealth beyond your comprehension?"

That last bit had been a mistake on his part. Prue's temper lit like a match to kindling. "Well, if it's beyond my comprehension, you can hardly blame me for not understanding the great honour you bestow upon me," she replied acidly.

Of all the arrogant, conceited....

"Don't be obtuse," he snapped. "Or I shall consider your mental abilities lacking, which was the one thing I had not believed below par. I have neither the time nor patience for sarcasm."

She gaped at him, astonished by the insult. Any guilt she may have felt at casting the man as her villain, with little in the way of disguising him, vanished in an instant.

"Why did you come and propose at all, if that's the case?" she demanded. "I never implied I invited your attentions, did I? I am aware I am no beauty, not do I have fortune or connections, I already told you as much. I have no pretensions to any. It is you who has forced this ridiculous situation upon us both, for reasons I simply cannot fathom."

"My reasons are sound, I assure you," he said, biting off each word with precision. "I have less conviction of yours, however. Give me one good reason you would refuse an offer which, as you have said yourself, your cousin would snatch at with both hands."

"Fine," she snapped, quite out of patience with the aggravating creature now. "Because I will never put myself in a man's power. I am not, as you so blithely suppose, as close to destitution as you may believe. I will soon be an independent woman, and I will not relinquish that independence for anyone. Certainly not *you*!"

The atmosphere in the room prickled with tension.

"I see," he replied, his expression fierce. "So, I am at least absolved of any particular wrongdoing, or at least any that would stop you marrying me. My greatest crime is my gender. Is that correct?"

"If it makes you happy to couch it in such a fashion, yes. That's correct."

There was a muscle ticking in his jaw, a frown tugging at those dark eyebrows, and his gaze upon her was insistent and unwavering. Good lord, why didn't the bloody man just give up and go home?

He didn't, though. He kept frowning and then looked away from her, pacing the length of the room and back again. Brooding.

Prue thought he was rather good at it; the brooding villain was a role he fitted into all too neatly.

When he finally spoke, she was so intent in her study of him that she jumped in surprise.

"Don't you believe in love?" he asked. Something in the question made her believe he was genuinely curious.

Though taken aback, Prue did not need to consider the question. She let out a breath and shook her head. "No. Love is for literature. They are fairy tales for grown-ups, stories we long to believe, but which never come true."

Emotion flashed in his eyes, a glimpse of something she couldn't read.

To her surprise he sat down, as though all the energy had left him. She watched, startled and unsure as he rubbed a weary hand over his face and let out a breath of sound that was not quite laughter.

"God," he muttered, giving the impression he was speaking to himself. "How I wish that were true."

Her heart lurched at the truth in the words, as though in that moment the role she'd cast him in fell away, exposing the actor beneath. He was hurt, she thought. Hurt and vulnerable.

A moment later and she hardly believed she'd seen it at all, for he stood again, embracing the role: a duke in full panoply, haughty and disdainful, an implacable expression on his face.

"This is ridiculous," he said curtly. "I need a wife. A wife who will embrace her own independent life, but do so discreetly and cause me no scandal. I have enough of those for one lifetime already," he added with a dark expression. "Charles believed that you were that woman, and after meeting and spending some time with you, I concur. You have my assurance I will never interfere in your life. You may be as independent as you desire, but with the safety of my name and wealth to ensure it." He clasped his hands behind his back, like a man who knew with absolute certainty he was right. "It is a situation that can only benefit us both, and it would be foolish of you to refuse without at least considering the idea."

Prue's mouth fell open in astonishment. What did she have to do to make the man understand?

"Then, your grace, you may call me a fool," she retorted.

He stared at her and shook his head.

"I believe you are acting on emotion, and not with the benefit of reason, so I will not discuss this any further with you today," he said. "My offer stands, despite your refusal. Please, may I request you think on it? You could have all the independence you desire, and so much more. I think an offer of such magnitude is worth some consideration, at least."

She threw up her hands. The man was mad, there was no other explanation.

"You may give me a few days, a few months, or a year. My answer will not change."

He gave her a considering look and then shrugged. "That is your right," he allowed. "But may I request we revisit this discussion once more, nonetheless?"

"Fine!" she said, shaking her head. "If it pleases you to be refused again, by all means."

He nodded and then gave a stiff, formal bow. "Good day to you, Miss Chuffington-Smythe."

Chapter 7

Another ball! Another opportunity for father to demand why I haven't married a duke or an earl. Oh, how sick of it I am already, and we've barely begun. If only something exciting would happen.

—Excerpt of a letter from Miss Ruth Stone to Miss Prunella Chuffington-Smythe.

***

18th April. Lord and Lady Hartington's ball. London. 1814

At the Hartington's ball, later that same day, Prue was still in a state of nervous agitation. The scene with Bedwin had been so extraordinary she'd not been able to keep from replaying it over and again. She'd been so agitated she'd been unable to find a single pair of gloves—where did the ridiculous things go to? Did they migrate during the season? She'd been thoroughly scolded by Aunt Phyllis because of it.

What had the man been thinking? Proposing to *her*, of all people!

It was outrageous.

Then she wondered why she believed it so outrageous. After all, she was perfectly marriageable. Not as beautiful as Minerva, but she was passably pretty, intelligent, in good health, and from a decent family. There was no impediment to them marrying, she supposed.

It might as well be her as anyone, and if he'd been looking for someone who was not a social climber and would avoid societal events like the plague, well, she *was* a sound choice.

She scowled, irritated. That his uncle, Baron Fitzwalter, had supported the match was another reason he'd thought it a good idea, no doubt. Likely the duke had expected her to swoon with joy at her good fortune. She almost felt sorry for him. Almost.

He'd been abominably rude and had proven himself a man who would not take no for an answer. That, if nothing else, would have sealed his fate, in her opinion.

She glowered over the scene before her: pretty silks and satins in every colour, whirling about the floor, each paired with a man in immaculate evening dress.

"Don't you believe in love?"

His question echoed in her brain. No. She did not. Her mother had been in love with her father, a man who had belittled and abused her both physically and emotionally. Except then he would cry and beg forgiveness and promise it would never happen again. They would be happy for a few weeks, months even, and then it would start over afresh. If that was love, unwavering obedience and blind devotion to a man who was not fit to kiss her mother's boots, then she wanted no part of it.

Yet, his response to her denial had surprised her. *"God. How I wish that were true."* There had been real anguish in those words. Regret.

She thought back to their previous meeting, of her demand to know how many innocents he had lured to his lair.

"Perhaps it was I who was tempted in, did you ever consider that? Perhaps I await rescue?"

Prue frowned. Was it possible he had loved his first wife? Had all the stories about his cruelty to her, his affairs, had none of them been true? His behaviour since her death had done nothing to still the tongues of the *ton*. He hadn't even made a token effort to refute the stories.

Damnation. Either way, it was none of her concern. She had her own plans, her own dreams. His were nothing to bother herself with. Good lord, if he discovered she was the author of the story about him, he'd likely have her flayed alive. He wouldn't be repeating his proposal, that was for certain.

She stared at her lap, pleating and un-pleating the folds of her gown in her agitated fingers, unable to keep them still. *Just stop thinking about it*, she scolded herself. She'd just have to tell him no, if he was so blind to propriety that he'd dare ask her again. It was simple enough.

Cursing herself, she tried to turn her attention to the conversations about her. The wallflowers were grumbling too, cursing their parents, cursing ugly dresses, lack of funds, and the lack of anything resembling a decent dance partner. All at once, she was in a foul temper and wretchedly irritated.

"Then do something about it," she snapped, turning to Kitty Connolly, who had been bemoaning the boredom of endless balls and being seated without dancing for hours at a stretch.

Kitty stared at her, dark eyes wide. She was a lovely girl with thick black hair and, on the face of it, she ought to be popular and never without a dance partner. She was of Irish descent, however, and this enough to put her in company with the rest of the misfits. Kitty might be in possession of a decent, if not bountiful, dowry, and chaperoned by English relatives, but her accent proclaimed her heritage.

"Do what, exactly?" Kitty demanded, her lovely eyes flashing with indignation. "Demand the English treat me with as much respect as other young ladies? Ah, yes, I'll be off and do that right away, Miss Chuffington-Smythe, why did I not think of it before?"

Prue clamped her mouth shut before she could make things worse, aware that her ire ought to be directed at a certain irksome duke and not the surrounding ladies.

"I see you are still among our numbers," Kitty added, a dangerous glint in her eyes as she folded her arms. "What have you done to change your lot?"

"More than you know," Prue retorted, wishing she could tell them the truth. "But I can't explain. Suffice to say I'm not sitting about waiting for some man to ask me to dance, or to marry. I'm taking my future into my own hands."

Kitty snorted, shaking her head so that her black ringlets danced. "I don't believe a word. You sit here meek and well behaved, just like the rest of us."

"An act," Prue said, with a deceptively sweet smile curving her lips. "I'm brave enough to know what I want, and to reach out and take it."

The girl considered her, a challenging light in her eyes. "Prove it."

"What?" Prue said, taken aback. "I can't, at least not yet. By the end of this year though, then you'll see."

"That's too long to wait," Kitty said, and Prue could see the other young women watching the exchange with interest. "Show us how brave you are. I dare you."

Prue blinked, wondering what on earth had just happened. This was the bloody duke's fault, she decided, gritting her teeth. If he'd not put her in such a bad temper, this argument would never have arisen. However, Prue was nothing if not stubborn. She might not be able to reveal her secrets yet, but she was damned if she would back down. These girls could sit about bemoaning their lot if they wanted; she was doing something about it.

"What do you have in mind?" Prue asked, wondering just what she was getting herself into.

Kitty shrugged, considering. "We think of a dare, you do it."

Prue shook her head. "You think you're all as brave as me," she said, knowing she'd been backed into a corner, but she was damned if she'd be there alone. "So, we all get a dare."

There was no way all the girls would rise to the challenge. This ought to get her free. Poor Alice was so shy she couldn't even open her mouth in public. A dare was certainly beyond her.

Without even looking at the other girls, Kitty nodded and held out her hand. "Agreed."

"Don't you need to consult with the others?" Prue asked, a little taken aback.

Kitty shook her head. "Oh, no," she said, a blithe smile curving her lovely mouth. "We're all up for a challenge, aren't we girls?" She turned and glared at each young woman in turn, none of whom dared to contradict her.

At last she looked at Alice, and Prue held her breath. To her astonishment, Alice turned scarlet but gave a tiny but defiant nod.

Good heavens.

Kitty grinned, triumphant.

"Oh!" she exclaimed. "This will be marvellous. So, this is what we shall do. All of us will write out a dare… no, two dares, so that there are plenty of options. Then we'll put all of the dares in a hat and pull them one by one until we've all taken a turn."

Prue sucked in a breath, rather alarmed. "But people might put in something extraordinary, you can't just dare a person to dance with Prinny or to swim the Thames, there must be rules."

Jemima Fernside looked down at her dress, which was several seasons out of fashion, and sighed. "I'd get nowhere near Prinny, and I can't swim."

Ruth nodded, laying a hand on Kitty's arm. "She's right," she said, her voice serious. "We must have nothing which is too outlandish or unachievable, and nothing which would put anyone in physical danger."

Kitty scowled a little but acknowledged the sense in this. "I suppose that's fair, but there's no point in having a dare if there is no risk to it. If the dare is only to have tea with your Aunt Margaret, then it's pointless."

"I don't know," Matilda said, her tone dry. "I have an Aunt Margaret. She's perfectly terrifying."

A nervous chuckle ran over the group, but Prue could feel the excitement behind it, the hope. The girls wanted this, she realised; they wanted to change their lives, even if it frightened them. That, she could well understand. Perhaps she could help them, encourage them by setting an example of what women could do if they dared.

"Very well," she said, grinning at Kitty. "Where and when?"

Ruth spoke again. "Why not have another meeting of the Peculiar Ladies. We can have the book club tomorrow as usual, and then this can come under any other business."

"Acceptable?" Kitty asked, turning back to Prue.

"Acceptable," Prue agreed, wondering if she'd lost her mind in the moments after being proposed to by a duke. The blasted man had a lot to answer for.

***

Robert skulked at the edge of the ballroom, feeling like the spectre at the feast. With frustration, he remembered a time when he'd been welcomed and fawned over, everyone vying for his attention. Now, even though his lofty title held considerable allure, he was too dark, too damaged a figure to be approached without caution.

Young ladies whispered about him behind their fans and conversations stopped abruptly when he drew near. There were one or two friends who had greeted him with smiles and good humour, but he seemed to have lost the knack for polite conversation and found himself forced to walk away within moments of greeting them, before things got too awkward and they regretted their association with him.

What the devil was he doing here?

With frustration, the answer to that question presented itself as his gaze drifted to the wallflowers and the outrageous Miss Chuffington-Smythe. He was still smarting from her defiant refusal of his offer. It had occurred to him he might meet with resistance, but only on account of the rumours about him. As the young lady in question had shown no fear of him and had already told him she refuted the worst gossip she'd heard, he'd hoped that would not be too much of a problem to overcome.

Robert had believed that a few outings together would show her he was not the cold-hearted villain he was purported to be, and could be trusted to behave himself both in and out of her company. He'd done little to aid himself in that cause by acting like an arrogant arse. Her refusal had been so curt, though, so lacking in a moment's consideration or awareness of the honour he was doing her in offering the title of duchess to a lady considered unmarriageable by many. It had annoyed him, to the point he'd become rude and unfeeling, and he knew he'd have to work to turn that about.

The obvious option was to forget her and try to find a bride of his own. He had toyed with the idea, looking over the season's crop of eligible females. With little enthusiasm he had sought a few invitations of introduction. He'd encountered eyes wide with terror, blushing and stammering and—even more unappealing— covetous glances that suggested they'd marry him whether the rumours had foundation or not.

The truth of the matter was he had neither the patience nor the inclination to make the effort. Miss Chuffington-Smythe met all his criteria and had the benefit of her character being well known by his uncle for the past five years. She was the one. All he had to do was persuade her of that fact.

As he returned his attention to the lady in question, he saw her get to her feet and move towards the refreshments room. It was likely his only chance to get her alone this evening, so he followed her.

He found her in the crush about the refreshments table, trying without success to move forwards.

"Miss Chuffington-Smythe," he said, gaining himself a start of surprise, as he'd spoken from behind her. She turned, looking up at him and flushing. "You would like a glass of lemonade," he guessed.

She nodded and he moved towards the table, the crowds parting for him with murmurs of unease, a predator scattering the herd. He returned a moment later, glass in hand.

"Thank you," she said, taking the proffered glass. "It was like watching Moses before the Red Sea. What had been an impenetrable ocean for me, reduced to a puddle at your feet."

He wasn't sure if she was mocking him or speaking with admiration, her tone was too even to tell.

"There are some benefits to having a murderous reputation," he said with a wry smile.

Robert thought perhaps her lips twitched a little at that, but she said nothing.

"Perhaps, when you have finished your drink, you will do me the honour of dancing with me?"

She met his gaze and sighed a little. Had that been regret or irritation?

"I don't think that is a good idea. It will only start tongues wagging and, besides, Minerva will accuse me of chasing you and stealing her thunder."

"Your cousin," he recalled, remembering a beautiful blonde. "The one who would snap my hand off."

"The very same," she replied with a sweet smile that was not sweet at all.

She lifted the lemonade to her lips, the movement drawing his gaze to her hands. They were long and elegant, but her fingers were ink stained.

"You've been busy writing."

She choked on her drink and he hurried to take the glass from her, wondering whether smacking her on the back would be taken as an act of violence. A moment later she had composed herself again.

"Excuse me," she said, having gone a remarkable shade of white. "It went down the wrong way."

"It's of no matter," he said, smiling and returning her glass to her. "I was just observing you've had a busy day writing letters?"

"Oh! Yes," she said, as though suddenly understanding the conversation. "Yes, writing letters. Lots of letters. I'm a copious letter writer."

"You have family to keep in touch with?"

She blinked up at him, her expression a little panicked. "Er… no… friends. I write to friends. I have no family outside of my aunt and cousin." She smiled then, glancing down at her inky fingers with a rueful expression. "I seem to have an aversion to gloves, or perhaps they have an aversion to me," she added, looking thoughtful. "They never seem to be where I expect them to be. I was toying with the idea that my gloves migrate during the season. They certainly don't seem content to return themselves to my drawer and remain there. In fact, they turn up in the most extraordinary places."

"All by themselves?" he queried, rather amused by her fanciful notion. She was a strange creature.

"Oh, certainly," she said, her expression grave. "Do you know, a few weeks ago I found one of my best ones outside hanging from the raspberry bushes in the kitchen garden. Only one, mind. The other was in my room. Now how on earth could it have got there, do you suppose?"

She looked genuinely curious as to his opinion and he frowned, thinking it over.

"I suppose you are not prone to raspberry picking with your best gloves on?"

A scathing look met this suggestion.

"It's too early for raspberries, for one thing, and no, of course not. I've never even worn them into the garden." She gave a bewildered looking shrug. "It's most perplexing."

"A phantom?" he suggested, finding himself entertained and enjoying the strange topic for no reason he could think of.

What an odd conversation.

Her eyes widened to saucers. "Oh," she said, sounding a little breathless. "Do you know, I hadn't even considered that."

Robert forced his expression to remain serious with difficulty. "Have you lived in the house long?" he enquired. "And is the glove phenomenon of recent duration?"

He had guided her out of the crush of the refreshments room as they spoke, walking back towards the ballroom.

"My aunt rents the cottage. We've been there a little over five years and, do you know, I can't remember when it began?"

"Who lived in the cottage before you? Did anyone die there, perhaps?"

He started in surprise as she clutched at his arm.

"Oh, a romance gone wrong," she exclaimed, her eyes alight with excitement. "She died of a broken heart when her lover did not come to the church as arranged. All he found of her was a single glove, alone and abandoned at the foot of the altar, just as she had been."

Robert watched, startled by the sudden flight of fancy as she pressed her hand to her breast, covering her heart and sighing with pleasure.

"Oh, the poor dear."

"Perhaps he found the glove and hurried to be with her," he said, a little unsettled by the tragic tale, and finding his attention riveted to the long fingers laying over the curve of her breast. "He may have had a good explanation. Perhaps they lived happily ever after?"

She raised her eyebrows at him, gaze sceptical.

"It's no more unlikely than your tale," he said, a trifle defensively.

A smile curved over her mouth. It was a generous mouth, with a full lower lip. Somewhat surprising when the rest of her was so slender, and her face was, in all other aspects, quite severe with those high, angled cheekbones. Her mouth hinted at a softness which nothing else about her suggested. Her eyes were tip-tilted, rather feline and extremely alert. They were a light hazel, flecked with gold and green and, he suspected missed little. They were watching him now, a considering look in them which gave him pause.

"Are you a romantic, your grace?" She said it as if it was an accusation.

To his horror he felt the colour rise on his cheeks. "Certainly not," he said in his best aristocratic tone, which was enough to quell most of the *ton* with ease in his experience. All he got from Miss Chuffington-Smythe was an enigmatic smile.

"What the devil is that supposed to mean?" he demanded, irritated.

"What?" she asked, blinking up at him innocently. "I didn't say anything."

"No," he said, frowning down at her. "You smiled at me."

"I smiled at you?" she repeated, smiling wider and sounding amused.

"Yes," he said, wondering why he sounded like a fool. "It was most unnerving."

She at once schooled her face into something graver. "I do beg your pardon," she said, with great sincerity. "I will try not to frighten you so again."

Robert snorted and let out a huff of laughter. "You are peculiar," he said.

She grinned at that and he felt rather pleased for no reason he could think of.

"Is that a compliment, or an insult?" she asked. "Not that I'm disagreeing in the slightest you understand."

He stared at her, realising he didn't know the answer to that question himself. Before he could think about it too much, he held out his hand to her again.

"Please, will you dance with me?" The words were soft, the question inviting, something in his voice he didn't entirely like. It sounded… needy.

Her amused expression faded at once and she looked from him to his hand and back again.

One, tiny shake of her head gave him his answer. "Forgive me," she said, and hurried away before he could speak again.

Chapter 8

Alice, are you quite certain you wish to be involved in this mad venture? I don't think you should come to the next meeting, just in case. Heaven alone knows what kind of scrape we shall end up in. I fear Kitty has a vivid imagination. It matters little to me as I have no intention of ever marrying, but for you dearest? Please, have a care.

—Excerpt of a letter from Miss Prunella Chuffington-Smythe to Miss Alice Dowding.

***

19th April. Upper Walpole Street. London. 1814

"Miss?"

Prue looked up as her bedroom door opened a crack and Sally poked her head in.

"Miss, there's a parcel for you."

The maid hurried into the room and closed the door behind her.

"For me?" Prue repeated, frowning. "Who on earth would be sending me parcels?"

"I don't know, Miss," Sally said, shaking her head. "That's why I hid it from the others. I thought it... well, maybe it were personal, like?"

Prue felt a flush of heat creep up her neck for no good reason. All at once, she knew who the gift was from. She stared down at the thin, elegant box, tied with a lovely green ribbon, and her heart pounded. With a little tug the ribbon came undone and she lifted the lid. Inside were fourteen beautiful pairs of gloves, each pair a different colour. Seven pairs of long satin evening gloves and seven pairs of short kid gloves for the day. There was a card, the Duke of Bedwin's crest emblazoned on one side. Prue swallowed and turned the card over.

I believe these are happily matched pairs who show no signs of migrating south for the season. With my compliments. B

"The duke sent you those," Sally breathed, her voice full of awe. "Oh, my lamb. Whatever will you do? He's got his sights on you, he has."

Prue flushed harder and returning the card to the box, placed the lid back on with shaking fingers. "Well, he'll just have to turn them elsewhere," she said firmly, before sending the woman an anxious glance. "Don't tell them, will you, Sally?"

Sally looked affronted at the idea. "As if I would!"

Prue smiled and gave her a quick hug. "Forgive me. I don't know what came over me. Only that this wretched man puts me all out of sorts. What is he playing at, sending me such gifts? It's quite inappropriate."

"Well, he intends to marry you. That much is clear," Sally replied, her expression dithering somewhere between wistful and apprehensive.

"Over my dead body," Prue muttered and then blanched as she remembered his first wife's fate. "Well, perhaps not. But it isn't happening, and the sooner I get that across to him the better."

She hurried about the room, determined to get the wretched man out of her mind.

"Now, where are my gloves?" she queried, looking at the top of her dresser where she thought they ought to be.

Sally rolled her eyes. "Wherever you left them, Miss," she said dryly. "Which is to say, anywhere you've been."

Prue scowled a little. "It's not my fault. They walk off, and of their own accord, I'd swear it. How did that single glove end up on the raspberry bush before we left home, I ask you? Explain that to me."

"You spilt your tea on one of them in your room, washed it in the basin and left it on the windowsill to dry. The wind caught it and blew it into the garden. You didn't notice for two days."

"Oh," Prue said, a little deflated. "Is that how it got there?"

"Yes, Miss," Sally returned with a long-suffering sigh. "I'll look downstairs."

"Thank you," Prue called after her. "I shall be late if I don't leave soon."

And then they'll think I've lost my nerve.

Sally paused in the doorway. "You could wear one of those lovely new pairs," she suggested.

Prue pulled a face at her and the maid chuckled and hurried away.

***

As Prue walked the short distance to Miss Ruth Stone's front door, she glanced down at her oldest pair of gloves and sighed. Her best pair had migrated to wherever it was her gloves took themselves off to. It would have been nice to wear one of the lovely pairs the duke had sent her, she thought wistfully, but quite inappropriate.

Despite her best intentions, her thoughts returned to their conversation of last night. It had been rather fun. She'd never have been able to hold such an odd conversation with any other man, she realised. Indeed, she'd tried, which was one reason she'd discovered herself so thoroughly unmarriageable. Men thought she was odd. As she had no intention of losing her independence, she'd grown to accept the fact. She had become used to looks of bewilderment and even concern if she dared to pursue her rather eccentric thoughts to their conclusions.

Not that she cared.

His grace had looked a little bewildered himself, but he'd gone along with her, even adding to the conversation, entering into the silliness with no show of discomfort.

Was he so desperate for them to marry he'd even make himself ridiculous to please her? The idea was so outrageous she laughed aloud, earning herself a look of reproach from an elderly couple who passed her.

Bedwin didn't seem to care for her, past the fact she met certain criteria and that his uncle approved of her. She supposed she'd heard of people marrying for far worse reasons, but still. He'd just have to turn his attentions elsewhere.

For the first time, she felt a pang of something that might have been regret. Prue stopped in her tracks, earning herself a curse of reproach as a man almost ploughed into the back of her. He gave her a glare and hurried on. She watched the fellow continue on his way, startled by the sudden jolt of emotion.

Marriage had never been a part of her plan, and she'd never regretted that fact. Her mother's existence had been illustration enough of all the reasons putting one's entire life into a man's power was a terrible idea. Yet she had never allowed herself to consider what it might be like with the right man, with a good man.

She almost laughed aloud again. *A good man?* The Duke of Bedwin? *The Damned Duke* himself! What nonsense. Prue might not believe him guilty of murder, but that he had spent the last years haunting the gaming hells and revelling in vice seemed to be common knowledge.

Forcing herself to move forward again, as she was attracting unwanted attention, she wondered if his character had been the same *before* he'd married. She'd never remembered hearing anything of him before the grand wedding which had been the talk of the *ton* for weeks, amongst the rumours that the man had been caught like a fish on a line. The gossip that had circulated after the wedding, via his wife, was of cruelty and abuse. Had that been retribution for ensnaring him in such a way? Could the duke be such a man?

Prue's father had always appeared jovial, kind, and good natured in public. It was only in private that the manipulative monster raised his head. Even if her mother had protested and sought help, Prue was aware no one would have believed her. Even if they had, they would not have helped. She was her husband's property. His to do with as he saw fit.

No. The whole situation was best avoided. She would miss out on a family and she would never know what it was to have anything resembling a romantic attachment, but she had always viewed such things as brief moments of infatuation. Such feelings would likely not endure, but burn out, leaving two people with some pleasant memories and a lifetime stretching before them. Besides, she could always take a lover, she supposed. Remaining a single female living alone with nothing but a maid for propriety would make her a figure of scandal, even ridicule. She may as well make the most of it.

Her musings were at an end as Ruth's grand address came into view, and she hurried forward to join her friends.

***

Prue stared into her teacup, silent and distracted, as the girls discussed *The Damned Duke*.

"I saw him at the Hartington's ball last night," Bonnie said, sighing a little. It was a wistful sound that made Prue smile, her attention drawn back to the conversation.

"He isn't *The Damned Duke*, you know," Prue said, not knowing why she said it. Only that the more she spoke with the man, the more she suspected, or perhaps hoped, he wasn't the terrible character she'd made him out to be.

"Well, of course he is," Kitty exclaimed, looking astonished. "The Duke of Bedwin and the Duke of Bedsin? That's a feeble disguise if ever there was one."

Prue flushed a little and turned her attention back to her teacup. A stab of guilt pierced her, and she forced it away. It was only a silly story; entertainment, not the truth.

"Well, Bedwin is very handsome," Bonnie continued. "Compelling, even. All that dark hair and dark eyes. Sinful, he is." Another heartfelt sigh escaped her, and Prue frowned, unsettled by the resentful sensation that filled her at her friend's words.

"He spoke to Prue again, didn't he, Prue?"

Prue blushed and looked up, turning to Ruth, who had spoken. Her friend was smiling a little, her expression curious.

"That's the third time he's sought you out, isn't it?" Matilda asked, her voice nonchalant as she lifted her tea cup to her mouth. She looked at Prue over the rim, her beautiful blue eyes alight with mischief.

"His uncle is a dear friend of mine," Prue retorted, sounding far too defensive. "We were speaking of him. There is nothing at all intriguing about it."

Wide eyes focused on her from every quarter and she fought not to let her blush deepen further.

"Now, about this dare," she said in a rush. Anything to get their minds from Bedwin. "Are we all ready?"

"Oh, yes!" Kitty exclaimed, almost squealing with excitement. She bustled to the corner of the room and lifted a rather battered hat box. She shoved the tea tray to one side and set the box down, lifting the lid and removing a man's top hat. With a grin of triumph, she moved to Ruth. "Your dares, if you would please, ladies."

Ruth swallowed, looking like she might be sick, but reached into the folds of her gown, searching for the pocket beneath and drew out two tightly folded scraps of paper. She took a deep breath and dropped them both into the hat.

Kitty moved around the room and Prue watched as Lucia, Bonnie, Matilda, Jemima, and Harriet all followed suit. She was a little surprised to see them all taking part, despite their agreement last night. Kitty moved towards Alice, who had gone a deathly shade of white. For a moment, Prue thought she might back out but, at the last moment, she opened her reticule and snatched up her dares, throwing them into the hat with some force.

"Bravo!" Kitty said approvingly, and Alice flushed and beamed.

Prue sighed.

Kitty added her dares to the hat and Prue reached for her bag, retrieving her own folded pieces of paper. She looked up at Kitty, whose dark eyes were alight with excitement, and dropped them in.

With all the drama of a magician about to produce a rabbit, Kitty stirred the dares in the hat.

"I feel like we ought to have a drum roll," Ruth quipped, though she looked anxious and rather unsure of whether this had been such a good idea now. Prue could only agree with her.

Before she could open her mouth to suggest that this might not be such a wise course of action, Kitty had made a theatrical bow and extended the hand that held the hat so that it was squarely before Prue.

Well, dash it all.

There was no way of backing out now, not with all her friends watching with such expectations. Drat her big mouth and drat the blasted duke for putting her in such a temper that she'd spoken without thinking.

Prue took a deep breath and sunk her hand into the hat, the little folded slips of paper rustling around her fingers. *Please, please, be nothing ridiculous*, she prayed. With a sense of inevitability, and a deeper one of foreboding, she plucked a folded slip from the mix.

"I think two should pick at a time," Kitty said, as the assembled ladies held their breath. "Who else will try?"

The silence was absolute, and for a moment Prue thought she might get a reprieve. After all, if no one else was brave enough, there was no way she'd go through with it.

"I will!"

The voice was high and squeaky with mingled terror and determination. Prue stared in astonishment.

"Alice?" she exclaimed, staring at the tiny redhead.

The fragile, elfin young woman looked like she might faint at any moment, except there was a glint of determination in her eyes that Prue had never seen before.

"I'll do it," Alice said again, sounding a little surer now. She stared back at Prue, unblinking.

Kitty offered her the hat, and everyone watched in awed silence as Alice plucked out a strip of paper with trembling fingers.

"Well then," Matilda said, flapping her hands at Prue. "What did you get?"

Prue swallowed and unfolded the narrow strip of paper. She didn't recognise the handwriting, the owner of it having gone to some lengths to disguise themselves with bold capital letters. Just as well, as Prue would have been sorely tempted to box their ears.

"Well?" Ruth said, clutching as the sides of her chair with white-knuckled hands.

"Dance in a garden at midnight," Prue said, her tone sour.

"Oh!" Jemima said, the sound somewhere between awed and wistful. "What did you get, Alice?"

Prue turned to Alice who was staring at her slip of paper like it was a venomous snake.

"K-Kiss a man in the moonlight," she stammered, her pale cheeks now blazing crimson.

"Oh, for heaven's sake!" Prue said, leaping to her feet. "This is it? These are your dares? We are all intelligent young women, and all you can think of is men? Dancing and kissing? What a farce!" she seethed.

It was one thing for her to take such risks, but Alice longed for marriage, for security, and there was no way she'd be able to induce a man to kiss her in the moonlight unless she took a dreadful and possibly dangerous risk with her reputation, even her safety.

"You see," Kitty said, smirking a little. "I told you she'd not go through with it."

Prue felt her temper flare, and she turned on Kitty. "Oh, I'll do it. I'll make good on the stupid dare, no matter how ridiculous, and it *is* ridiculous, but you leave Alice out of this."

"No!"

Prue swung around, a little taken aback by the vehemence of that one word. Alice was standing, fists clenched, staring at her.

"It's my dare, not yours, Prue," Alice said, her voice quiet but firm. "I knew what I was doing, what I was risking. It's my choice, not yours. I may be small, but I am a grown-up, not a child, and I'm sick of people treating me like one."

Prue drew in a breath, realising that Alice was right. She was a woman with a brain in her head; the risks would be as obvious to her as to Prue. If she wanted to go ahead with this mad scheme, well, it was her affair.

"I'm sorry, Alice," Prue said, nodding at her. "You are right, of course only—"

"I'll be careful." Alice smiled. "Don't worry."

Prue nodded again, sick with guilt. This was her fault. If she hadn't got into that stupid argument with Kitty, if she hadn't said such awful things with no thought for the consequences.... Now one of her best friends would put herself and her reputation at risk, and for what? For a stupid dare? To kiss a man in the moonlight?

She looked around and could tell some of them thought it a romantic idea. Prue swallowed down her anger and regret, though the guilt had lodged in her chest and would not shift.

"How long do we have to complete these *dares*?" she asked, unable to keep the scathing quality from her voice.

Kitty shrugged and looked around at the others. "A week or two?" she suggested.

The women looked from one to the other, each of them nodding in turn.

"Very well," Prue said, standing and picking up her reticule. She needed to get out of here and away from her friends before she said something she regretted. Everyone else was milling about now, the women talking in excited, low voices as many of them huddled about Alice. "Good afternoon, ladies," she said, receiving some half-hearted replies as most of them returned their attention to Alice, offering advice or asking questions of her.

Prue restrained herself from rolling her eyes and headed for the door.

"Prue."

She turned to find Matilda following her. The beautiful blonde reached out a hand and took hers, giving it a brief squeeze.

"I know what it is to lose your reputation," she said, her expression grave. "Please, don't worry about Alice. I will see she comes to no harm. You have my word."

Prue looked back at her, a little surprised. Matilda and Alice had never been close, Alice too awed by the ravishing young woman to speak with her.

Yet, Matilda Hunt did know what it was to be ruined.

According to Ruth, who was closest to her, she had been ruined through no fault of her own. It had been her brother's doing, indirectly at least. It changed nothing, though. Whatever the truth, she had been caught alone with the Marquess of Montagu in a men's gambling club. Inevitably, Matilda *Hunt* had been dubbed evermore *The Huntress*, for trying to trap the marquess into marriage. That she swore she had intended no such thing was a poor defence against the tattling voices of the *ton*. Either way, Montagu had refused to be caught, and Matilda was ruined.

"How will you manage that?" Prue asked, not disbelieving as much as sceptical.

Matilda returned a rather enigmatic smile. "I have my ways," she said, glancing back at Alice, who was blossoming under the attention of the rest of the group. She looked happy and rather excited. "So, don't fret. She'll be safe."

Prue nodded, believing her. "Thank you," she said, and bade Matilda goodbye.

Chapter 9

Dear Alice,

Would you like to come to tea with me tomorrow? We so rarely have the time to talk and I should like to get to know you a little better. Do say you'll come.
—Excerpt from a letter from Miss Matilda Hunt to Miss Alice Dowding.

***

Dawn. 20th April. Upper Walpole Street. London. 1814

Prue stared up at her bedroom ceiling. London was awakening and even on their quiet street, the bustle of the city was audible.

The words of the dare turned in her head.

Dance in a garden at midnight.

Of course, by the letter of the dare, she had no need of a man. It simply said *dance*, not who with, or with anyone at all. If she were being clever, she could dance all by herself, and no one would ever be the wiser.

Yet, another idea had taken shape in her mind; one that, once considered, she was having considerable difficulty in putting aside.

The Duke of Bedwin wished to dance with her. He had asked her twice, in fact. He'd sent her fourteen pairs of gloves with a funny little note, all tied up in pretty ribbon.

Prue frowned, remembering the odd and rather unpleasant sensation that had assailed her when Bonnie had sighed and mooned over him. It had been a rather possessive emotion, something horribly close to jealousy.

She winced in the dim light of her room. Oh no.

No. No. No.

She was not, repeat *not,* developing feelings for the Duke of Bedwin. *Good heavens.* After everything she had promised herself about keeping her independence, about never, *ever* allowing herself to end up in a situation akin to her mother's.... There wasn't a worse choice of husband in the entire country, if that was her goal.

Yet she could not deny Bonnie's words. The duke was a handsome man, compelling even, and when she spoke to him, she found it hard to equate him to the man his reputation suggested he was.

Just like your bloody father, she told herself. *Men are liars. They show the world one face; their nearest and dearest see quite another.*

Despite her words and her certainty, her heart was a belligerent creature and she felt the denial of that truth echoing there. *He's not like that,* the foolish organ told her.

He's different.

Prue snorted. If there was one thing she knew was not to be trusted, it was anything resembling romantic feelings. Sentiment could twist good sense around its little finger and lead the most intelligent woman on the road to their own destruction. She'd seen her mother on the twisting road time after time, each time with the same outcome.

No.

The duke needed to be put off, put in his place. He needed to see that Prue was far from his ideal of quiet and sensible and scandal-free. Then he would leave her alone, and she could be comfortable again.

She didn't need him coming in and upsetting her plans, making her doubt them and unsettling her peace of mind. Prue certainly did not need him to awaken her heart to the kind of romantic dreams she had never allowed herself to consider. That was the most dangerous thing about him, and she needed it to stop before she found herself discontent with her lot and yearning for things she'd long forbidden herself to contemplate.

So, she had a plan. If you could call the nonsensical idea by such a grand name. Prue shook her head and sighed. Well, whatever it was, it was her way to get what she wanted. She would complete her dare, show the duke she was far from the well-behaved miss he wanted to marry, and perhaps get some more ideas for her story. She was reluctant to admit it, but the next chapter was eluding her.

Her hero seemed an insipid creation, far less interesting than the duke, whom everyone seemed to be desperately in love with. What strange creatures women were. Why did they love *The Damned Duke* so, when he was so obviously rotten to the core?

Except, the more she went back and reread what she'd written about the blasted man to date, the more she saw his motivation. He'd lashed out because a woman had hurt him. She had broken his heart, humiliated him in public, and he sought revenge for it. His actions were selfish, and certainly ill-judged, but perhaps understandable. Was he really as evil as she had intended to make him? After all, he must get his comeuppance. She had contrived a wonderfully gruesome death for him, too.

Now, however, she felt the first stirrings of anxiety that there might be a backlash from heartbroken women the length and breadth of the country if she killed him off. Worse than that, she wasn't even sure she *wanted* to kill him off. There was a strong part of her that would far rather murder the dull hero, for whom she could never find as much empathy, or interest in, as she could the duke.

Oh, what a muddle.

Well, perhaps if she was outrageous enough with the real-life duke, he'd be so disgusted and disappointed in her that he'd show her how obnoxious he could be. Perhaps he'd behave as badly as he ought to and show her his true colours? Then everything could go back to normal. She'd have inspiration for the ending of her story, complete her dare for her friends' edification, and get on with her life.

Yes.

It might not be a grand plan, but it had merit, and she would put it into action at once.

***

Prue, for perhaps the first time in her life, took pains with her appearance that night. Instead of dragging a comb through her hair and arranging it with more haste than judgement, she allowed Sally to take the time to curl it and create a style for her. She chose her best dress, a deep emerald green satin, and even applied a touch of perfume. At Sally's insistence, she added a delicate pearl necklace and matching ear-bobs.

At the last minute, and ignoring the wide-eyed expression of her maid, she sought out the gift box, and chose a pair of long, white satin evening gloves.

"Well," said Sally, staring at Prue with sparkling eyes. "I never saw you look so well, Miss. You look right pretty, you do indeed."

Prue smiled, turning to take a last look at the glass on her dressing table.

"Not too shabby, at least," she returned, grinning. She felt rather pretty, it was true. Oh, she'd never climb the height of beauty that lovely Minerva could claim, but she could not help that and felt no desire to lament the fact.

Once downstairs, Prue smiled at the astonishment on the faces of both her aunt and Minerva that she was not only ready, but looking presentable. She even had gloves on.

"Why, Prue," Minerva said, getting to her feet. "You do look nice."

Prue stilled, a little startled by the compliment. "Thank you," she said, smiling at her cousin. "Not as lovely as you, of course, but it's nice of you to say so."

Minerva beamed and looked down at her gown, which was a rich pink and very becoming. "It's a lovely colour, isn't it?" she said, though when she looked up there was a glint of anxiety in her eyes. "I hope it was worth it."

Prue decided she'd not ask how much the dress cost. She could take a good guess, and that was frightening enough as she knew how slender her aunt's purse was.

"Still hoping to catch a duke?" she asked, the words soft rather than mocking.

For a moment Minerva stared at her, an adversarial light in her eyes, but then she sighed and shook her head. "I don't think so," she said, glancing over her shoulder to see if Phyllis was listening.

Prue watched her with curiosity, wondering for the first time how afraid Minerva was of her mother. How much of her behaviour was motivated by her own desires, and how much by her mother's ambitions?

"You certainly look like a duchess tonight," Prue said, wanting to reward Minerva's honesty with her own. Though the thought of her anywhere near Bedwin made that unpleasant sensation stir in her chest again.

Minerva smiled at the compliment, more delighted by it than Prue might have credited.

"I don't think he's interested," Minerva admitted. "Though please don't tell mama I said so," she added, blanching a little.

"Of course not." Prue shook her head and reached out to squeeze her fingers. "I would never do that."

Minerva looked relieved and gave Prue a searching look, as though she was debating this new *entente* between them. "Mr Bradbury was very nice to me, and most attentive," she offered, brightening. "He's very rich," she added with a wistful tone.

"*Mr* Bradbury?" her aunt said in disgust, entering the conversation as Minerva jolted with alarm. Neither of them had heard her approach. "We are not about to throw away your assets on a mere *Mr*," the woman exclaimed, shaking her head and giving Minerva a scathing look. "You must try harder with the duke, girl. If you were a little more forthcoming, he'd take more notice of you."

Minerva flushed, a rather belligerent look in her eyes. "Yes, Mama," she said, though there was a rigid set to her jaw.

Their aunt hurried from the room to fetch her cloak and Prue hesitated. She'd never been close to Minerva, the two of them chalk and cheese, but she knew her Aunt Phyllis was a rather difficult woman to countermand.

"Is he nice, your Mr Bradbury?" she asked, studying Minerva's face.

Minerva shrugged, all the sparkle gone from her eyes. "Nicer than the others. He speaks to me, converses *with* me rather than talking at me or just… just looking…." She blushed and gave another shrug. "I'd better fetch my cloak."

Prue watched her go and wondered what would become of Minerva. She would not catch Bedwin, that was for sure. The duke had looked almost disgusted when she'd suggested it to him, though she couldn't fathom why. Minerva was beautiful and, once out from under her mother's influence, Prue suspected she'd be rather easier to live with. Still, it was their business, not hers. She'd be gone soon enough, out from under their roof, and she doubted either of them would want to have anything to do with her once that happened.

She had other things on her mind this evening, in any case. With a sudden rush of nerves, Prue gathered her own cloak and followed her aunt and Minerva out to the waiting carriage.

***

8pm. 20th April. At a ball given by Jasper Cadogan, the Earl of St Clair.

By the time Prue entered the ballroom, she felt sick and jittery. Despite telling herself that faint heart never chased away an aggravating duke, her stomach had tied itself in knots and she felt all on edge.

She realised two things over the following hour.

Firstly, she'd never been so nervous in all her life. She cared little for people's opinions, and other than finding the season rather a waste of time, she was content to people watch and gather ideas and information for her work.

Secondly, she discovered that when she was nervous she talked too much.

Prue was certain she was speaking utter nonsense, but the strangest thing was that it seemed to be gaining her attention. The more she babbled and laughed, the more people were drawn to her. She was asked to dance no less than three times in a row by quite presentable, even eligible young men. They had come to flock about Minerva, of course, but Prue ended up filling her dance card just as fast as her cousin.

Minerva looked over at her, a little startled. "You're in high spirits tonight," she said, her astonishment obvious. "I've never seen you enjoy yourself so much. Usually you're moping about with the wallflowers."

Prue frowned. Was that what she did? Moped? She'd never thought so, and... *was* she enjoying herself?

At that moment a rather earnest young man with large ears and freckles held out his hand to her. "My dance, I believe Miss Chuffington-Smythe?"

She took it, recognising him as a good-natured fellow with whom she had chatted earlier in the evening.

"So it is," she replied, smiling at him.

Yes, she decided, feeling more than a little surprised by the realisation. Yes, she was enjoying herself a good deal. She looked back at Minerva, who waved at her, grinning as the Earl of St Clair sought her hand for the next dance.

Prue beamed, pleased for her cousin and feeling almost affectionate towards her. She and the earl made a rather dashing couple. No doubt Aunt Phyllis was already making plans for the wedding breakfast, she thought with a chuckle. He wasn't a duke, perhaps, but still… an earl wasn't *such* a comedown.

It was close to ten o'clock when she made her way to the refreshments room. She had known Bedwin would not appear much before eleven. He always arrived late. It was a good couple of hours before supper, though, and all the unexpected dancing had given her a thirst. That being the case, she gave a start of surprise as the duke appeared before her, holding a glass of lemonade.

"I suspected, after your strenuous activities this evening, that you might require refreshments," he said, offering her the glass.

Prue stared at him. She realised she was surprised, not only by the thoughtful gesture, but also that he had been here for some time, and that he'd been observing her.

"Thank you, your grace. You are most kind."

His eyes fell to the gloves she wore, and he smiled a little. Not the spontaneous, boyish smile that had stolen her breath some evenings earlier, but a smile that touched his eyes, chasing back some of the cynicism and wickedness that seemed to linger in his expression.

"They pleased you?" he asked, his voice soft.

"They did," she said, nodding. "Though quite inappropriate, as I'm sure you well know."

He held her gaze, unblinking. "But my intentions are honourable, as *you* well know."

Despite herself, Prue felt a rush of heat under his piercing gaze. He was devilishly handsome tonight, those dark eyes full of promises, and that sinful mouth…. Desire bloomed in such a low and intimate part of her that she blushed.

With a jolt of shock, Prue tore her gaze away.

"Do excuse me," she said, in a rush. "My dance partner will be looking for me."

Prue turned, hoping to hurry away. Though she would need to see him again tonight for her plan to be put into action, she had to hold him off until midnight.

"Am I to be denied the honour of dancing with you yet again?" he demanded, and Prue turned back to him, noting a glint of irritation in his eyes.

She spread her hands out in an apologetic gesture. "I'm afraid you're too late, your grace. My dance card is uncharacteristically full," she said, smirking a little. She held his gaze, forcing her expression into something she hoped was flirtatious and feeling quite idiotic. *Hold your nerve*, she thought to herself. Prue gave a heavy sigh and glanced up at him from under her lashes. "But perhaps something could be done about that… if you want to dance with me so very badly?"

A flicker of surprise registered in his expression and she laughed, surprising him further as she tossed her blonde curls and hurried away.

***

Robert watched Miss Chuffington-Smythe rush away from him, feeling more than a little perturbed. Not that it seemed to be an unusual sensation in the young woman's presence. She never quite said or did what he expected of her. He wasn't certain if that was a complaint or not.

Something about tonight was different, though. Something about *her* was different.

Perhaps it was her hair. Whenever he'd seen her before now, it always appeared a little haphazard, as though she'd dealt with it as a matter of urgency. It was one thing that appealed to him about her, strange as that was. There was nothing remotely vain about her. She was herself, with a quiet sense of style that seemed to care little for fashion, though he knew economy had a good deal to do with that outlook.

He remembered Lavinia then, and the eternity she'd take preparing for a ball. She had spent hours gazing at herself in the looking glass, trying out first one style, then another, and asking endless questions as to which one became her most. God help you if you didn't answer correctly or showed any sign of boredom. Of course, at first, he'd been content to gaze upon her like a besotted moon calf… until it had come home to him that her efforts were not made on his behalf, or even just her own.

Lavinia's father had used her like a pawn in a game, manoeuvring her this way and that to get her the title of duchess and, by default, get himself close to a man with such wealth and power.

Once she'd achieved his end, Lavinia had refused to acknowledge her father ever again. Robert had sympathised with this and encouraged it once he'd discovered the plot. He'd forgiven her for it and told her she was free of her father now, that they could be happy despite the way they'd begun, but Lavinia wanted none of it—wanted none of *him*. She'd never cared for him, she said; she thought him a bore. His love of the countryside was tedious and she needed constant entertainment. Lavinia wanted parties and life, she wanted to be admired and loved and fought over. Well, by god, she'd got what she wanted. Right up until the day she'd broken her lovely neck.

"Evening, Bedwin."

Robert looked around and nodded as Jasper Cadogan, Earl of St Clair and the host of this evening's festivities, hailed him.

"St Clair," Robert replied, his smile warm.

The earl was one of the few men whose friendship he'd kept throughout his disastrous first marriage. Despite a reputation with the ladies, St Clair had never betrayed their friendship, though Lavinia had tried hard to snare him. There was no question why she'd wanted to. He was one of the biggest prizes among the *ton*, handsome, wealthy, and titled. Jasper Cadogan was Robert's opposite in every way. He was light to Robert's dark, and not simply in their colouring. Where he glowered, St Clair laughed. He was popular and well liked, unlike Robert.

Not that it had always been that way.

"Rumour has it you're in the market for a wife?" St Clair remarked, a cautious look in his usually smiling eyes.

Robert shrugged. "An heir and a spare. You know the rules. What choice do I have?"

The earl leaned against the marble pillar at his side, the picture of aristocratic nonchalance. "You have someone in mind?"

"Perhaps," Robert replied, noncommittal.

St Clair followed his gaze. Miss Chuffington-Smythe was dancing with some lanky looking fellow with large ears. Not handsome or well made, Robert noted with some pleasure, though the two of them seemed to be having a fine time. She was laughing, her eyes sparkling with pleasure. What the devil had got into her tonight?

"Who is she?" St Clair demanded. Robert glanced at him. He was watching her, a considering glint in his eyes. "I don't remember seeing her before, let alone inviting her."

"Miss Chuffington-Smythe," Robert said, strangely reluctant to give the information over.

St Clair smiled. "Oh, yes. Isn't she one of the odd ones who lurk on the outskirts? I wouldn't have recognised her."

Robert bristled a little at the description but agreed she was, irritated to realise he'd been thinking much the same thing.

"She's a lively one tonight, though," St Clair mused. "Something's changed. Perhaps she's fallen in love."

A jolt of something unpleasant shot through Robert and he frowned. He wasn't vain enough to suppose that the girl had fallen in love with him. She wouldn't even dance with him, damn her. Was that because she was already taken? She'd never given that as a reason for her refusal to marry him, though.

He didn't get another opportunity to speak to her, however. Miss Chuffington-Smythe danced every dance and gave him a wide berth wherever she could. It was close to midnight before he got anywhere near her. He'd hoped to arrange things so he could sit with her at supper, which St Clair had told him would be informal and was being served at half past the hour. Yet as he moved to seek her out, she found him.

She appeared from out of the crowds, flushed from the exertions of the evening, her eyes sparkling, almost feverish. Robert thought for the first time that she wasn't as plain as he'd believed. In fact, she was attractive.

"Do you still wish to dance with me?" she asked, sounding breathless, her voice an urgent undertone.

"Of course," he replied, a little startled. "But the dancing is over."

She shook her head, a determined movement as he became aware she had pressed a slip of paper into his hand.

"I dare you," she said, and then gave a little laugh, as if she couldn't believe she'd said it. Before he could reply, she'd hurried away.

Robert curled his fingers about the paper and moved back, seeking a private spot away from prying eyes. Once he was certain he was unobserved, he raised the crumpled slip to read the strangely bold writing.

Dance in a garden at midnight.

What the devil?

He stared at the message, nonplussed. Why on earth would she want to do such a thing? Most women would want to dance with him in full view of the *ton*. A duke, even one whose reputation was as tarnished as his was, could only elevate their consequence. Dancing with him alone in a garden, however… she'd be ruined if they were discovered. Why risk it when he had offered her marriage? What did she have to gain?

Unless the illicit nature of it gave her a thrill.

A shiver of unease rolled down his spine. That was exactly the kind of thing Lavinia would have adored. He knew that all too well. He'd caught her at it.

Robert crumpled the note in his hand. There was something going on here. Something he didn't understand and liked even less.

Furthermore, she could have been a little more specific. The gardens around St Clair's vast London home were bloody enormous. How the devil was he supposed to find her? Feeling increasingly irritated, he considered the grounds. There was a private garden, a beautiful spot with a fountain that any woman with romantic notions would surely approve of. He'd just have to try there first.

Chapter 10

Do you ever feel like your life is spinning out of control? That all your careful plans are unravelling and coming apart like a torn hem? What if you can't mend it? What if you discover you're not even sure you want to?

—Excerpt from a letter from Miss Prunella Chuffington-Smythe to Miss Matilda Hunt.

***

Midnight. 20ᵗʰ April. A garden. At a ball given by Jasper Cadogan, the Earl of St Clair.

You're an idiot, Prue cursed herself as she lurked in the shadows. *What on earth made you think this was a good idea? Even if he comes, he might not find the right garden. Why didn't you give him instructions, for heaven's sake?*

Though, surely, this was the obvious choice. It was a lovely spot, small and intimate with a large three-tiered fountain at the centre. It was closed in on all sides by thick hedges, and lit by lanterns, their soft light warming the darkened space, and making shadows dance as a breeze rustled the leaves. There were only two ways in and out of the garden, and Prue lingered in a shadowy corner on the opposite side she expected the duke to arrive from, assuming he found her. Assuming he came at all.

He came.

Her breath caught as he entered the space, looking somehow larger and broader than she'd ever seen him, which was utterly nonsensical, she assured herself. He was the same size he always was. Her reassurances did not stop her heart from pounding, though, or her eyes from denying the truth. He was larger and broader, more powerful than she'd ever noticed before, and she was an idiot for ever thinking this could be a good idea.

"Are you going to hide there all night?" he said, his tone suggesting he was bored by her already. "I thought you wanted to dance?"

"You are the one who wanted to dance, your grace," Prue said, finding her courage rise with indignation at his cool manner. She had the sudden urge to shake him out of it, to make him angry. That was why she was here, after all, to give him a disgust of her, so he'd leave her be. "I have done nothing but give you the opportunity. If you don't wish to take it, I am not about to delay you."

There was a taut silence.

"Come where I can see you."

Prue folded her arms. "I'm not yours to order about."

She heard a sigh of irritation and smirked in the darkness. "You ordered me to come here didn't you? If you can do it, so can I."

"I did not order you," she said, the words precise and clipped. "I dared you. There is a significant difference."

"Very well. Miss Chuffington-Smythe, please would you reveal yourself? I cannot dance with a shadow."

Prue swallowed down her nerves and stepped into the lamplight. "You're always in the shadows, though," she said, watching him, the golden glow illuminating the harsh planes of his face. He did look a devil tonight. "Your life of late is lived entirely in shadow, in the gambling dens, with ladies of the night."

"Is that so?" he asked, the bored tone still lacing his voice. "I see you know everything about me."

She laughed then, shaking her head. "I know nothing about you. Only the parts you wish the world to see and judge you on."

He scowled at that. "You think I want them to judge me?"

Prue smiled, pleased that the affectation of boredom had slipped, revealing a thread of anger in his voice.

"I think you believe they already have. You've just been giving them what they expect."

He stepped towards her and she faced him, her certainty he had not increased in size shaken further by his proximity.

"My God, you're not a bleeding heart, thinking I'm really romantic and sweet and that I've been misunderstood all this time?"

He sounded revolted by the idea, and she laughed.

"Not in the least. I think—murder notwithstanding—that you've done plenty to earn your reputation, your grace. I'm just not certain you enjoy it as much as everyone would like to believe."

He let out a breath, holding her gaze. "You're remarkably perceptive."

Prue said nothing in reply, feeling her heartbeat as an erratic thud in her chest.

"Well then, are we going to dance?" he asked.

"I don't know, you've not asked me to."

He snorted and folded his arms. "I've asked you several times and been refused."

"I won't refuse," she replied, a little annoyed that the words had sounded rather breathless, almost eager. Almost as if she wanted to dance with him.

She watched him step closer, holding out his hand to her. "Miss Chuffington-Smythe — that really is an awful mouthful, you know," he said, startling her a little.

"I know," she said with a sigh. "You have no idea what a burden it is. It's possibly the only thing that would induce me to marry, just to be rid of it."

"The only thing," he repeated, staring down at her. "I do not understand why you are so opposed to the idea."

Prue looked up at him then. "Would you wish to marry again, if you didn't need an heir?" He opened his mouth and she raised her hand, stopping him. "Tell the truth," she demanded.

For a moment she thought he wouldn't answer.

"No," he said at last. "No, I don't believe I would if I didn't have to."

She nodded, satisfied. "There you are, then."

"No, it's not the same," he objected. "You've never been married."

Prue shrugged. "No, but I've had first-hand experience of what it can mean, how it can trap a woman. I'll not be trapped. Not ever. Not by anyone."

"You'll be trapped if anyone discovers us here," he pointed out, curiosity glinting in those dark eyes now. Prue stared up at him, wishing the shadows would lift, wishing she could see the green that seemed to change depending on the light. They were far darker now, almost black; "We'll have to marry then."

"No, we won't," she said, smiling at him. "I'll just be ruined. It's not at all the same thing."

"You'd rather that?" He looked shocked, perplexed, and possibly even a little hurt. "You'd rather ruin yourself than take a chance with me?"

"Yes," she said, the answer simple enough. "I would."

His jaw tightened a little, but he said nothing further on the subject.

"Will you dance with me?" he asked then, and she could read neither his expression nor his tone.

"Yes."

He moved her into the position for a waltz, though there was no music and, for a moment, Prue felt ridiculous... until she didn't. Until she was all at once terribly aware of him, of the heat of him burning through his clothes, of the scent of fresh linen and soap and leather. Many of the men she had danced with tonight had worn more perfume than she did, the scents rather dizzying at close quarters. The duke smelled strangely wholesome in comparison, which was the last thing she'd expected.

What *had* she expected, she wondered? Should he have smelt of sin and sex? Yes, she thought, a frisson of something she did not wish to put a name to shivering over her.

"You're cold," he murmured, drawing her a little closer.

Prue shook her head. She wasn't the least bit cold, not now, but she moved closer to him all the same.

"Your parents."

She frowned at his words, looking up at him. "What of them?"

"Your parents were not happily married."

"No." Prue looked away from him. "No, they were not."

He paused then, and she felt the weight of his gaze forcing her to lift her head, to meet his eyes.

"My father was a bully," she said, wondering why she felt the need to tell him, but believing she perhaps owed him some explanation for her refusal, for her words of rejection. "A manipulative bully."

"He...." She watched as he reconsidered his words, perhaps wondered if he should voice them at all. "He hurt your mother?"

Prue nodded, her throat tight.

"I'm sorry," he said, such regret in those simple words that she felt the sting of tears. Such emotions froze however, as he lifted one hand to her face, stroking her cheek with his thumb. "If that is what holds you back... I would never hurt you. I would never, ever, lift a finger to you. I give you my word."

Prue blinked, her throat working as she tried to steady herself. "That's what my father said, after every single time he hurt her. He would cry and beg for forgiveness, tell her how much he loved her, that he would never, ever hurt her again, he'd rather die. They'd be happy for a while—a few weeks, a month—and then he'd do it again."

He nodded, understanding in his eyes. "You don't believe me."

"Men lie," she said, with rather more venom than she'd intended.

"Not all men," he countered, and there was something soft in his expression, something that, in that moment, she longed to believe in, to take at face value... but she didn't dare.

The dance moved them in slow sweeps around the garden, the movement hypnotic, their only music the soft splash of the fountain, the rustle of her skirts, her heart beating far too fast.

"Of all the men I might risk giving myself to," she said, needing him to agree with her, at least to understand her. "Do you think one with your reputation for cruelty is my best choice?" There was no condemnation in the question, no intention to wound, only a simple query of truth.

He stared down at her, his expression shuttered and his reaction impossible to gauge. "And if I swore to you that every word was a lie, that I have never raised a hand to a woman, that I never would, it would mean nothing to you?"

"How could it?" she said, wondering why she wanted it to mean something, why she could hear the truth so clearly in his words and yet could never trust them. "I don't know you."

"Perhaps you should get to know me better, then?" he suggested, and her breath caught as he moved closer, lowering his head towards hers. "Give me a chance, at least."

"And find myself falling for a bad man?" she retorted, though it didn't sound at all like a retort, it sounded frightened and unsure and breathless.

"Could you fall for a bad man?" he asked, something urgent in the question.

"I—" She stopped, arrested by the look in his eyes. "Are you going to kiss me?" she exclaimed, too surprised by the desire she was seeing not to say it aloud… too loudly, in fact.

The flicker of a smile glinted in his eyes. "I was considering the idea, yes," he admitted. "If you will allow it," he added, the words husky. "I would like to."

Prue swallowed, alarmed and excited, and knowing this was the worst idea she'd ever had—daring him to dance with her in a garden at midnight aside. Yet she wanted him to kiss her, more than anything. Her gaze fell to his mouth, and she could do nothing but lick her lips as longing flooded her.

"Yes," she whispered.

He closed the distance between them, and she hardly dared breathe, *couldn't* breathe as his lips brushed hers. It was the barest of touches, like the faintest press of silk against her skin. Goodness, his lips were soft. She'd not expected that.

The movement came again, that gentle press of his mouth to hers, a little firmer this time, and then again. This time he kissed her upper lip, then the lower, and then she sucked in a breath at the

---

warmth of his tongue. She opened to him without even thinking about it, about what they were doing, or about the consequences.

Her thoughts were scattered and gone, nothing in their place but instinct and some heated force within her. It flamed to life as his tongue teased and invited, urging her to join this intimate exchange. It was an invitation she could not resist, her own curiosity and need reacting to instinct. She raised her arms and threaded them about his neck as he deepened the kiss further, her fingers finding the warmth and silk of his hair.

Prue pressed closer to him, some faint voice in her head urging her to have caution as another, far louder demand insisted on more, *more, take more.*

The duke made a harsh sound, his arms tightening about her, one hand dropping to her hip and pulling her close. He wanted her. The realisation was startling somehow, which was odd, as he'd been pursuing her from the beginning, though she'd known it had been because she fit his criteria. That was the only reason. The practical need for a no-nonsense girl who would not cause him trouble. She almost laughed. Little did he know.

But whatever his criteria, he wanted her, and the feeling was powerful. It fed her own wants, her own desires, and the truth it revealed startled her. She wanted him too.

That thought brought her back to reality and she drew away, pushing at his chest. He released her at once, though one hand still rested on her hip. He was breathing hard, his hair ruffled, his mouth reddened from their kiss. Prue felt a jolt of desire so fierce she had to step further away, raising her hand to her mouth as if to assure herself it still belonged to her, that it would still obey her will.

His hands fell to his sides, and he made no attempt to return her to his embrace.

"I-I must go now," she said, her voice unsteady, her breathing as harsh and erratic as his.

He nodded his understanding, his eyes never leaving hers.

Prue licked her lips, disheartened to discover she didn't want to quit his company. Good lord, but this man was dangerous. With difficulty she forced herself to remember why she was here, why she'd done it at all.

"May I have something of yours?" she said in a rush. She needed proof of this meeting for the girls or they would never believe her. "Just to remember this evening by."

He looked surprised at that, something that might have been pleasure in his eyes and she experienced a pang of remorse. "For example?"

Prue shrugged. She hadn't thought this part through. What could he give? To her surprise she didn't need to answer as he drew off his ring, the one that bore the Bedwin seal.

"Oh, no," she protested. "That's too precious. I—"

"You can give it back," he said, smiling as he held it out to her. "Next time we meet. I'll exchange it for something more appropriate."

Prue stared at him, the warmth of his words and that smile easing over her like the heat of a fire, welcoming and comforting.

Next time we meet.

Except that there wouldn't be a next time. She couldn't allow it. The risks were becoming too high. She'd find another way to return it to him.

"Thank you, your grace," she said, unsettled, aware that there was too much deception here, a hidden agenda of which he was unaware,

Her thoughts were in turmoil, regret and guilt and heaven alone knew what else flooding her, overwhelming her senses. She wanted at once to run as far as she could from him, and at the same moment to launch herself back into his arms and demand he kiss her again.

"Robert," he replied, reaching out one hand to touch her face for a moment before dropping it and stepping back. "My name is Robert."

"Robert," she repeated, finding it strange to think of him as anything other than *your grace,* or *the duke.*

"Prunella," he said in return, smiling and looking amused. "If I may?"

She grimaced and shook her head. "Prue, never Prunella."

"Prue, then," he said, and the sound of her name shivered over her, said low and intimate as it was. "I shan't ask you again tonight but... does this mean you will consider me a little less harshly?"

She stared at him, suddenly afraid, afraid that this charming, handsome man could trap her as her mother had been trapped. Fear overrode desire, bringing her back to reality with a bump.

"No," she said, the word harder and more definitive than perhaps she'd intended, but there was no point in saying it any other way. "I have to go," she mumbled, unwilling to meet his eye, afraid he might see something in her expression that would prove her a liar.

She didn't dare stay a moment longer but walked to the gap in the hedge she had come through and hurried away.

Chapter 11

Dearest Prue,

I don't know what has happened to plunge you into confusion, but I know this; life is uncertain, and we must take our opportunities where we can, how we can. If you find something true, even if it is not where you expected to find it, for heaven's sake grab hold of it and don't let go. Change your plans! Who cares if it rips at the seams of propriety, of what is expected of us? Who cares if it is not what you thought you wanted? What use are plans if they do not adapt when things change around you? Love and happiness are too precious to risk losing. You may not get another chance at it and a lifetime is too long to spend regretting.

—Excerpt of a letter from Miss Matilda Hunt to Miss Prunella Chuffington-Smythe.

***

Long after midnight the same night. 21ˢᵗ April. A garden. At a ball given by Jasper Cadogan, the Earl of St Clair.

Robert watched Prue hurry away from him, unsure of what it was he was feeling. That determined little *no* had hit him harder than he cared to admit. At least he understood her reasoning now. She wasn't just afraid of him, she was afraid of any man ever having control over her, over her life. If he wanted them to marry, he would need to prove himself trustworthy.

He sighed as he realised; he wanted them to marry, though his reasoning was not as clear cut as he'd imagined. That kiss had shaken him.

The one thing he'd not needed, hadn't wanted in his next marriage was anything resembling love or lust. For practical reasons, he had no intention of marrying a woman he neither liked nor could find anything attractive about. He needed an heir for heaven's sake, and a woman to raise his children, but Lavinia had taught him the dangers of being blinded by desire.

Not that it was anything like that with Prunella—Prue, he corrected—but that kiss had still rattled him. The passion of it had taken him by surprise. *Her* passion had surprised him. Tonight's odd behaviour—*odder* behaviour—aside, Prue had been ensconced firmly among the wallflowers since her come out, according to his uncle. He had expected a chaste little peck on the lips followed by furious blushing.

What he got had stolen his breath and made him want to tumble her into a dark corner and stay there until they were both coming apart at the seams.

Robert drew in an uneven breath. Miss Chuffington-Smythe was full of surprises, and he wasn't entirely sure that was a good thing. What, for example, had she wanted something of his for? At first the idea had charmed him, and he'd wanted to please her, to make it a romantic gesture by giving her his ring. It had seemed appropriate as he intended to propose again soon, yet her reaction hadn't been as he'd hoped. Then that hard little "no" in answer to his question had baffled and hurt him. It seemed a little peculiar, that demand to remember the evening when she refused to consider him as a suitor.

As if she was playing games.

His jaw tightened, anxiety tensing his muscles. Robert didn't like games. He'd lost too many to Lavinia. He'd wanted Prue to be straightforward, for their courtship to be simple and no nonsense, and short. Now he felt he was part of something he didn't understand, and he didn't like it one bit. Though he had liked her kiss... he'd liked that a good deal.

Frowning over the strange events of the evening, he returned to the house, making his way back to the dining room and determining to question his uncle once more. He knew Prue better than Robert could pretend to; perhaps he could shed light on her behaviour. Until they met again, it was all he could do.

***

The morning of the 21st April. Beverwyck. London. 1814

Robert greeted his uncle as he sat down to a late breakfast, and Charles smiled at him.

"Good morning, did the St Clair ball entertain?" Charles asked, accepting a cup of coffee from a footman.

Robert frowned, looking down at his plate. "It was certainly a lively affair," he said, wondering how to broach the subject of Prue's behaviour with him. The old man had implied that he was exceedingly fond of the young woman and regarded her in the light of a favourite grandchild. How he would react to the events of last night, Robert was not at all sure, but he needed advice. "Miss Chuffington-Smythe was there," he said, avoiding his uncle's eye.

"Ah, and which way does the wind blow in that quarter?" Charles asked, smiling a little as he helped himself to a serving of kedgeree.

"From Arctic to Saharan and back again," Robert replied, deciding that honesty was his only choice if he wanted to hear anything helpful.

"Arctic doesn't entirely surprise me," Charles said, looking up with a curious glint in his eye. "Your reputation precedes you, my boy. Saharan, though?"

For a moment Robert hesitated, unwilling to damage Prue's reputation before one who cared for her.

"Spit it out," Charles said, shaking his head. "I do not believe Miss Chuffington-Smythe to be either a paragon or a temptress, and I do remember what it was to be young." This last was said with just a touch of severity and Robert gathered his courage.

"You remember everything we discussed," he began, sitting back to meet his uncle's eye, "about the kind of wife I wanted this time?"

"Of course," Charles agreed, nodding.

"Miss Chuffington-Smythe dared me to meet her at midnight, in the gardens, and dance with her."

"Did she now?" His uncle's eyebrows lifted a little, the corner of his mouth twitching up. "And?"

Robert cleared his throat. "And... I met her. We danced. We also talked and I discovered the reasoning behind her reluctance to marry."

He watched as Charles' face darkened. "Her father," he said, with obvious disgust. "Now there was a bastard. Married above his station and never forgave his poor wife for being better than him. And no," he added, his voice harsher still, "I'm not a snob and neither was she. He was. A nasty piece of work if ever there was one. Handy with his fists, too, from what I heard."

"Prue said as much." Robert felt his guts clench. Of all the things the *ton* had accused him of, that one had hurt him the most, somehow more than murdering his wife. Murdering a flighty and spiteful creature like Lavinia in a fit of passion was an idea he could find some sympathy with after what she'd put him through. Beating his wife without provocation and on a regular basis, though....

The rumours of cruelty had begun shortly after their marriage and had been blatant lies. Raising his hand to any woman for any reason was something he'd always believed repugnant. To be falsely accused from his wife's own mouth, through rumour and gossip... that had been intolerable.

"Prue?" Charles repeated, smiling now at the familiar use of her name. "You mentioned a Saharan wind I think?"

Robert snorted. "I kissed her and—" Damn it, how did he explain this without making her sound like she was no better than she ought to be? Yet, wasn't that precisely what he wanted to reassure himself about? "And she did not behave as I expected. What did she mean by daring me to meet her, to dance with her, and then kissing me like… like…?" He trailed off, appalled to feel heat creeping up his neck. "I'll not make another mistake, Uncle. I… I just can't."

Charles looked at him, sympathy in his eyes. He at least had never been fooled by Lavinia. He'd seen through her from the first.

"Miss Chuffington-Smythe is everything I told you she was, Robert," he said firmly. "She will make you a fine wife, and be a good and loving mother. I know she would be a faithful wife, loyal to her husband, especially if she has given her heart to him. I realise, however, that you'll have a fight on your hands to gain it. Her father has given her a deep mistrust of men and no desire to marry. Yet, she is a young woman like any other; no doubt last night's frivolity was a desire for romance. Women like to be courted, Robert. Indeed, everyone, you included, needs a little romance in their lives."

"That is the last thing I need," Robert snapped, annoyed now. "I told you I wanted none of that. I told you I did not want a woman to love, or to love me. I simply need a wife I can tolerate, with whom I can agree on the raising of our children, of my heir, and that's all."

Charles let out a breath; a pitying look accompanied the sound, and raised Robert's hackles still further. "Then find your own bride and leave Miss Chuffington-Smythe alone. If you can't be bothered to do the thing properly, to secure your own and her happiness, then I'll have no part in it."

"You never implied I must make the blasted girl love me when we spoke," Robert protested, stung by the remark. "You said she was a sensible young woman!"

"As she is!" his uncle threw back with more force than Robert had been expecting. His anger was palpable. "Sensible enough not to tie herself to a man who doesn't give a snap of his fingers for her happiness. Now, do as you will, Robert, it's your affair, but leave me to eat my breakfast in peace. You're giving me indigestion."

Robert got to his feet in silence. Only his uncle would ever dare speak to him so, leaving him feeling rather more like a scolded boy than the Duke of Bedwin. He knew he could make the point of his rank, and Charles would be forced to apologise. If he did so, however, he would damage one of the few close relationships that mattered a damn to him, and so he held his tongue. He was halfway to the door when Charles spoke again.

"I'm fond of that girl, Robert, and I think you two could be happy together, but if you hurt her, I'll never forgive you."

Robert bowed his head in acknowledgement, and left the room.

***

The morning of the 21st of April. At the residence of Miss Ruth Stone. Upper Walpole Street. London 1814.

"Well?" exclaimed the young women in varying tones of breathless excitement as Prue joined the rest of the Peculiar Ladies.

"Well what?" she asked, all innocence as they hurried to get her settled down with a cup of tea, impatient for her news.

"Oh, stop it, Prue," Matilda begged, looking as if she wanted to stamp her foot. "We can see you have news. For heavens' sake, tell us before we all burst of curiosity!"

Prue smirked, rather enjoying herself. She still thought the dare had been a grand piece of folly, but could not help congratulating herself on having achieved it so swiftly. Kitty's eyes were on her, narrowed in suspicion.

"You danced in a garden?" the young woman said, her scepticism blatant. "At midnight?"

"I did," Prue replied, not beyond crowing a little, as a triumphant smile curved over her mouth.

"I suppose you followed the letter of the dare and danced by yourself," Kitty grumbled, folding her arms and looking sulky. "We ought to have rewritten it before you left. Everyone should have been more careful with their wording," she added, glaring about the assembled company.

"I was not alone," Prue replied, taking a nonchalant sip of tea. The room exploded with squeals of delight and intrigue, and Prue almost upset the cup entirely as Bonnie clutched at her arm.

"Who was it?" she demanded, almost bouncing with excitement. "Tell us!"

Prue frowned a little and stared about the room, meeting each woman's gaze.

"I must have an oath first, an oath on our friendship, on the loyalty of each Peculiar Lady to one another. Anything said within the sanctity of these meetings, anything to do with the dares we accept, or their outcomes, we will take to our graves."

"Agreed!" said everyone at once, but Matilda shook her head and raised her hand.

"I think we should also swear an oath," she said, her voice firm. "That no matter what, we support each other. If ever one of us is in trouble, each and every one of us will drop everything and come running, that we will never leave one of our number out in the cold to face the wolves alone."

"Agreed," Prue said without hesitation, smiling her approval at Matilda.

After a moment's hesitation, everyone followed her example, their voices grave and sincere, and Matilda smiled, then turned to Prue and clapped her hands together with glee.

"Tell us everything!"

"And don't leave out a single detail," Bonnie added, grinning.

Prue sighed and took pity on them. "Last night, at the St Clair ball, I danced in the private garden, at midnight, with…." She drew it out, aware that the entire room was holding their collective breath. "The Duke of Bedwin."

The room erupted.

Prue laughed and shook her head, refusing to answer any further questions. What had happened outside of the dance was between her and the duke and she had no intention of sharing the details.

"How do we know she's telling the truth?" Kitty demanded, looking no less sceptical than she had before Prue's revelation.

"Because if Prue say's that's what happened, that's what happened!" Alice said with considerable heat.

Prue smiled at her, touched by her timid friend's defence. "Thank you, Alice, but I thought Kitty might be difficult to persuade, and I took the precaution of bringing evidence."

The room fell silent once more as Prue reached into her reticule and pulled out the duke's ring with a flourish. Everyone gasped.

"Oh, Prue," Matilda said, her voice filled with wonder.

Prue looked back at her friend's shining eyes with consternation. "What?"

"He gave you his ring," she said, sounding awed and as if she might swoon.

"Yes," Prue said, looking at the heavy gold signet ring which bore the Bedwin crest. "I can see that."

"But, Prue," Matilda said incredulous now, "can't you see the significance of that?"

Prue looked around and discovered that if she couldn't, everyone else could. They looked stunned.

"What?" she said again, perplexed.

"He wants to marry you, you goose," Kitty said, rolling her eyes now. "Honestly. Why else would he give you something so precious?"

Prue flushed. She knew, of course, that Bedwin—that *Robert*—wanted to marry her, though not for any of the romantic reasons she could see shining in her friends' eyes. She hadn't, however, wanted anyone else to be privy to that information. How foolish of her to accept his ring, of all things.

"Oh, Prue," Alice breathed, her sweet face alight with excitement. "Has he asked you?"

Prue swallowed, wanting to deny it, but finding herself unable to do so in the light of her friend's honest pleasure in the idea.

"Yes," she said with reluctance, sounding as though she was admitting to having caught lice rather than gaining a proposal of marriage from a duke.

The shrieking began again. Louder.

"I told you he was fascinated with you!" Matilda exclaimed, staring at her in wonder.

"Oh, what did you say?" Jemima added. "I mean he's a duke and awfully handsome, but... but they do say—"

"Oh, Prue, they say he... his w-wife...." Alice stammered.

"He's got a dreadful reputation."

"... a gambler and a libertine...."

127

"They say he beat her…."

"…locked her in her room."

"He fought a duel with a man just for looking at her!"

"She died at his hands…."

"Enough!" Prue shouted over the cacophony of gossip and intrigue. "There's not a shred of evidence he did any of those things. It's all malicious tittle-tattle," she added, feeling strangely defensive of the duke for no good reason she could think of. She had gossiped about him more than they ever had, defamed his character more thoroughly than anyone, with her scurrilous tale of *The Damned Duke*.

The guilt she'd felt before rose again, more insistent this time, as she remembered the sincerity in Robert's eyes, the truth she'd heard in his words.

"I would never hurt you. I would never, ever, lift a finger to you. I give you my word."

Had he made his first wife such a promise? Had he kept it?

She turned her attention back to her friends who were staring at her with undisguised impatience.

"I already refused his proposal," she said, a rather odd sensation settling in her chest at the words. "So, there is no need for all this hysteria, but I don't think he's nearly as black as he's been painted."

"You turned down a proposal from a duke?" This was from Lucia; the gorgeous young Spanish woman whom she might have thought would disapprove of such a piece of impertinence from one as low on the social scale as Prue was. Instead, Lucia looked more than a little impressed.

"I did," Prue admitted, shrugging a little and wishing the strangely unsettled feeling besetting her would leave her be.

She felt the sudden need to get away and be by herself, to think about what she'd done and to remind herself of all the reasons she'd done it. Besides, she had a chapter to write. A chapter which ought to have been posted days ago. Yet her *Damned Duke* kept trying to redeem himself and she wasn't sure she was ready to let him. At least there were two chapters still to publish before she was in trouble with the magazine.

There was no need to panic.

No need at all.

Prue swallowed as something cold and closely resembling panic stole over her and made her feel shivery and rather ill.

The women were all still talking, weighing the merits of marrying a duke against the dangers of marrying a man with Bedwin's reputation. Prue let their words wash over her, replying to their questions with noncommittal answers.

Some of the women got up to investigate a tray of cakes they had ignored during the excitement of Prue's arrival and Alice sat beside her as a space appeared. She covered Prue's hand with her own.

"You look awfully pale. Are you all right?" she asked.

Prue nodded, forcing something approaching a smile to her face.

"Of course," she said, infusing the reply with a bright tone she was far from feeling. "But dancing at midnight takes it out of a girl, you know. I'm a little worn out. I might go home and have a nap," she said, gathering her things and ensuring Bedwin's ring was safely back in her reticule. "Never mind me, in any case," she added, hoping to turn the conversation away from her and the duke. "How is your dare coming along?"

Alice blushed and looked awkward, and Prue wished she'd not asked.

"Oh... I-I haven't... that's to say...." Alice turned her teacup around and around on the saucer in a distracted manner. "I'm having tea with Matilda tomorrow," she said, rather more brightly. "She's going to help me."

Prue looked over to Matilda, who returned a bland smile.

"Well, then," Prue said, feeling a little relieved. "You're in good hands."

"Yes," Alice replied, the one word rather faint, as Prue reflected that Matilda had been ruined after being found alone with a marquess.

Chapter 12

Dearest Prue,

Tell me more about Bedwin! What was the duke like? Was his proposal dreadfully romantic? Did he kiss you?

—Excerpt of a letter from Miss Bonnie Campbell to Miss Prunella Chuffington-Smythe.

***

23rd April. At Lord and Lady Faversham's garden party. Hambleton House. Beside the Thames. Richmond. London.

You had to give Aunt Phyllis her due. She managed to keep in with all the best people.

The invitation to the Hambleton House garden party was one of the most sought after of the season and, by dint of Lady Faversham being an old crony, Phyllis had secured them all a place.

It was a glorious event, and one of the few that Prue heartily enjoyed, so she indulged Phyllis' constant crowing over her success and applauded her efforts. It would have been easy enough for a widow to be overlooked on such occasions, but Phyllis was not a lady who would allow such a thing. She might have been clinging to respectability by a thread, but cling she did.

Prue's mother had been the daughter of a viscount, but her marriage to a man far beneath her social standing had made her a pariah. This had isolated her further than ever when the marriage soured, and she was left with no one to turn to. As far as the viscount had been concerned, his daughter had made her own bed, and she could lie in it.

Though Phyllis' connection to the viscount was rather vague, her breeding was still impeccable and, being the widow of a respected military man killed in battle and with a lovely and vivacious daughter, she was acceptable company.

Prue was included in the invitation as a matter of politeness.

It was a glorious day. The spring sunshine felt warm upon Prue's back as they walked the grounds, admiring the thousands of spring bulbs that carpeted great swathes of the garden, and which were the reason for the party itself. Although she'd still not resolved her thoughts on the chapter that was still outstanding, and despite feelings that ranged from guilt and regret to annoyance and irritation, Prue was in good spirits. It was hard not to be in such lovely surroundings, and with the sun shining down on her. It was spring on parade, showing its colours and promising new beginnings.

New beginnings, she reminded herself.

She would have a new beginning. The offer to publish her story as a novel would surely come soon, along with a demand for at least one other story from *The Lady's Weekly Review*, hopefully more. That she was doing it at the duke's expense was the only thing souring her good mood, but she pushed it away. She wouldn't think on that today, having spent too much time already dwelling on the rights and wrongs of it.

Prue had made an excuse not to attend the last ball two nights previous, begging off and pleading a megrim. It had been a grand affair and she'd known the duke would attend, known he would seek her out. She wasn't ready to see him again.

The taste of his kiss still lingered upon her lips. It had kept her from sleep and made her mind wander down paths she'd refused to consider before he'd made his ridiculous proposal.

For heaven's sake, why was she getting in such a tizzy about it? It wasn't as if he cared a jot for her. He just wanted a wife who would keep her head down and not cause him any trouble. On the face of it, that was Prue... but he didn't know the truth.

She'd hoped that her outrageous behaviour in the gardens that night had put him off, but the kiss they'd shared, and his words after the event, had not given her that impression. Prue was not a fool. She knew the kiss had meant nothing to him. His reputation was such that she doubted the kiss had lingered in his memory for more than a minute or two, let alone kept him from sleep.

If only she could say the same.

Good lord, she needed him gone from her life. He was upsetting all her lovely plans and she couldn't allow it. Of course, she could just tell him she was Miss Terry. That should put a dent in his ardour—feigned or otherwise—fast enough. The idea made her heart give an unpleasant little flutter in her chest, and not because he'd be furious. She didn't want him to know it was her who had cast him in such a wicked light. Mainly because she now suspected she'd got it terribly wrong.

Trying to force her attention away from the blasted man who had occupied far too much of her time of late, she turned to look at Minerva. Her cousin appeared the picture of spring today, in a pale yellow dress and matching bonnet.

"You look like a daffodil," she said, smiling as Minerva turned to her in surprise.

"Oh, thank you," she said, looking pleased by the comment. "I thought it was a sunny colour."

"It is. It suits you."

Minerva pulled a face and Prue took her arm, surprised. "What is it?"

Emma V. Leech

The young woman looked over her shoulder at her mother, who was walking close behind them. "Nothing," she said with a sigh.

They walked on in silence for a while as Prue considered her.

"Tell me the truth. Do you *want* to marry Bedwin?" she asked, wondering what had possessed her but gripped by the sudden desire to know.

Minerva looked just as startled by the question and glanced back again, relieved to see that her mother had paused to speak to someone else and fallen behind. She shrugged.

"It's what Mama wants," she said, before giving Prue a sharp look. "Why? Do you not think I could? Am I not clever enough?"

Prue paused, a little taken aback by the comment. "I think you could catch just about any man you set your heart on, Minerva," she said, with complete honesty. "If you were yourself, and stopped trying so hard, whether or not you do it to please Aunt Phyllis. Why not consider your own feelings?"

Minerva frowned and Prue waited, wondering if she was about to face a torrent of abuse in thanks for her reply.

"She'd never let me marry for love," Minerva said scathingly, as though Prue was an imbecile for even considering the idea. "She wants a title and she says I have the face to catch one."

Prue nodded. "You do," she said, smiling at her cousin. "And would that make you happy?"

Minerva stared back at her and then took a breath but, before she could speak, Aunt Phyllis' voice cut through the air like a blade.

"Look who I found, Minerva, darling!"

Prue turned with a dull sense of foreboding to see her aunt bearing down upon them with the Duke of Bedwin.

***

134

Robert greeted both young ladies, too aware he appeared stiff and awkward. He *felt* stiff and awkward, and completely off balance. It did not improve his already erratic mood. There had been a large part of him that wanted to damn the blasted title and forget the whole idea. There would be a distant cousin somewhere who would be dug up in the event of his demise, no doubt, and the name would lurch forward again. Christ knew they couldn't sully it any further than he had already.

Yet there had been another emotion, one he'd not been able to bury, even though he'd tried.

Excitement.

He wanted to see Prue again. It had been disturbing to realise how disappointed he'd been not to find her at the last event he'd attended. Her aunt and cousin had been there, and he'd left before they could bear down on him. If Prue wasn't there, he had no interest in staying.

Robert watched her now, watched her expression as she looked around and saw him approaching. Well, that wasn't encouraging.

Mrs Butler prattled on, extolling the beauties of the garden and making far too many obvious allusions and comparisons to her own daughter. Feeling belligerent, he refused to act the gentleman and make the obvious replies she set him up for. Miss Butler looked increasingly mortified and he felt like an arse, but he was tired of being manipulated, even in such a minor way.

"Oh, I do beg your pardon."

Robert looked up, returning his attention to Prue, who had just interrupted her aunt's endless monologue. Unlike Mrs Butler, Prue hadn't spoken a word to him past her initial greeting. Now, she was looking at them all with an apologetic smile.

"I've seen someone I must say hello to," she said, far too brightly. "If you would excuse me."

His jaw tightened as she all but ran away from him. What the devil was going on? She was the one who had sought him out and dared him to dance. She was the one who had come alive in his arms, returning his kisses with such passion he'd not been able to sleep a wink since for thinking of it.

As quickly as he could without being too obvious about it, he divested himself of Mrs and Miss Butler. He passed a dull hour speaking to acquaintances and making small talk, all the while looking out for Prue, who seemed to have disappeared.

Disgruntled and annoyed—mostly by how much her evasion bothered him—he took himself off for a walk along the river at the far reaches of the garden. Most of the guests lingered close to the house, and so he hoped he might get a few moments peace to gather his thoughts.

A long alley of close-cropped yew hedging blocked out the spring sunshine, plunging him into gloom as he followed the path towards the shimmering water he'd seen off in the distance. Halfway along the path, he paused as voices reached him.

"What happened next? Did the hero come and rescue her?" came a little girl's voice, all high-pitched wonder and excitement.

"Of course he did," said a rather gruffer, indignant tone: that of a boy who was evidently far from impressed.

Robert smiled and was about to move away when he was arrested by the next person who spoke.

"No, he didn't."

"Oh!" said the little girl, rather deflated.

"What?" demanded the first boy, echoed by several other voices Robert had not heard speak before.

"The princess would not sit about waiting to be rescued by some half-witted prince," returned the familiar voice.

Robert felt a smile curve over his mouth as he imagined the revolted expression on Prue's face as she spoke.

"She paced the dark confines of the dungeon, looking around for things she could use to make her escape."

"Ooooh," said the little girl.

"Pffft," said several of the boys. "It's a locked dungeon. She can't get out."

"Well, that shows what you know," Prue retorted. "The princess, finding nothing of use, knew she'd have to rely on her own quick thinking, and began to talk to herself in a rather loud voice, exclaiming that *'no, she really didn't wish to be rescued and would the handsome stranger please go away.'*"

"But you said she was all alone?" the girl pointed out.

"And so she is," Prue said, and he could hear the smile in the words. "But the guard did not know that and demanded, *'who are you talking to in there?'*"

Robert chuckled at her attempt to convey a deep, masculine voice.

"Oh, it was a trick!" the girl exclaimed, delighted.

"Yes, it was. The princess replied, *'Oh, no one. There's no one here but me,'* and hid herself behind the door. Well, the guard was suspicious and burst into the room. Quick as a flash, the princess ran through the open door and slammed it shut, locking the guard inside."

The little girl squealed and clapped. "And did she marry the handsome prince?"

There was a long pause and, for no explicable reason, Robert held his breath.

"No," Prue replied, her voice decisive. "The princess decided she thought the hero was boring because he wanted her to stay at home and look after him. She married the villain instead, and they travelled the world together, getting into mischief wherever they went."

Robert smiled, and all the ill humour, doubts, and annoyances of the past days vanished as his heart gave an unsteady thump in his chest. It was ridiculous, he knew that, but those words had given him hope, foolish as it may be.

"Prue, Prue! William's kite has got stuck in a tree."

There was the sound of scuffling and movement beyond the hedge and Robert moved forward, looking around an opening in the yew hedge that led into an orchard and then to meadowland beyond.

Prue and her entourage were hurrying to the edge of the orchard, where a bright blue-and-red kite had caught in the upper branches of an apple tree. The tail of the kite trailed down, disconsolate in its branch-bound prison.

With amusement, Robert stood and watched as a group of five children—one girl and four boys—stood around, considering the kite. He was a little alarmed but, after hearing her version of a fairy story, not the least bit surprised when Prue hitched her skirts and climbed the tree. A moment later and the kite plummeted to the ground to cheers and cries of thanks. The children ran off to play with their prize, leaving Prue still clinging to the upper branches of the gnarled old tree.

It was too good an opportunity to miss.

He reached her in time to hear a surprisingly impressive string of curse words and get a lovely view of a well-turned ankle.

"May I be of any assistance?" he enquired, his voice grave.

"Oh, no!" she wailed, looking down at him with obvious horror. "Oh, it had to be you, didn't it?"

Robert returned a wounded expression. "But Prue, darling, I have only come to give you my support, in any way you may require it."

"I am not your *darling*," returned a tart voice from above him. "And you can give me your support by going away, please."

"But, as a gentleman, I could not leave a young lady alone and in danger."

"I'm in no danger, I assure you," she replied, sounding a little exasperated. There was a breathless quality to her voice and he squinted up, having difficulty in seeing her as the sun was at her back. She appeared to be twisted around, tugging at the back of her dress, the delicate muslin quite unsuitable for the endeavour she had been attempting. Somewhere along the bodice and in several places among the skirts it was hopelessly caught in the branches. "Just go away," she muttered, "and I shall get down by myself."

Robert frowned, a little concerned now. "Prue, you've got yourself into a tangle. Let me come up and help you, you goose."

"No!" she exclaimed crossly. "I don't need your help, I can do it myself."

He gave a frustrated sigh. "Oh, come along, even your quick-thinking princess married the villain, you can at least allow *your* villain to untangle you from a tree, can't you?"

A rush of peculiar warmth assailed him at the thought of being *her* villain. Good lord, he was losing his mind.

There was a mortified groan from above as she realised he'd been listening and he smiled, his heart giving a hopeless little jolt in his chest at the sound. Dear god, she was adorable.

"I didn't mean to eavesdrop, but the story was so riveting I couldn't leave," he said, by way of apology.

"Well, the princess rescued herself, and so shall I," she retorted. "And I'm not marrying anyone, so you can just take yourself off and find another lady to play the hero for… or the villain… or whatever you are," she said, sounding increasingly vexed.

"But I want to play with you," he said, his voice soft.

There was a rustle from above and he saw her cat-like eyes staring down at him, wide and startled.

"You… you shouldn't say such things," she said, returning her attention back to the branches and almost twisting double in the attempt to unhook herself.

"Why not? It's true," he said, unable to keep the smile from his face or his voice. "I want to kiss you again, too." He didn't know why he'd said it, other than it was true. That kiss had haunted him, kept him from sleep, and flavoured his lips in such a way he couldn't help but lick them whenever he thought of her, trying to chase every lingering taste of her so he would never forget it.

She stilled, and then the tugging and cursing began again, more frantic than before.

"Let me come up and help," he said, shaking his head at her stubbornness. "I can untangle you. If you keep doing that, you will tear—"

There was a shriek and the sound of ripping fabric as she fell. Robert cried out and began to climb, but she'd stopped falling, holding out one hand to keep him where he was.

"Oh, dear," she murmured.

She was a great deal lower in the tree now, her feet on the bottommost branch. Robert reached out, grasping hold of her ankles as she swayed and tried to look at her, squinting into the sun.

"Don't look up!" she squealed, panic threading the command.

Robert immediately snapped his gaze to his boots but didn't let go.

"Why not? What's wrong?" he demanded.

There was a taut silence. "I… I appear to have ripped my gown."

With a great deal of effort, Robert schooled his expression into something solemn, even though she couldn't see his face. He was less successful with his voice, which trembled slightly.

"Oh, dear," he said, fighting not to laugh. "Where? And… how badly?"

"At the back," she said crisply, sounding irritated. "And quite ruinously, I assure you."

Robert sobered at once, realising she was speaking quite literally. If anyone saw her in such a state of undress, it *would* ruin her.

"Ah," he said, trying to figure out the best course of action. "We need to get you out of here without anyone seeing you."

"You don't say?" she replied on a huff.

He let out an impatient breath. "If you hadn't been so damn pig-headed, I could have got you down without incident." In hindsight it might have been more gentlemanly not to have pointed that out, but he had been cast as the villain, after all. He might as well play the part.

"I didn't want your help," she retorted. "If you hadn't insisted on staying, I would have been fine."

Robert let her go as she seemed steady on her perch now and folded his arms. He gave a snort to illustrate his incredulity. "Yes, you'd be in exactly the same predicament, *alone*."

"See?" she said triumphantly. "A huge improvement on my current situation."

He couldn't help but laugh. "Oh, Prue, you impossible creature."

There was far too much warmth in the words, but he couldn't help it. She said nothing, but he could feel her glowering at him.

Robert looked around them, trying to get his bearings. "The hothouses are over there," he said, pointing to the glass gables.

"I'm sure I saw the rooftops as we came up the driveway. If we can find a way out to the front of the house, I'll be able to smuggle you into my carriage with no one any the wiser."

"Into your…. Oh, no… I don't think—"

"If you have a better plan, I'm listening," he said, trying to be reasonable. "Do you want to see your aunt in this state?"

He could almost hear her teeth grinding as she realised there was no option.

"Very well."

Robert forgot himself for a moment, he was so relieved by her agreement, and glanced up.

"Don't look!" she snapped, clutching at her bodice which seemed to be rather loose, one shoulder of the dress sagging down her arm.

Turning away at once, he couldn't help but chuckle. "Scandalous as it is, I believe it still covers everything, er… crucial."

"Only if I hold on to it," she admitted, as a surge of heat rushed through him.

Don't think on it, he instructed himself. *You're not that much the villain.*

"Won't you let me help…?"

"No."

A moment later and she was on the ground, her arms wrapped about her chest to keep the dress in place. He stared at her, flushed, her hair in disarray, her hazel eyes alight with irritation. His breath caught.

"What?" she asked, the irritation receding as doubt coloured her expression in its place. Her slender hands reached for her hair, forearms still pinning the dress as she bent her head, finding the pins escaping and her hair all tumbling down. "Good heavens. I must look a fright," she muttered, her mortification obvious.

"You look perfectly charming," he said, meaning it with all his heart. The unbidden thought came to him that Lavinia would always have looked nothing less than perfection. His late wife would also have been just as delighted as Prue with the dark little nook beside the yew hedge, though she would have seen it as perfect for an illicit rendezvous. Gathering a group of children together and telling them unlikely fairy stories about independent princesses would never have crossed her mind.

The dangerous realisation that this woman was getting under his skin, charming him with her peculiar conversation and frustrating him by keeping him forever at arm's length, hit him hard and fast. She hadn't wanted to keep him at bay when he'd kissed her, though. When he'd kissed her, she'd pressed closer; she had clung to him like ivy to a tree, as if she never wanted to let go.

The desire to kiss her again, to press his lips against that indignant little pout, was all consuming.

She made a disgusted sound of incredulity at his compliment, and he was taken aback by how determined she was to disbelieve him.

"Save your charm for someone who wants to hear it," she said caustically. "I don't need pretty falsehoods, thank you."

"But it was true," he objected, running into a cool look of disdain. "You do look—"

"I think it safe to say," she said, interrupting him. "That any interest you may have in me does not stem from an infatuation of my great beauty." She lifted one pale eyebrow to underscore her sarcasm. "So, don't embarrass us both by trying to flirt with me in such a manner."

Robert stilled, watching her, seeing both the fierce expression she wore and something else, something vulnerable, something that would not allow her to trust him. He reached out and tucked a little curl of honey blonde hair behind her ear.

"I'm not a man who flatters women for the sake of it," he said, holding her gaze. "I don't dally with nice ladies of the *ton*, I don't do flirtatious conversation, and my polite manners are all used up. Ask anyone. They'll tell you I'm a cold bastard with no time for small talk, and less for propriety. They'll tell you I prefer gaming hells to *Almack's*, and I never do anything I don't want to. I certainly don't bother saying things I don't mean." He smiled at her then, allowing the warmth to show in his eyes, feeling it in his expression, in a way he'd forgotten was possible. "I said you look charming because you do. Charming and innocent and perfectly lovely. Just the kind of sweet creature a villain would enjoy carrying away from a party to ravish in private."

He watched an intriguing blush of colour as it rose over her neck, flushing her cheeks.

"But I promise not to ravish you unless you invite me to," he added, not wanting to give her any concerns about going with him. Robert forced himself not to allow his gaze to drop to her bare shoulders as she clutched the front of her dress to her bosom.

"Should I have a look and see what can be done?" he asked, gesturing to the back of her gown.

He watched her throat work as she swallowed, and then gave a sharp nod.

Moving behind her, he inspected the damage. The tie at her waist had only come loose, though the skirts were badly ripped in several places. He tied the loose ribbon. The top tie at the neckline, however, had snapped, the ribbon pulled completely free of the casing. There was no way to repair it.

"It's beyond saving, I'm afraid," he said, giving her a sympathetic smile as she huffed her displeasure. "Come," he said, realising they'd already been missing for too long. "We'd best get you out of here."

Prue nodded, silent now, and followed him through the orchard and over a stile. Robert glanced behind them, assuring himself there was no one about. They were out of sight of the house here and, though he could hear the children playing, they had returned to the gardens on the far side of the orchard.

Climbing the stile proved challenging, as Prue kept an iron fist clutched at her neckline. Crossing the field afterwards was not too troublesome as the grass was short yet, but there was a thin line of woodland to traverse before they came close to the drive that led to the front of the house. The muslin skirts of her dress, already having proven themselves fragile, caught and snagged on every bramble, twig and dead fern until Robert cursed aloud.

"This is taking too long," he said, shaking his head. "Forgive me."

Before she could open her mouth to ask *what for*, he'd picked her up. "It's only for a moment," he assured her, regretting that fact as they soon reached the edge of the tree line and the carriages lined up in front of the house became apparent. He liked the feel of her in his arms, liked the fact that, for once, he could at least try to play the hero. It made a refreshing change. That being the case, he didn't try to hold on to her for longer than he ought but put her down. "Stay here," he instructed. "Stay out of sight until my carriage arrives. I'll get it to wait here and it will block any view of you from the front of the house. No one will see you get in. I'll be as quick as I can."

"But Aunt Phyllis and Minerva," she objected. "I can't just disappear."

He frowned at that, nodding. "Did I see you talking to a friend? A Miss Hunt, wasn't it?"

She nodded, shivering now in the chill of the shadowy woods and he wished he could give her his coat, but if he was seen it would draw attention he did not desire.

"Do you trust her?" he asked.

"Yes."

"Very well. I shall have to explain the circumstances and ask her to cover for you. I will ask her to tell your aunt you have been taken unwell and she has lent you her carriage home. A megrim, perhaps," he suggested, unable to resist quirking one eyebrow. "You seem prone to those."

Her silence and answering look of guilt confirmed his suspicions. She'd not been ill at all, but avoiding him.

"We shall discuss your sudden ill health when you are in less danger of ruination," he said, somewhat bitter as he realised that he'd hoped he'd been wrong. "I'll be as quick as I can."

Chapter 13

Prue!

Whatever happened to you? Tell me everything! I'm dying of curiosity. The duke swore me to secrecy and was so fierce about it. Not that I would have breathed a word anyway, but I certainly wouldn't have dared refuse anything he asked of me. Is he in love with you? He seemed like a man who wanted very much to be your hero. Did he achieve it?

—Excerpt of a letter from Miss Matilda Hunt to Miss Prunella Chuffington-Smythe.

***

23rd April. Still at Lord and Lady Faversham's garden party. Hambleton House. Beside the Thames. Richmond, London.

Prue shivered. Her arms were prickling with gooseflesh by the time the duke's carriage paused beside her. The door swung open and Robert leapt down, helping her the short distance to the carriage and hurrying her inside. Once she'd sat down, he rapped smartly on the roof and the carriage pulled away.

She watched, a little alarmed, as he stripped off his coat and moved to sit beside her.

"You're cold," he said, by way of explanation, slinging the coat around her shoulders.

The warmth of his body still burned in the silk lining as it slid against her chilled skin, Prue shivered again, though pleasurably this time. It seemed intimate, that sharing of body heat, even though he wasn't touching her. She kept her gaze cast down, fighting the flush of colour that the thought of his hard, masculine form was inviting, but that didn't help as the scent of him rose from the fabric of the coat. Crisp and clean and something faintly citrus. Lemon soap, she guessed, and felt an illicit thrill at having such a personal detail revealed to her.

"Better?" he asked.

"Yes, thank you," she said, and looked up, wishing she hadn't as she was confronted with those green eyes, for once not the cold reflection of deep water he usually wore, but as soft and inviting as a mossy bank. Tiny flecks of gold glinted amid the green, almost yellow as the sun shafted through the window and illuminated her perusal. Like primroses in the grass, she thought, smiling as she realised the absurd thought would revolt him.

"What?" he demanded, a curious look in the dark forest jade of his gaze.

"Nothing," she said at once, turning to stare out of the window. At once she was too aware of him, of his large presence so close to her on the plush velvet seat, and of the fact they were alone together in his carriage. She would be ruined if they were discovered.

"You'll have to marry me now," he said, his voice gentle and amused. "You're ruined."

Prue stiffened, alarmed by the way he'd all but read her thoughts. "I'm only ruined if I'm discovered," she corrected. "Are you going to allow anyone to find out about this?"

"No, of course not," he said, folding his arms and sitting back, resting his head against the squabs. "But it doesn't change the fact you are alone with a man in a carriage, looking very much as though you've been thoroughly ravished." He smirked. "Any whisper of my name will have everyone believing you've been debauched, most likely against your will," he added, his tone souring a little.

She stared at him, hearing the bitterness behind the words, and marking the sardonic twist of his mouth.

"But you would never do that, would you."

It wasn't a question for, rightly or wrongly, despite her awareness of his proximity and of the strength contained in those broad shoulders and powerful limbs, she felt no fear of him. Her father had been a smaller man than this powerful duke, yet the damage he had wrought had been enough for Prue to swear off men for good. This man, though… despite his terrible reputation, he'd done nothing to hurt her.

He stared at her, his gaze unwavering.

"No," he said, that one word firm and full of certainty. "Only a weak man would use his fists, or his strength, against someone who has no means of defending themselves. Only the worst kind of villain would take what has not been offered freely. I am many things, Prue, and I've done plenty I am not proud of, that I am rightly vilified for, but I was never cruel to a woman, not to my wife. I never laid a hand on her, and I did not kill her. I would have made her happy—or tried to, at least, if she'd allowed me to—but she didn't want that from me."

"Why not?" she asked, wondering if he would answer such an indelicate question.

He shrugged and looked away from her. "She was as trapped as I was, for all that it was her who caught me. Her father had manipulated her since she was a child. Her only purpose in life was to catch herself a title. Once she'd done that, she refused to play his games any more. She wanted to taste freedom and pleasure and be wild after years of being the perfect daughter."

"You sound sympathetic," she said, surprised.

"Now, perhaps," he said, with a derisive snort. "I've spent plenty of my life loathing her, loathing what she did to me, despising her for how she wrecked everything." He shrugged. "Age and time give perspective, I suppose. She was unhappy, lonely too, in her own way. We were unsuited, and I was blinded by her beauty. I didn't take the time to get to know her. What happened was as much my fault as hers. If I'd have been thinking, I would have gained her trust. I would have discovered her heart, instead of allowing my baser instincts to rule me, and accepting her invitation to meet in secret."

"You don't know me, either," she pointed out. "And you met me in secret. Have you not learned your lesson?"

He chuckled at that. "No, perhaps not," he admitted. "But I'd like to know you. My uncle would rhapsodise about you for hours. I believe he knows you well—he certainly thinks so—and there is no one whose opinion I trust more than his." His voice lowered, shivering over her, far too intimate in the confined space of his carriage. "I have seen enough to believe it would not be a mistake. Far from it. I… I think we could be happy."

Prue felt something shift in her chest: an ache for something she'd long ago told herself was not for her. *Don't believe it,* she warned herself. A snide voice whispered that he wanted something from her, that he was just lulling her into a false sense of security.

"But you just want a brood mare," she said, deliberately coarse and accusing. "You need only to secure the line. When you proposed marriage, you implied that once I'd provided your heir, I would be free of you, that I could live an independent life as long as I caused you no scandal."

He frowned and looked away from her.

"Yes, that was what I told you."

"And is that untrue?" she asked, drawing his attention back to her, unsettled by his expression. He looked less the gentleman without his coat on. He'd run his hand through his hair and the thick locks were dishevelled, the shadow of his beard visible even though he was clean shaven. The interior of the carriage had grown gloomy, shrinking somehow as a large cloud blocked the sun.

Robert's eyes were dark and intense, the hard planes of his face severe in the dim light.

"It was true then," he said, the words careful, considered.

Prue's heart picked up. "And now?" she asked, startled by the breathless quality of her voice. "What is true now?"

He shifted closer to her on the bench and she drew in a sharp breath as he reached out and touched her chin with a fingertip, lifting her head a little.

"The truth is," he said, his voice low and slow and heavy with promise. "I don't know, but I can't get the idea of kissing you out of my mind. I'm desperate to do it again." He inched a little closer, still touching her nowhere but the fingertip that burned beneath her skin, the slight contact electrifying. "I want to take you home and take you to my bed. I want to ruin you. Not in the eyes of the *ton*, not for society, not to force your hand… I want to ruin you, so you'll want no one else but me."

Prue swallowed, her breathing erratic. *Good lord.* She was alive with anticipation, with temptation, and with desire, whilst a teeny tiny part of her brain also longed for pencil and paper so she could write down what he'd just said in precise detail, as it was the most spectacular thing she'd ever heard.

"Well?" he said his gaze hot and urgent.

Prue racked her brain, trying to figure out if there had been a question there. She was distracted by his mouth, so close, remembering how it had felt against hers, soft and warm, tender and demanding.

"Er…." She felt as if she was on quicksand, sinking into a situation where her grasp on control would slip through her fingers at speed, and lead her into danger. *Oh, danger,* she thought with a sigh, staring up into those wicked eyes, thick, dark lashes framing desire and the promise of decadent pleasures. *Yes, please.*

"That was not an answer," he said, his breath fanning over her. Her body was on fire, every inch of her skin alive with his proximity. Liquid, molten heat pooled in her belly, and there was a strange aching sensation between her thighs that was startling and strange and... not unwelcome.

"W-What was the question?" she stammered, licking her lips and trying to tamp down the urge to throw her arms around his neck and just agree to whatever it was he would offer her. She was not that woman.

Prue wrote about reckless women, women who gave into desire and fell into dramatic circumstances, but Prunella Chuffington-Smythe was not the kind of woman to be swept away by love and romance and passion. Certainly not. She was too sensible, too level-headed, too....

"Shall I kiss you?" he asked, interrupting her train of thought.

"Yes, please."

The words were out in a rush, before sensible, level-headed Prue could even consider her answer. Somewhere inside her, another, braver, fiercer Prue had raised her head and taken charge, taken what she wanted. As his head lowered, his lips meeting hers, she couldn't find it in herself to regret it.

Kissing was not something Prue had a great deal of experience with. There had been a boy at a party. They'd been young, barely thirteen, and he'd been cheeky and sweet and had stolen a kiss. Such innocence in that kiss, a dry press of lips. There was nothing innocent about this, or about this man. The more he kissed her the more she wanted, *needed,* him to continue. His mouth took and gave, all at once, sometimes gentle and caressing, then deepening, demanding things her body seemed to understand without question.

The thoughts that arose as that kiss grew wilder were shocking and delicious.

Prue knew the facts of life. She'd long ago decided she could not write about romance, sin, and temptation if she didn't know the mechanics of what drove men and women to take such terrible risks with their reputations, their lives, and their souls. Yet discovering how two bodies fit together was no more helpful than reading a recipe. Prue might know the composite requirements, eggs, butter, flour… but she couldn't smell the decadent perfume, couldn't taste the sweet, tart, soft, crisp textures and flavours.

She couldn't experience it.

She hadn't had the slightest idea.

His breath was hot and urgent, her own coming in short, desperate little gasps, overwhelmed and wanting more. Good lord, what was she doing? Yet, if she was never to marry, this might be her only chance to experience this thrilling insanity. How could she write about passion without ever having tasted it?

Robert groaned, a low, wild sound deep in his throat that made fire chase through her veins. She was powerful, she had power over him in this moment, and yet she was out of control, driven by her own desire, which was far fiercer than she'd ever suspected.

Thoughts clamoured in her feverish brain, thoughts of the heat of his skin against hers, of the weight of his body over her, his hands on her. Madness. Utter, bewildering, divine madness. There were only two options: dare to face her own desire and succumb to it, or listen to reason and stop this at once.

Reason would have her accept the first offer of marriage she gained, no matter from whom.

Reason would never have allowed her to lift a pen and write a romantic story.

Reason would keep her polite, within the bounds of propriety.

Obedient.

Decision made.

"I want you," he murmured as his hands caressed and kneaded. He kissed and nipped and traced patterns with his tongue as Prue shivered and sighed. "I need you closer."

Robert tugged at her, trying to achieve just that but it was awkward in the carriage, the two of them side by side. *Drat it,* she thought, why hadn't he chosen a better place to seduce her? Surely a villain of his calibre should think of such things? She almost giggled at that, but was hit instead by a wave of sadness.

This complicated, marvellous man would never be hers, not as a husband, not as anything more than she could have in this moment. Her plans for the future did not, *could not* include him. She had used him, used his misery and his terrible reputation for her own ends and that was to be her punishment. Yet, there was no reason he should suffer further for her actions. She could give him something in return. He wanted her closer, and she wasn't about to deny him.

There had to be a way.

Prue shifted, bracing one hand on his shoulders she pulled back from his kiss, delighted by the look of him. Rumpled and heavy-lidded, he looked thoroughly villainous. She smiled, taking a steadying breath to bolster her courage before standing.

"What—" he began, surprised until she returned to him, putting a knee on the bench on either side of his thighs. "Oh, Christ," he muttered, pulling her closer, his hands sliding under her skirts, pushing them higher until he grasped her hips and tugged.

"Oh," she exclaimed, both at the warmth of his hands through the fine fabric of her drawers, and the sudden intimacy of her position, the breathless sound of surprise muffled as he kissed her again.

He's mad too, she realised, pleased to recognise the same desperation in his eyes. The thought scattered as he pulled her hips closer, their bodies touching. He was hard beneath her, his arousal rubbing against her sex and sending pleasure spiking through her like a delicious little lightning strike. She thought she'd known what to expect, having seen medical illustrations of a man's member in various states of stimulation.

Somehow, even through the fabric of his breeches, the neat little drawing had not done the matter justice.

Prue sighed and shivered as he moved against her again, the hard, thick length snug against her body, making her ache for more and sigh and move without thought, clutching at his shoulders.

Robert discarded the coat, taking it from her shoulders and tugging at her ruined dress, exposing her breasts to his gaze.

"Christ, Prue," he said, and that sensation of power rolled over her again at the undisguised lust in his eyes, and in the rough quality of his words. He kissed her again before pulling back. "I want to be inside you," he said, his voice unsteady, rough with desire. "For god's sake, Prue, tell me you'll marry me."

She stilled, bewildered as she stared down at him, frowning. "I thought you wanted to ruin me," she pointed out, a little disappointed in the less-than-villainous statement.

He grunted, skimming his hands over her sides, cupping and squeezing her breasts, toying with the nipples as she gasped and ached at his touch.

"I've already ruined you," he said, sounding rather irritated. "And I told you that wasn't how I meant it. I just want you to want me, more than anyone else."

A little exasperated by this, Prue raised an eyebrow. "Surely you've proof enough of that?" With a rather unexpected show of her own wickedness, Prue rubbed against him, sighing with pleasure and sinuous as a cat.

His head tipped back, and she felt a thrill of exhilaration as he groaned, clutching at her hips, stilling her.

"Stop, for God's sake, before I spend in my breeches," he said, pushing her back a little to put distance between them.

Prue laughed, shocked to her bones and delighted all at once. Never in her life had she considered herself a temptress, and even with his words and the physical evidence, it was hard to credit.

"Stop looking so damn pleased with yourself," he grumbled, though there was something suspiciously like affection behind the words.

That, more than anything, brought her to her senses. He deserved better than this. As much as she'd been trying to give him something he wanted, she realised in that moment, that it wasn't this. He didn't want something brief and sordid, a few moments of shared pleasure with a woman who had already taken so much from him. If he knew what she'd done he'd not want anything from her at all.

"Of course," she said at once. "I should never...."

Good lord, what had she been thinking? They could be only ten minutes from her home. What would have happened if the carriage had stopped and they'd been... been....

Prue flushed scarlet and moved off him, but he held her fast, pulling her back.

"Where do you think you're going?" he asked, frowning.

"I apologise, your grace," she said, numb with horror at what she'd been about to do.

"Your grace?" he echoed, his eyes dark with surprise and something that looked unnervingly like hurt. "I think we've moved past that, don't you? We're to be married."

She shook her head, realising just how badly she'd behaved. Of course, he'd think she would agree after... after....

"No," she said, shaking her head and dismayed to note the reluctance she felt in saying the words. For a moment she wondered what it might be like to marry such a man, and pushed the dangerous idea far away. "No, we're not."

He let her go then, his face shuttering up, his expression cool and unreadable. Prue rearranged her clothing as best she could, feeling her stomach twist as the warmth she'd seen in his eyes snuffed out. She looked away from him, not wanting to see the change. He'd change a great deal more than that if he ever discovered the things she'd written about him, the terrible things she'd implied. Oh, lord, why had she done it? Why had she been so blatant?

She'd thought she was righting wrongs and vanquishing a foe. Yet even if he'd been every inch the villain she'd first believed him to be, she'd had no right to vilify him further, to make assumptions about him and use them to entertain the *ton*.

She felt sick, and increasingly as though she might cry.

"Why not?" he asked, with self-possession in the words, although he was still breathing too hard, too fast.

"You don't know me," she said, wishing she could sound calmer, and wishing the thread of panic running beneath her reply was better concealed.

Robert was quiet for a long moment, and then let out a breath. He shifted beside her and, when she dared look at him again, his expression had softened.

"Then let me in, Prue," he said, reaching out to stroke her cheek with the back of one finger. "Let me know you. Give me a chance to gain your trust."

The sensation made her breath catch as longing rose inside her, and she recognised too late the danger she was in. This was a man who could upset all her plans with ease, and she'd allowed him to get too close. She'd known he was best avoided, but not the extent of the risk she was taking in being in his company.

Now, at last, she had some small understanding of what her mother had felt when her father had been at his most charming. She recognised the yearning to believe in his lies, to allow his soft words to soothe the bruises he'd inflicted, to look into his handsome face and allow him to make it better. It had never been better, though, and her mother had been trapped. She had been merely a possession, with no recourse against an owner who treated her carelessly at best, and more often with cruelty.

There was always the possibility that Robert was a good man through and through, that he would never bully or hurt or ignore her thoughts and feelings. The more she knew him, the more she believed it possible. Yet, if she was wrong, she'd have a lifetime to regret, caught in his cage with no way of escaping him.

No.

She couldn't look at him. "You don't know me," she repeated. "And if you did, I'm not sure you would like what you found."

He let out a soft breath of laughter. "If you wish to compare sins, I'm at your disposal. I assure you, I will win any attempt at self-flagellation you wish to attempt."

To Prue's relief, her aunt's cottage came into view, and she remained silent until they had drawn to a halt. Then she turned, looking him in the eyes and knowing she would always regret not taking the chance he offered, even as she knew it was for the best.

"I'm afraid you're wrong," she said softly, forcing herself to look in his eyes as she came as close to revealing the truth as she possibly could. "Some crimes are secretive and insidious, but no less grievous to those who are victim to them. Thank you for bringing me home. Good day to you."

Chapter 14

Why must men be so pig-headed? Why not just accept that I have made up my mind, and my answer is no? Why does he insist on believing there is a possibility of doubt in my mind?

Why is there doubt in my mind?

—Excerpt of a letter from Miss Prunella Chuffington-Smythe ... never sent.

***

25th April. A meeting of The Peculiar Ladies. Upper Walpole Street. 1814

"How does one create a scandal?" Prue asked.

Alice choked on her tea, the cup clattering back to the saucer as Matilda paused, a dainty little macaroon suspended in front of her mouth in long, elegant fingers.

"Oh, darling," she murmured, her lips twisting in a wry smile. "It's easier than you think."

The Peculiar Ladies were gathered for another meeting of their book group, though so far they had discussed not a single title, excepting a brief squeal over the latest chapter of *The Dark History of a Damned Duke.*

They had aimed all conversation at Prue and her disappearance from a certain garden party. Though Matilda had kept her confidence, she had implied that there was something mysterious afoot. *The wretch.*

They hadn't given her a moment's peace since, hence her urgent desire to change the subject. Besides which, she really wanted to know.

"Why would you want to create a scandal?" Ruth asked.

Prue turned to look at her, studying her friend's face. It was an uncompromising, no-nonsense face, not pretty, but not unattractive either. Handsome, Prue decided. Ruth was the woman who would always know what to do in an emergency.

"Oh, not a large scandal, nothing unwieldy, just a small one. Enough to rid myself of an unwanted suitor," Prue replied, deciding she may as well tell them the truth. "Of *any* unwanted suitors, come to that." She trusted these women, trusted in the oath they'd taken to keep each other's secrets, to come running if things went awry.

The problem was, things had already gone awry, and they couldn't help her put her plans back together. Only she could do that.

Bonnie stared at her in dismay. "He's asked you again!" she exclaimed, wide-eyed and appalled. "And you refused him… *again*?"

"Oh, the poor man," Alice said, holding a hand to her heart and sighing.

Prue tutted with indignation. "Why are you pitying him? He's *The Damned Duke*, the one with the terrible reputation for cruelty and vice. You should do everything in your power to keep the scoundrel from my door!"

She now suspected the duke she'd been on far too intimate terms with, and the man whispered about behind his back—the one that had inspired her villain—were not at all the same person, but still, *they* didn't know that!

Alice frowned and shook her head. "I don't know," she said, sounding hesitant. "I was speaking to a cousin of mine a few days ago, and she knew the woman he married. Lavinia Bradford, she was then. The most beautiful woman you ever set eyes on."

Prue felt a vicious stab of jealousy at Alice's words, and cursed herself for a fool. What nonsense. She had no business being jealous of his wife. His *dead* wife, at that.

"What else did she say?" Jemima prompted, sitting forward on her seat. "My neighbours knew the family and their son said she was a…." She faltered, clearly unwilling to voice the word aloud.

"I heard that, too," Matilda said, smirking a little. "My brother met her once at a dinner party. She tried to seduce him before they'd got past the fish course. Her husband was at the same dinner."

Gasps echoed about the room.

"And don't ask me," she added with a grimace. "I don't know, and I don't want to."

Prue swallowed as her stomach roiled. Poor Robert. What must he have endured? Yet he hadn't condemned his wife when they'd spoken; he'd pitied her loneliness, her unhappiness.

Alice's voice brought her back to the conversation. "My cousin knew her as a child and she said, well… I'll not repeat it word for word, but she said she was wild and unkind and… spiteful."

"The poor man," Bonnie said, shaking her head and looking back at Prue once more. "How can you refuse him? He's handsome and rich—he's a duke, for heaven's sake—and he's clearly not the monster we've been thinking him all this time. Oughtn't you give him the chance to prove himself, at least?"

Prue felt an unpleasant lump sit heavily in her throat as the echo of Robert's words filled her mind.

"Let me know you. Give me a chance to gain your trust."

She couldn't, even if she wanted to... and, too late, she'd realised how much she *did* want to. But how could she marry him without revealing what she'd done? How could she let him know her without telling him about her writing? Even if she didn't reveal the truth, he'd figure it out soon enough. Either she told him, or he would discover it, and both outcomes ended in him hating her, in him being hurt by what she'd done, and all the dreadful things she'd written.

How stupid. She'd thought to lash out at a bully, at the vile monster who had terrorised her mother in the only way open to her as a woman. With stealth and her own intelligence as her weapons of choice, she would expose and cut down a powerful man in a way she'd never achieved with her own father. She hadn't saved her mother, but she could warn other women to stay clear of this weak, vile tyrant.

Except she'd been wrong. Her aim had been true, her intention just, but she had caught the wrong victim in the crossfire. She'd judged a man and allowed him no defence, no chance to prove her wrong, and that made her as much of a vile bully as she'd believed him to be.

Shame burned in her heart.

Prue jolted as Alice laid a cool hand over hers. "Are you all right, Prue? You look rather pale."

"Fine," Prue said, forcing energy she was far from feeling into the word and attempting a bright smile. "I'm fine."

Except she wasn't. She was tired and heartsick, and so tangled up she couldn't think straight.

The Lady's Weekly Review had written to her, demanding the next chapters of her story. They had one more which would be published in three days, and she still hadn't sent them the next... hadn't sent it because she hadn't written it.

She didn't know what to write. Her villain wasn't a villain and the innocent maid he'd been hunting was neither so innocent nor as hunted as she'd believed. Nothing was as black-and-white as she'd supposed it to be. People weren't so easily cast into their rightful roles of villains and heroes—as temptresses, little innocents, or saintly heroines—as she'd imagined.

The revelation had cast everything in shades of grey, a heavy, dull fog that Prue could not fight free of. It sapped her energy and made her rethink every decision, every dream and plan and ideal. She felt lost and aimless, and she didn't know how to recapture her future, how to reshape it in the light of her own stupidity.

"If you want a minor scandal, just ask a fellow to dance," Bonnie said sourly. She shrugged as the women all turned to look at her. "Worked for me. It's why I'm here," she added with a sigh. *"To learn propriety, ye wee hellion,"* she said, thickening her Scottish accent, no doubt to imitate her formidable sounding ward. "I dare ye, try it," she added, grinning at Prue.

Prue raised her eyebrows though and regarded Bonnie with interest. "Yes," she said, giving a decisive nod. "That should do it." Surely such unladylike behaviour would be the last straw for a man with a dukedom to consider. "I accept."

Bonnie stared back at her, startled. "B-But, Prue," she stammered, "I was only teasing. I did it at a local dance and there was no one there who cared overmuch. If you do it in front of the *ton*—"

"I'll finally be regarded as completely unmarriageable," Prue said, wishing her heart wasn't thudding in such an unpleasant way. "I'll stop having to make excuses to get out of going to endless balls and ridiculous affairs I haven't the slightest interest in. It's perfect."

The words tasted bitter, the finality of them making her stomach clench.

There was no other way, she assured herself. This was what she must do. She'd be free of the duke, and he'd be free of her. She'd retract her story, even issue an apology. The editor would be furious, but she'd make things right with *The Lady's Weekly Review.* She'd offer them another story, a better one, one with more honesty, more thought.

There was no point in lamenting that she'd made a mistake; she had to stop feeling sorry for herself. It had come as a shock to discover she was the real villain of the piece but, just as her villain had been maligned, she was not a bad person. She would make things right, but first... first, she needed to cut herself free of Robert, before he tempted her into lying to him, accepting everything he offered and pretending she deserved it.

He'd had such a wife once before. She'd not be guilty of tricking him into a second.

***

The evening of the 25th April. The Cavendish Ball. Mayfair. London. 1814.

Prue stared about the vast ballroom of Cavendish House, filled to bursting with the great and the good. She snorted at that. How many of those she'd believed wicked characters were merely misunderstood, or at least more complicated than she'd realised? How many of the sweet-faced debutantes were hiding vile secrets? Good lord, she was losing her mind.

She sighed and pressed her fingers against her temples, massaging the tender flesh as a headache raged. Ironically, she thought she really might be on the verge of a megrim for the first time in her life.

Prue looked up as the Marquess of Montagu entered the ballroom. *Ah,* she thought with a sigh, as the world righted itself, *there's a proper bastard,* and she was not referring to his impeccable lineage. The marquess was a cold man, haughty, powerful, and ruthless, and he was the reason Matilda Hunt was so thoroughly ruined. He'd accused her of trying to trap him into marriage—wrongly—and had thrown her to the wolves. Matilda would never find a match now. The only offers *The Huntress* got were not the sort ever voiced to a respectable female.

Now that was cruelty of the highest order, to ruin a woman who was simply in the wrong place at the wrong time.

Robert would never do such a thing. He'd not allowed himself to take her innocence—which she'd been quite prepared to hand over without a murmur—unless she agreed to marry him first.

Aware of a sudden thrill of interest in the room, Prue looked up, feeling her heart give an unsteady jolt in her chest as she saw him.

God, he was magnificent.

He was tall and dark, that thick, curling hair of his just a little too long. One untameable lock fell across his forehead as he moved. Broad, powerful shoulders filled a perfectly tailored coat and he radiated masculine vigour and potency. Was it any wonder the women still swooned over him, despite his reputation… or perhaps because of it? His eyebrows were heavy and added to the wicked, almost devilish appearance, the sharp green eyes beneath assuring anyone who dared meet them that he'd make good on his promises.

She smiled a little, saddened as she realised he wore that persona like a cloak, keeping everyone at bay. The aggressive expression, the contemptuous sneer that made women duck behind their fans and whisper in hushed voices… it was all a façade.

Better to be believed a villain than to be pitied.

"Perhaps it was I who was tempted in, did you ever consider that? Perhaps I await rescue?"

Her throat tightened as the desire to cross the room and go to him pushed at her heart. She wanted to take hold of his hand, to tell him he had a friend, someone who believed in him… but she couldn't. The only thing she could do was get herself free of him, and make him believe her every bit as scandalous as his wife had been, so he would stay away. She felt sick as she saw him greet the Earl of St Clair, the two men falling into conversation.

Get it over with, she told herself, watching the dancers skipping up and down the ballroom in a longways country dance. *Just do it and you'll both be free, then you can move on.*

Far from encouraging her, the thought only made her want to cry, and she pressed her damp palms against her dress, surreptitiously wiping them dry. Prue took a deep breath, but it didn't help. It only made her dizzy and unsettled, her head pounding ever harder as the headache took hold.

She forced her feet to move, forced herself forwards, keeping her gaze locked on Robert as she moved around the dance floor and headed towards him. She was perhaps ten feet away when he saw her, and the change to his expression in that instant made her stop.

There she stood, in full view of everyone, staring at him like a fool. Yet, he looked nothing like a rogue, or a *Damned Duke*, or anything close to villainous in that moment. As he set eyes upon her she saw that carefree, boyish smile she'd only glimpsed once before, and her heart had leapt for joy. Prue knew then, knew that she was lost, knew that it didn't matter what happened next. He'd found his way into her heart. The realisation sank into her, but brought her no happiness, no warm feelings.

She couldn't have him, no matter what her heart was telling her, and she would always regret not being able to take that risk with him. Love was always a risk, she realised then; there was never any guarantee. You could only follow your instincts, and your heart.

Except... she couldn't. Not now.

Numb with anxiety, she closed the distance between them and curtseyed.

"Your grace," she said, hearing the tremor beneath the words, though she was determined to force them out. "May I request the honour of the next dance?"

Prue held out her hand in the imperious manner often used by men who were too certain of their lady's answer.

Robert gaped at her, his eyebrows hitting his hairline as the Earl of St Clair gave a startled bark of laughter. All around them, gasps of shock rippled around the room as the first strains of a waltz filled the air.

Prue watched his face, sick with apprehension as she awaited his reaction but forcing herself to remain in place. She'd done it. She had burned her boats. Now she must face the consequences. Slowly, and to her chagrin, a smile curved over his mouth.

"Another dare, Miss Chuffington-Smythe?" he said, smooth as silk, one eyebrow quirking. "I accept."

He took her hand, leading her onto the floor as Prue's head spun. *Er... now what?* She'd expected him to be furious, to take her to task, maybe even to cut her. This hadn't been in the plan. Drat the man, why was he always overturning her plots and rewriting things?

Any possibility of coherent thought fled as his hand settled at her waist and memories of the last time he'd touched her rushed into her mind. Heat swept over her, prickling across her skin, tightening and awakening her body.

"You're blushing," he murmured in her ear as he moved them into the dance. "Whatever are you thinking about?"

Prue swallowed and opened her mouth to give some devastating retort, but none came. Her mouth was dry; not a problem she was experiencing elsewhere, she realised with mortification.

"Stop holding me so close," she managed, her voice sounding jerky and odd.

"I want you closer than this," he said, amusement rumbling through his chest. She could feel that somehow, feel the words sink into her, melting into her bones. "I want you as close as you were in my carriage, closer even. I want to be inside you, to hear you moan and sigh with pleasure."

"R-Robert," she stammered, glancing about, certain that everyone must be able to hear his breathless whispers.

"I didn't sleep for thinking about it, for imagining what might have come next if you'd agreed to marry me."

"As we were minutes away from my home, I can only be grateful I did refuse," she said, doing her best to sound tart and snappish and only managing flustered and on the verge of swooning.

The scent of him was all around her, clean, masculine, with just a hint of cognac on his breath. She wanted to know if she could taste it on him too, wanted to press her mouth to his and chase the flavour across his lips with her tongue.

"Ah, but it's an easy thing to ask the driver to go around the block," he murmured, chuckling, low and wicked, as if he knew with certainty his words were setting her aflame. "And around and around."

"Good gracious," Prue exclaimed, quite giddy but unsure if the cause was his proximity, his outrageous words, or the fact she was thrumming with desire. "It's like dancing with a randy stoat. You're living up to your reputation tonight, your grace."

He smiled, though there was a glimmer of unease in his eyes

"A randy stoat?" he repeated, a little incredulous, and then gave a sigh. "I can't deny it. That's exactly how I feel."

Me too, Prunella did not say, because she was a liar.

He gave her a look of sheer challenge before lowering his head and whispering in her ear. "Come closer and I'll illustrate just how appropriate your description is."

He lifted his head and gave her a wicked grin and Prue mis-stepped, treading on his toe and stumbling. He righted her at once, his arms strong about her. She glared up at him, cheeks blazing as he returned a bland expression, all innocence. Torn between laughter and a jolly good cry, she knew she had to end this. Sooner or later this man would persuade her into his bed and, if she went, he would be relentless in his aim of making an honest woman of her. She couldn't do that to him… to either of them.

Frustration and misery burned inside her, chasing away any desire to find the situation amusing. It wasn't; it was tragic.

"Why aren't you furious with me?" she demanded, forcing herself to look at him again. "I asked you to dance in front of the entire ballroom. I've pretty much ruined myself. I'll be labelled a fortune hunter, no better than I should be… certainly not fit to be a duchess."

Though they were moving, going through the motions of the dance, she felt him go very still. His muscles grew taut under her fingers, his expression freezing in place.

"So, that's why you did it," he said dully, and she felt her heart ache at the loss of the teasing warmth she'd heard just seconds before. "You really would ruin yourself to escape marrying me." He gave a humourless huff of laughter. "Am I such a terrible prospect, Prue?" Hurt blazed in his eyes now. "Do you trust me so little?"

Prue stared at him, her throat tight as the music ended and the dancers all swayed to a halt. "My father was a bully and a liar," she said, forcing the words out, making herself say it even though she wanted to cling to him and beg his forgiveness for giving him a moment's pain. "I'll not swap a tyrant for a villain."

Eyes burning, she moved out of his hold and hurried away.

Chapter 15

My goodness, Prue, what did you say to him last night? As you walked away, he looked like you'd stamped on his heart.

—Excerpt of a letter from Miss Matilda Hunt to Miss Prunella Chuffington-Smythe.

***

The morning of the 26th April. Beverwyck. London. 1814.

"You might at least pretend you're pleased to see me."

Robert looked up, finding the amused green eyes of his sister regarding him. He smiled and reached out, giving her hand a brief squeeze.

"Of course, I'm glad to see you. You can't doubt it, surely?"

Helena pursed her lips and picked up a knife, intent on piling copious amounts of marmalade onto a piece of toast. "I can, when you stare into space with that morose look on your face, but it seems I'm not to blame for your ennui, so... tell me everything."

She waggled her eyebrows at him before taking a large bite of toast with even, white teeth.

"There's nothing to tell," he said, doing his best to force Prue's words from his mind.

"I'll not swap a tyrant for a villain." As they'd been echoing there all night, he didn't expect them to budge an inch.

"It's a woman," Helena said, dropping her toast and clapping her hands together with excitement. "Oh! At last," she squealed. "Who is she? Will I like her? Are you in love?"

Robert rolled his eyes at her. "I just said there's nothing to tell," he pointed out, bewildered, as ever, by his sister and her uncanny knack of knowing what he was thinking.

"Yes, and for a man with such a terrible reputation you're the most hopeless liar. There is clearly a great deal to tell." She took another bite of toast, staring at him and making *go on then* motions with her free hand.

"I suppose you'll tell me every detail of your romantic affairs when you finally come out, won't you?" he said dryly.

Helena dropped her toast and stared at him, wide-eyed. "Why of course, Robert, dearest. I'd never keep anything from you."

He snorted, shaking her head. "I'll admit, you're far better at that than I. I pity your poor husband." A troubled look crossed her face and he cursed himself. "Helena, I didn't mean—"

She smiled then, quick and bright, like a sudden shaft of sunshine. "I know," she said. "And you do know I'd... I'd never lie, not about anything important. Not unless.... Oh, I don't know, unless there was simply no other way. To protect someone, perhaps, where the truth would cause heartache. Do you know what I mean?"

Robert frowned, considering her words. "Yes. I know what you mean."

He'd thought Prue such a woman. He'd thought he'd felt a connection to her, something he'd never dared hope for. She was funny and vivacious, and said the most peculiar and outrageous things, and every time he was in her company, he didn't want to quit it. She was like no one he'd ever met before and, every time she walked away from him, he grew increasingly impatient for the time when he would see her again. Except, she'd made it clear she wanted no part of him. He sighed with frustration and then caught Helena watching him, her eyes full of sympathy.

"You've not gone and fallen for someone unsuitable again, darling?" she asked, such concern in her eyes he cursed himself for causing her such worry.

Lavinia had not only blackened his name; Helena would always be associated with her brother, *The Damned Duke*.

"No," he said, with a brief smile. "This time she is eminently suitable, handpicked by Uncle Charles, in fact, but…." He shrugged. "She's not interested."

"But how can that be?" Helena demanded, so obviously baffled that Robert could only laugh. "Well?" she pressed, shaking her head. "If Uncle Charles recommended her, then she's a sensible girl who would never listen to gossip, so it can't be your reputation."

Robert frowned. "No. No, it's not that."

She'd challenged him about his reputation to begin with, but she'd never seemed afraid of him. Not past the first few minutes of their acquaintance at least. He felt sure she didn't believe the worst of him any longer. So why had she flung that accusation at him last night?

He realised then she'd only said it when he'd failed to be angry at her asking him to dance. Thinking about it now, he supposed he *ought* to have been angry with her, but he'd only been charmed that she wanted to dance with him enough not to wait for him to ask her. Her boldness thrilled him. Her bravery made him want to be brave too, to spit in the eyes of the gossips and tattle-mongers and not give a farthing for them or their approval, propriety be damned.

She had gone out of her way to make him angry, though, to hurt him, to make him stay away. Why had she done that? It was only now he considered how she'd looked as she'd walked away from him. At the time he'd been too hurt, too raw to consider anything else but his own feelings, his own disappointment. Now, though….

She'd been close to tears.

What the devil was she playing at?

He looked down as Helena laid a hand on his arm.

"Let me help you," she said, eyes glinting with mischief. "If anyone can discover what is holding her back, it will be me. You know how good I am at winkling out secrets."

Robert frowned at her for a moment, but then nodded. "I'd appreciate that."

Helena gaped at him, so astonished he couldn't help but laugh.

"I never thought you'd agree," she said with delight. "I thought I'd have to torture you into it."

He shook his head, unable to hide that he was in a quandary. "I... I think she could be the one, Helena. I feel like I...." He trailed off, unable or perhaps unwilling to put it into words. If he said it aloud there would be no denying it, no taking it back. "I'll take all the help I can get," he said instead.

"Oh!" His sister leapt to her feet and moved around the table, throwing her arms around him. "Oh, Robert! I'm so happy. I'll do anything to help, you know that. I will like her though, won't I?" she asked, a flicker of doubt in her eyes.

"I think you'll love her," he said, knowing it was true. "And if you can make her love me...."

He shrugged and gave her a crooked grin.

"Robert," she said, giving him a stern look as she straightened. "If I know you, the poor girl is already besotted, so what on earth have you done to frighten her off?"

"I don't know, I swear it!" He threw up his hands in frustration. "One minute I'm certain she's at least halfway in love with me and there's no way she'll refuse my proposal, and the next... well, the next she does!"

She gave him a doubtful look. "How many times have you proposed?"

He rubbed the back of his neck, feeling awkward at the admission. "Once, officially, but I've repeated the offer several times in less… formal circumstances."

"And she *keeps* saying no?" Helena said, his ego somewhat mollified by her astonishment.

He nodded.

"She's got something holding her back."

"Her father was a brute," he said, his voice low and angry. "He beat her mother and certainly terrified Prue. She says she'll never be any man's property."

"And you've explained that you'd never… *ever*—"

"Of course!" he said impatiently. "And I think she believed me. I thought she'd begun to trust me, and that hurdle had been overcome but… apparently not."

He watched his sister as she pursed her lips and felt a swell of tenderness for her. He hoped to god there was a good man out there for her. She so deserved it. Never had she reproached him for Lavinia, even though his wife had not been the kindest sister-in-law at times.

"Or," she said, tapping one elegant finger against her chin. "There's something else, something you don't know about."

Robert nodded, looking into his sister's eyes and finding them filled with curiosity and energy. "Yes."

She smiled at him and sat back down again, replacing her napkin and reaching for another slice of toast. "Let me see what I can do," she said, her voice firm. "What is the lady's name?"

"Prunella Chuffington-Smythe."

Helena's knife clattered to the table. "Oh, dear me," she exclaimed. "The poor girl."

Robert snorted and gave her a rueful smile. "She told me once that the only reason she might ever be induced to marry was to rid herself of her name."

"Well," Helena said thoughtfully as she concentrated on piling marmalade onto her toast. "That's something to work with, I suppose."

***

27th April. The Dowager Countess St Clair's Spring Art Exhibition. London. 1814

Prue sighed and stared at an uninspiring portrait of a plump lady in an unlikely hat, as Aunt Phyllis chattered with one of her cronies. She wasn't entirely sure why she was here. The invitations for them all to attend a private exhibition had come out of the blue that very morning from the Earl of St Clair's mother. The dowager countess was a notable art lover, and her spring exhibition was quite a select event. Prue had no notion what they were doing here.

Aunt Phyllis had, of course, been beside herself with glee, and had almost forgotten to spend a large part of the morning reprimanding Prue for her appalling behaviour at the Cavendish ball. The only way to face scandal, in Aunt Phyllis' opinion, was to meet it head on and act as though nothing had happened. So, far from being given the chance to languish in her room and mope, Prue had been hustled out of the door and into a carriage.

Minerva looked about as pleased as she was to be here, and stared with an air of fatalistic gloom at a still life of flowers in a large crystal vase.

Prue stared at her cousin, wondering what was troubling her, and was about to walk over and engage her in conversation, when a small, neat figure barrelled into her, forcing her sideways.

"Oh!" the young woman exclaimed, dropping her exhibition booklet and her reticule in a flurry. "Oh, how dreadfully clumsy I am. I do beg your pardon. Are you hurt?"

Prue sank to her knees to help the girl retrieve the booklet and a small container of smelling salts that had rolled across the floor as the reticule spilled its contents.

"No, not in the least. Please, don't worry." Prue got up and smiled, holding out the smelling salts and the booklet and then froze.

The young woman stilled, eyebrows rising. "Is something the matter?" she enquired.

"I-I …" Prue stammered before collecting herself. "No! No. Not in the least. Here you are."

She was a beautiful girl, with flawless ivory skin, thick dark curls, and the greenest eyes. Just like her brother's. For there was no possible way this young woman wasn't related to Robert. The resemblance was uncanny.

"I'm Lady Helena Adolphus."

Prue dipped a curtsey. "I'm very pleased to meet you, Lady Helena. I'm Miss Prunella Chuffington-Smythe."

"Oh!" the young woman exclaimed, her eyes growing round and wide. "It's *you.*"

Flushing a little, Prue shifted, unsure of what that meant. "It is?"

The young woman beamed at her, a smile of such startling enthusiasm that Prue felt a little winded.

"Oh, how perfect. I just knew I would love you, after everything Robert said. He told me I would, of course, but it's such a relief to discover he was right."

Prue glanced around them to be sure no one was listening in. She felt her heart pick up, as she wondered what on earth Robert had told his sister.

"Take a turn about the room with me," Lady Helena said, leaving Prue no escape route as she grasped her by the arm. "Such a happy accident to have bumped into you," the young woman continued, and then gave a chuckle. "Quite literally, too."

"Indeed," Prue replied, forcing a smile and wondering if Lady Helena's brother was here too. Good lord, had Robert told his sister he'd proposed to her? What was he thinking? Did she not know Prue had refused him, and several times over?

Prue turned her head, aware of being scrutinised, and found Helena looking her over, curiosity in her eyes.

"Why won't you marry him?" she asked.

Taken aback by the forthright question, Prue could only open her mouth and stare.

Apparently unperturbed by Prue's stunned silence, Lady Helena continued. "If it's his reputation, I would like to put your mind at rest. Robert is the most wonderful man. He's been a devoted brother, he's kind and generous, and so sweet… not at all like the man you've heard about, I assure you. I don't recognise him in those descriptions, you know."

Prue opened her mouth, but Lady Helena appeared to be something of a force of nature and lifted a finger to silence her.

"I'm not blind or naïve, however," she said, frowning a little. "He does have a dark side, but it's only ever himself he hurts. After Lavinia died…." She paused for a moment, considering Prue. "Does it bother you if I speak plainly?"

Privately, Prue thought it was a little late in the day to pose the question, but she smiled and shook her head. "No. I prefer it."

"Excellent." Helena was brisk and purposeful as she propelled Prue towards a door that led to the gardens. Once outside and away from the crowds, Helena carried on.

"Lavinia seduced Robert, and he believed himself in love with her. He tried his best, he really did, but Lavinia was not a girl who wanted home and children and a happily ever after. They had a terrible row the day she died, and Robert said a lot of things he regrets, but he never wished her dead. He never wanted her hurt, and the combination of his guilt, and all the dreadful gossip...." She trailed off and shrugged. "He was in a dark place for a long time and I worried for him. He didn't seem to care about anything, certainly not himself, but... but that's changed."

Prue held her breath, willing the woman to keep the next words to herself, desperate not to hear them.

"You changed him."

"No... I...."

Once again, the imperious hand rose, one finger lifted in a demand for silence.

"You did, whether you meant to or not, and I've never been happier to see the return of the brother I love so dearly. I'd do anything to make him happy. Wouldn't you?"

Prue felt the weight of silence descend around them, her heart thudding in her chest.

"Yes," she said, meaning it. "Which is why I won't marry him."

Lady Helena gave her a shrewd look. "Yes," she said, nodding. "I rather thought that was the case."

The two women stood, staring at each other, Prue unflinching under the young woman's scrutiny. At last, Lady Helena spoke.

"Come to tea with me tomorrow." Again, the finger rose, brooking no argument. "I shan't take no for an answer," she added with a twitch of her lips. "I promise we won't discuss Robert, and I won't try to influence you or set a trap where you find yourself alone with him," she added, smirking. "I would like to know you better, though. So, you'll come tomorrow for tea, yes?"

Prue opened her mouth to politely refuse and snapped it shut as Aunt Phyllis' voice cut through her.

"Prunella would be delighted to accept, Lady Helena. We'll escort her, of course. At which time would you like us to come?"

Lady Helena stared at Aunt Phyllis, somewhat taken aback, but to her credit she said nothing. She merely glanced at Prue, who returned a mortified look of apology and wished she could die.

With no other option than to accept the inevitable, Prue listened as Aunt Phyllis made the arrangements.

Chapter 16

I feel like I've been caught in a web of my own devising, the harder I struggle to get free, the tighter I'm bound. I've been such a fool, done such a dreadful, spiteful thing that there can be no forgiveness for it. The only way to cut myself free will be to tell the truth, but I'm too afraid of the fall, when there will be no one there to catch me.

—Excerpt of a letter from Miss Prunella Chuffington-Smythe ... never sent.

***

28th April. Beverwyck. London. 1814

Beverwyck was impressive. Aunt Phyllis was in raptures, while Minerva was, by contrast, white-faced, awed, and strangely sullen.

"Good heavens, think of what the seat of the dukedom must be like, if this is his London home?" Phyllis exclaimed, alight with excitement.

Prue pressed herself back against the seat of the carriage and willed herself invisible.

Once inside the vast building, Lady Helena was the perfect hostess, charming and welcoming, putting them all at their ease and giving them a brief tour of some of the highlights of the grand house before settling them down for tea. Under her informal and cheerful presence, even Prue relaxed. She felt confident that the young woman would keep her word. Though Aunt Phyllis pressed several times for details about her brother, *the duke,* Helena kept to the blandest of answers, turning the intrusive questions aside for other topics of conversation.

There was only one moment when Prue felt the question resurface.

She had risen, teacup still in hand, to look down at the gardens behind the house. It was hard to realise you were still in London and not the heart of the country as she stared outside at the beautiful vista. Spring colour was everywhere, the scene vibrant and welcoming, filling Prue with a longing to explore.

Lady Helena appeared at her elbow.

"My mother loved the spring," she said softly, before giving Prue a direct look which seemed to ask the unspoken question: *Why won't you let him share it with you?*

The clatter of a cup chinking too hard against its saucer had both Prue and Lady Helena spinning around. In her excitement, Phyllis had almost upset her tea—and as a large, dark figure filled the doorway—Prue could see why.

"Robert!" Helena exclaimed. "You promised," she added in a fierce undertone only Prue could hear.

Prue was relieved to discover that Lady Helena was as dismayed by his presence as she was. She would have been disappointed to know his sister had lied. Robert, however, had clearly broken his promise to her.

"I changed my mind," he said with a bland smile. "Ladies, it is a lovely day. Won't you take a turn about the gardens with me?"

***

Robert escorted the ladies outside, trying hard not to look directly at Prue. It had been obvious enough that seeing him enter the room had horrified her. He tried to push away the ache that bloomed in his chest, wishing he understood what he'd done, or what it was she feared he'd do.

He wasn't some green boy, he knew when a woman found him attractive, and Prue had wanted him badly that day in the carriage. Even the last night he'd seen her, when she had tried so hard to end things between them, the tension between them had been enough to make it hard for him to breathe.

She wanted him, and she liked him, too. He felt sure it was true in his heart, but his heart had misled him before. His confidence in his own judgement was severely dented, and he did not know what to do for the best. Perhaps he ought to have left Helena to it. She'd promised to help him, and he'd promised to let her, and not to interfere. Knowing that Prue was here, however, in his home….

He couldn't help himself.

Drawn to her presence like a magnet, he'd been powerless against the desire to see her again, to be in her company. He'd hoped he'd see the same desire returned in her expression.

He had not.

Robert looked around, dragging his thoughts back to his sister's guests as Prue's appalling aunt spoke to him.

"Minerva loves daffodils," she was saying, giving her daughter a fierce look when she didn't respond.

"Oh, yes, indeed," the young woman said, her enthusiasm quite obviously mechanical. "It's why I wear yellow so often."

"There were lots of young fellows at the Faversham's' garden party who said she looked like a daffodil in that lovely yellow gown. You even received a poem, didn't you, Minerva?"

"Yes," Minerva said, smiling though her voice sounded dull. "I did."

Her mother gave her a surreptitious jab in the ribs and Minerva started. "C-Could we go and see the daffodils over there, your grace? They look so lovely."

Robert glanced up to see a flash of impatience in Prue's eyes.

"Of course," he said, offering his arm. "Though I'm sure their loveliness will pale with you beside them."

Minerva blushed and looked down, the picture of maidenly innocence, and Robert forced himself not to look back at Prue.

He kept up a stream of inane chatter as they walked, liberally interspersed with fulsome compliments. With each one, Minerva looked more ill at ease—which might have been intriguing in other circumstances—while her mother looked as if she might burst with excitement.

It was the hardest thing not to look at Prue, though he could not escape a look of pure fury from Helena. His sister clearly believed he'd run mad, and he could do nothing to gainsay her. He *felt* mad. Mad and out of control, and desperate to understand what the hell was going on.

Of all the things he'd wanted, most of all it was not to fall for a woman who would lead him a dance and keep his heart on a string, and what had he got? Damnation, he was a bloody fool.

He returned his attention to Minerva, laughing heartily at some silly comment she'd made and feeling like a blasted idiot. Was this what he'd been reduced to? Trying to make the woman he wanted jealous, like some lack-witted schoolboy?

"I'm sorry, would…?"

He looked around at the sound of Prue's voice, finding her pale and unhappy.

"Would you excuse me? I don't… I feel a little…." She blushed, the colour vivid against the pallor of her skin, and then turned tail and almost ran back in the direction of the house.

"Miss Chuffington-Smythe!" he called after her, feeling like an utter bastard.

"Oh, don't worry about her, your grace," her aunt Phyllis said, with a blithe lack of concern. "She'll be fine. Probably a megrim. She's rather an odd girl, always scratching away writing or with her nose in a book. All that thinking isn't good for her, I've told her so. It's not good for the female brain. Is it any wonder she gets headaches, I ask you? No, no, such things are best left to the men."

"Mrs Butler, Miss Butler, do come and look at the folly with me," his sister said, encouraging them further into the garden.

Once they were on the path, Helena gave him a sharp gesture, and a glare, indicating he should move himself, fast.

Robert didn't need telling twice, and hurried after Prue.

With a little help from a gardener who had seen the path she'd taken, Robert discovered her on a bench in a private corner of the garden. It was one of his favourite spots, hidden out of view from both the house and the rest of the garden, but with the focal point of a statue of Artemis at the far end of a swathe of lawn, and deep borders on either side.

"Prue," he said, dismayed as she stiffened at the sound of his voice.

He hurried towards her before she could move, dropping to his knees on the grass and taking her hand in both of his.

"Forgive me," he said, his voice hoarse with regret. "I've been an utter arse, I know it. I wouldn't blame you if you held me in contempt for today's entertainment."

He looked up at her, ashamed to see there were tears in her eyes.

"Prue," he said, helpless to know what to say. "I know I'm an idiot, and you are at liberty to tell me so. I wanted to make you jealous, to punish you for hurting me. I don't understand what I've done to—"

2

"You've done nothing wrong," she said unsteadily. He watched as she swallowed and shook her head, one tear sliding down her cheek. "This is not your fault."

Robert stilled and took a breath, staring down at the ground before finding the courage to look up at her again.

"Prue," he began again, desperate to understand. "Will you answer one question, please, and swear that you'll tell me the truth? I understand it will likely not change the answer to the other question I've posed several times, but… but I should like to know…."

She wiped away the tear and gave a taut little nod.

Robert hesitated, and then asked, "Do you *want* to marry me?"

His heart crashed in his chest, loud in his ears as she closed her eyes. For a moment, he thought perhaps she wouldn't answer him.

"Yes," she said.

She spoke so low, the word barely more than a whisper. He almost didn't hear it. His heart leapt, and then he saw the bleak, fatalistic look in her eyes.

"But it doesn't change anything?"

"No."

Unsurprised, Robert bowed his head for a moment, and then pressed a kiss to her fingers before releasing them. He got up and sat beside her. They sat together in silence for a little while, both trapped in misery only she understood the reason for.

Robert took a deep breath.

"The morning my wife died, I'd found her in bed with one of my friends. It was at a house party, one of many I arranged during the summer… at her insistence. She did love to be entertained."

"Oh, Robert," Prue began, but he shook his head and she fell silent.

He needed to tell her this, so she'd know all of it. Even if she never changed her mind, he wanted the truth between them, his truth at least. He prayed one day she would trust him enough to give him hers.

"It wasn't a huge shock by that point, except that there wasn't even the slightest pretence at discretion. He was in her bed, in her room, the one adjoining my own. God, I felt like such a bloody fool. I started drinking, though in truth I'm not certain I'd sobered up from the night before. The whole group was going hunting that morning, though."

He paused, remembering the scene, remembering his fury and despair, and the sickening sense of being trapped. Watching them all laughing and raucous in their hunting pinks, he'd felt like the fox, hunted down and trapped with no escape. Lavinia was smiling and flirting with the man who had been his friend, utterly unrepentant that she'd seduced someone who had been a part of his life since he was a boy.

"I was drunk and furious, and I... I confronted her in front of everyone."

He let out a breath, staring down at his hands and not entirely surprised to find them trembling.

"I told everyone she was a slut and that they'd best take tickets for her bed, as she'd make her way through them sooner or later. She was angrier than I'd ever seen her and retaliated, of course, telling them... well, what a poor husband I was." He paused, appalled to find his throat tightening at the memory. "I'm by no means perfect, Prue, I know that, and I'm not proud of the things I said. I know I ought not have done it in such a manner, but I *had* tried to be a good husband to her. I had, truly."

He swallowed as she reached out and covered his hand with her own. Robert tucked her fingers into his and held on, wishing he could always hold on to her, wishing that she would let him.

"I told her that...." Pausing, he took a deep breath and tried again. "I told that I hoped she'd break her bloody neck, that I'd be well rid of her."

Robert heard the soft intake of breath, and knew he couldn't hide from her reaction.

"She did."

Prue stared back at him, horror in her eyes. Few people knew the truth of that day. They had hushed it up, but rumours surfaced, whispers and differing versions of events. He looked down at his hands again, at Prue's slim fingers held in his, seeing nothing but Lavinia's beautiful face, utterly still.

"I was a long way back on the field. In fact, I was far too inebriated to be anywhere near a horse, let alone out hunting, and I realised it soon enough. I was about to turn back when I saw her, riding hell for leather at a jump no one in their right mind would take, but she lived for the thrill of excitement, for the risk, for the moment of recklessness and the possibility of discovery, or death...."

Robert watched Prue's slim fingers withdraw from his and closed his eyes, knowing it was inevitable. He put his head in his hands for a moment and then forced himself to face her, to see the disgust in her eyes.

She had gone a startling shade of white, one hand covering her heart. Robert watched the elegant hand tremble as it moved to her throat. To his dismay, it was worse than he'd thought. She looked ill, as though she might faint or vomit and, before he could even begin to think of a way to tell her he was sorry—that he'd never forgive himself for his actions that day—she'd scrambled to her feet.

"I… I must go…. I…." The words were disjointed, her expression one of utter panic. "I need a hackney cab, at once."

"Prue, please, I know I don't deserve your forgiveness but—"

She cut him off, her voice impatient. "No. You don't understand. I don't… it isn't…. It isn't you. You're not the…. It's me," she said, her eyes filling with tears as her voice broke. *"It's me!"*

He watched as she backed up and then turned and ran.

***

Later that day. 28th April. Premises of My Lady's Weekly Review. Drury Lane. London. 1814

Prue sat still. It took a remarkable effort of will. The office on Drury Lane belonged to a Mr Richardson, printer and proprietor of *The Lady's Weekly Review*. He was due back at any moment, and so she had no option but to bide her time and wait for him.

She closed her eyes and pressed one hand to her stomach, praying she wouldn't have to face the ignominy of casting up her accounts before seeing a man she needed to beg a favour of. Though she had already written to him days earlier, asking for him to withdraw the remaining chapter of her story, he had replied, denying her. He had paid for the story in good faith, and he intended to publish it, but he didn't know how close she'd come to the truth of what had happened to the real duke's wife… how close and yet how very, very far from the truth.

This chapter all but accused him of hunting down his wife and killing her, if not by his own hand, then by her terror at needing to escape him. Terror that had forced her to risk taking a jump she knew she'd likely not make.

What had she done? What had she done?

Robert would be vilified all over again for something that had not been his fault. The guilt in his eyes over the part he had played that day had been so fierce, so heavy. The thought of adding to that burden, of making the *ton* stare in his direction and accuse him all over again made her want to curl up and die. Her stomach roiled, the sound audible as she took a deep breath, trying to steady her careening heart.

Coming here had been a risk. The printer only knew her as Miss Terry, and that was the way she liked it. If he had any sense, he'd guard her anonymity, but it would give him power over her if he was in any way unscrupulous. Not that it mattered now. She was ruined enough, and it was her that had done the ruining. Not by asking Robert to dance in full view of the *ton*, either, but by making such a mess of her own life, and damaging his so deeply, so callously, that there would be no going forward together.

How strange to realise that she would have done it—would have risked all her plans—now, when there was no possible way of taking the risk. Robert was a good man. Not a perfect one, by any means. He had made mistakes and he would have to live with them, but he had learned from them. He had a good heart and she felt she could have trusted him with hers, with her body and soul. She doubted such a man would ever come her way again. She certainly didn't deserve it.

"Well, the mysterious Miss Terry," came a dry and amused tone.

Prue leapt to her feet and regarded a stocky, balding man with piercing blue eyes and a craggy face.

"Good afternoon, Mr Richardson. Thank you for agreeing to see me."

"Not at all," the fellow said, looking her over with interest as he opened the door to his office and gestured for her to enter. "You've done remarkable things for my magazine, young lady, and I had been intending to ask for a meeting with you. You've just brought it forward a little is all."

He gestured for her to sit and Prue did so as he moved behind an ancient and heavily scarred desk, covered with papers and newspaper clippings. She leaned forward, her heart thudding hard.

"Please, Mr Richardson, I must ask you not to print the final chapter you have. The Duke of Bedwin is being badly maligned and…."

There was a dark chuckle and the fellow shook his head. He spoke before she could finish.

"Ah, but it's the Duke of Bedsin who's the villain of the piece."

Prue looked at him with impatience. "We both know that is a flimsy disguise, and that everyone believes the duke is the inspiration for the character."

"And so he is," Richardson said, smiling a little as he sat back in his chair and laced his fingers over the generous curve of his belly.

"Quite so," Prue admitted. After all, there was no point in trying to deny the obvious. "However, I have come to realise the real duke is nothing like the man I have portrayed. He played no part in his wife's death and has suffered the gossip and ill-natured prattling of the world as they painted him in the blackest of colours. That I have had a hand in this makes me burn with shame, and so I am begging you… *please*, sir, withdraw the chapter. I promise you will have another to replace it by next week. A new story, something—"

"No."

Her breath caught, tears prickling in her eyes.

"Please, Mr Richardson," she begged, appalled to hear her voice tremble and break, but she would get on her knees if she had to. Anything to stop that chapter being seen by the world… by Robert.

"Miss Terry," the man said, leaning forward towards her now, his voice gentle. "I could not, even if I wanted to. The magazine was printed days ago; it will be on sale tomorrow, and so has long been sent out to the various distributors. I'm very sorry, but what you ask is impossible."

Prue sat back, misery overwhelming her. Well, that was that, then.

Mr Richardson continued to speak, a fatherly tone to his voice now, with a hint of condescension that she was too defeated to take issue with.

"The duke is a grown man, a powerful one at that, and he's had a long time to get used to such notoriety. In fact, he's always done his best to live down to his reputation as far as I can see. Don't worry your pretty head so. There's no reason for him to know that it was you who wrote the piece; I'm certainly not about to give you away. Killing the golden goose is hardly in my interests. Which brings me to what I was hoping to discuss with you. I think we need to discuss a publishing deal, don't you?"

Prue got up, hardly hearing his words and certainly not caring. Nothing mattered past the terrible thing she'd done. Somehow, she had to make it right.

"I have to go," she said, with the disjointed sense of walking through a nightmare. The world seemed at once darker and filled with shadows, and she would have to grow used to them, to walk within them. That was where she belonged.

"But miss, we are talking about a good deal of money here. You'll be made——"

"Thank you, Mr Richardson," she said dully. "If you'll excuse me."

***

Later still that afternoon. 28th April. Upper Walpole Street. London. 1814

Prue sat at the tiny writing table in her room, staring down at the words which the world would read and exclaim over tomorrow morning. She always kept copies of the chapters she sent to the magazine, and so there was no escaping the scurrilous tale, no way of lying to herself and pretending it wasn't as bad as she'd thought.

It was worse.

How could she have written such things about a man she didn't know?

Except she'd believed she had known him. When she'd first begun the story Prue had believed the gossip and seen a man just like her father, a bully who would use his fists and his might to crush someone who ought to have been protected by that same might, and with that same passion. At the time of writing she'd felt like a pioneer, a champion for those women who could not stand up for themselves, showing the world the face of a tyrant who hid behind his title and his power and was untouchable, especially by someone whom he owned like he did a horse, or a teacup, or a pair of shoes.

Even when she'd begun to understand he was perhaps not the violent man she'd believed him to be, she'd been unrepentant, as he was clearly a libertine and a profligate gambler at best.

Except she'd been wrong about that too.

Robert was flawed, but no tyrant, and Lavinia had been no virgin sacrifice. Her father had already sacrificed her virginity to get him closer to a title, and she was tired of being a pawn. Neither was hero nor heroine, villain or villainess. Just two people with imperfect lives, muddling through and making more mess in the process as their anger and hurt drove them towards a terrible climax.

Prue had played judge and jury without even regarding the evidence. There had been *no* evidence, only deliciously dark whispers and murmurs of cruelty and vice. She'd listened to it with as much eagerness as anyone, fuelled with righteous indignation and ready to strike out at the villain, at the powerful nobleman who thought himself invincible, invulnerable, and would prey on those who were weaker than himself.

In a fit of anger and frustration, Prue swept the papers from the table. With a muffled cry of anguish, she put her head in her hands.

She did not hear the door open until Minerva was in the room. She and Aunt Phyllis must have come home, and she hadn't even noticed. Stupidly, she had also forgotten to lock her door, and now Minerva hurried in.

"Prue, wherever did you get to? I was so worried. Are you ill?"

Prue jolted, getting to her feet so fast that her chair tipped over and crashed to the ground. She lurched forward, snatching up the scattered papers as Minerva bent to help her.

"No! Don't!" she exclaimed, panic making her voice hard and angry.

Minerva jumped a little and straightened but she had a sheet of writing in her hand and, in the light of Prue's shout, she looked down at it with a frown. Prue's heart gave one erratic thump and she reached forward, trying to seize the sheet from Minerva, but she evaded Prue's hand, and then it was too late.

Minerva paled as her gaze rose from the paper.

"It's you," she said, her voice soft, her lovely eyes growing wide. "Y-You're Miss Terry!"

"Minerva," Prue said, her stomach twisting in horror. "Please, listen to me."

"You wrote all those things about Bedwin," she said, looking truly shocked. "And he's... he's not at all like people say he is, you know he isn't. He's been kind and... even when Mama is being so vulgar and awful, he never... he never crushed her, he never looked down on us, and...."

Minerva took a step back, as though being in the same room as Prue was something she couldn't stand to do.

"Minerva! Minerva, come at once, you have a visitor!" Aunt Phyllis almost screamed up the stairs, her voice vibrating with excitement.

Prue's heart skittered in her chest, as if one heartbeat had run directly into the back of the next, each of them stumbling and crashing about. Turning, she looked out of the window that looked down into the street. She couldn't breathe.

Robert was at the front door.

Oh, dear god, no.

Prue swung around to beg Minerva to hold her tongue, to make her understand that Prue would make it right. She would do that much before she confessed to her sins, but Minerva had gone, and she'd taken the page of today's chapter with her.

"Minerva!" Prue shouted, terror forcing her past the numbness in her mind and body, driving her into action. She ran to the stairs, but Minerva had already reached the bottom, and Aunt Phyllis had already shown Robert inside.

"Minerva, don't! Please—"

As though in a dream where the horror unfolded in slow, inevitable increments she saw Minerva hold the page out, delivering it to Robert, who frowned. He looked at Minerva, to Prue, and then down at the sheet of paper, taking it from her hands.

Prue froze, clutching at the banister, breathing as if she'd run for miles, her lungs burning, her skin turning to ice as she watched him read. The chill sank into her, into her blood and bones, freezing her so thoroughly that she couldn't move or speak. The inescapable cold reached her heart, and she was glad of it, glad for the way it numbed her against the pain of shock as he realised what he held, and who was responsible.

Those green eyes looked up, meeting hers.

Prue had written of broken hearts before, jotting down trite little sentences depicting pain and longing and hurt, but she'd never experienced it first-hand. She'd never seen a heart break before her eyes, never felt her own explode in that same moment, the icy shards tearing at her from the inside out, slicing clean through her soul.

Prue watched him drop the sheet to the floor, turn away, and leave.

Chapter 17

Oh, darling, Prue, what have you done?

—Excerpt of a letter from Miss Matilda Hunt to Miss Prunella Chuffington-Smythe.

***

May 4ᵗʰ Beverwyck. London 1814

Robert winced as the curtains drew back with a snap.

"I said to leave me alone, damn you!" he cursed, struggling to lift his head enough to glare at whatever idiotic servant had ignored his express commands.

"Speak to me like that again, and you'll be wearing the pot of coffee I've so kindly brought you," his sister replied. She stood over him, looking down at him with a wrinkled nose and an expression of deep disgust. "You smell like a wet dog," she observed.

"Good," he muttered, turning onto his side and away from her. "Just what I was aiming for."

"I meant it about the coffee," she said, her clipped, precise words jangling through his brain as she plopped several lumps of sugar into a cup with the silver tongs, being sure to clang and clank as much as she could as she poured and stirred it with pure viciousness. He'd never known pouring coffee could be so bloody noisy, or so damned vindictive.

"All right, all right," he cursed, groaning and clutching his head as he heaved himself upright in his bed.

Relenting a little, his sister helped to pile the pillows behind him, set the cup into his hands and perched on the edge of the bed.

"I don't smell that bad," he retorted, observing her pretty nose still crinkling. "I've not even been near a bloody dog, wet or otherwise."

"No," she allowed, folding her arms. "But I'm too much of a lady to say you smell like a whore's parlour."

"Christ, Helena!" he exclaimed, choking on his coffee in shock. "Where in god's name did you even learn such a word?"

She returned a scathing look. "Oh, please, my brother is *The Damned Duke*, I'd have to be deaf, blind, and utterly stupid not to know of at least some of your exploits, you idiotic creature."

At the reminder of what had sent him into this latest spiral into hell, a sharp stabbing pain hit him hard and fast, somewhere in the vicinity of where his heart used to reside. It had been a surprise to discover he still had one after Lavinia, and a bigger one to discover he was as much of a fool as he'd always been. God, would he never learn?

"I wasn't there to…." He cleared his throat, feeling appalled as Helena rolled her eyes and waved his excuses away.

"So, Prunella is the author of *The Dark History of a Damned Duke*?" she asked, getting to the heart of things like a surgeon with a blade.

Robert glared at her. It never ceased to amaze him that no one else realised his sister was far more ruthless and resolute than her brother had ever been. She never pulled her punches. The girl had the face of an angel, and the dogged determination of a bloodhound.

He remained silent, his jaw so tight it sent pain radiating through his head. Too hurt and angry to form actual words, he knew if he thought too much about what Prue had done—the things she had written about him—he'd need to destroy something… or cry. It dismayed him to realise the second option was more likely than the first.

"I knew I liked her," Helena said, smiling a little.

That got his attention.

"What? You think what she did was admirable?" he demanded, shocked and further hurt that his sister, of all people, wouldn't defend him.

Her expression softened and she reached out, taking his hand.

"When do you suppose she wrote that story, I wonder? I mean, the series began months ago. That was chapter sixteen and, as the magazine publishes an episode each week...."

She trailed off, giving him a look that urged him to keep up as Robert struggled to follow her train of thought.

"You mean to point out she must have written it before we met?" he said cautiously. Damned if he would believe there was a way to forgive her for what she'd done. He'd forgiven Lavinia for trapping him into marriage, for forcing his hand, and look where that had got him. "Or at least, much of it?"

Helena didn't answer, but held his gaze. "Tell me again what happened when you told her how Lavinia died. How did she react?"

"She looked like she would be ill, and ran away," he said sourly, remembering his guilt, remembering how he'd understood that she'd not want anything to do with him, that *he* wasn't worthy.

"Yes, yes," Helena said, waving that away with impatience. "But what did she *say*?"

Robert sighed, setting down his cup and folding his arms, doing his best to focus his aching brain on a scene he'd tried hard to forget. Somewhere through the haze of brandy, her words filtered back to him.

"She said I didn't understand," he replied, frowning as he tried to recapture her words. "She said it wasn't me, that I wasn't...."

Robert rubbed at the back of his neck, trying to remember, what *had* she said? "She said it wasn't me, it was her."

Helena stared at him as his heart thudded.

"I think your young lady is rather extraordinary, Robert, and I stand by what I said. I like her. I think she made a mistake with you; the same mistake most everybody does. She's guilty of believing gossip, but I think she knew that day. I think she realised how wrong she was, and she wanted to put it right. I think that's why she ran but, unless you see her, speak to her, you'll never know for sure."

Robert felt his eyes prickle, hot and alarming as he fought for composure, anger and resentment warring with hope in his chest... but hope had sent him down the path to his destruction once before, and he was afraid to repeat the same steps.

"She vilified me in front of the world," he said, the words uneven. "I was falling in love with her, and all the time...." He snapped his mouth closed as his voice broke.

Helena reached out and stroked his cheek. "I know, dearest. I'm not saying she's blameless. Who is? But she lived her life in the shadow of a monster she couldn't fight. You said that yourself. Perhaps she believed she was slaying a dragon." She smiled at that, a look of such affection cast his way that his throat tightened. "Only to discover he wasn't a dragon at all."

He closed his eyes, wanting her words to be true but not daring to believe them.

"You'll never know, Robert, if you don't ask. You'll never be sure. You'll always regret letting her go, if you don't hear her side of it. Go to her, for heaven's sake. At least let her explain. Then you'll know the truth."

Robert let out a shaky breath and nodded. "All right," he said, though it sounded begrudging. "I'll talk to her."

Helena smiled, patting his cheek and then pulling a face. "There's a good fellow, and for the sake of society, wash and change before you set foot outside or you'll be locked up for criminal offenses to nostrils, and for causing a danger to public health."

"Funny, Helena," he muttered, accepting a second cup of coffee. "Now, go and find yourself a husband, would you? So I don't have to be amused by your scintillating wit a moment longer."

Helena chuckled and got to her feet, blowing him a kiss. "I love you too, darling," she said, with a saccharine smile, before leaving him alone.

***

May 4th Mrs Charlton's musical Soiree. Berkeley Square. London. 1814

Prue shuffled herself a little further into the corner and out of sight. To say she was in disgrace was putting it mildly. Minerva hadn't spoken a word to her in days, and Aunt Phyllis was angrier than she'd ever seen her. She believed Prue had ruined Minerva's chances, that the duke had been on the verge of proposing, and Prue had wrecked everything. Minerva did not contradict her, perhaps believing it too. Prue didn't know. She almost welcomed their anger; it felt as if she was receiving her just desserts. She well deserved her punishment and would not try to escape it.

She would, however, try to escape this terrible evening.

Everyone was talking about the last chapter of her wretched story. Everyone was lapping up the sordid tale and wondering how much of it was based on the truth, for surely the author must know something… there was no smoke without fire.

Prue had stepped in to defend Robert a few times, to say the author was likely someone with a grudge, that there was no evidence at all of his wrongdoing, and this was merely vindictive gossip. There were some who'd agreed with her, and others who weren't about to let the truth impede a delightfully salacious story.

Now she was tired and dispirited, and drowning in guilt that made her stomach churn and her heart hurt. She swallowed hard, afraid her misery might force her to sob into the fronds of the potted palm she was cowering behind.

When the next chapter published tomorrow, she hoped she would have gone some way towards making amends, but she wouldn't see it happen, wouldn't see the reaction to her words first-hand. She'd be gone by then.

Prue had already written a letter to her aunt and Minerva, explaining as best she could, and apologising. She had only to return home to leave the letter and pick up her carpet bag, stuffed with all she could carry, and tiptoe out of the house.

Her new beginning awaited.

There, at least, she had been lucky. There had been a dear little cottage she had longed to rent. She had seen it advertised in a local paper when they were still in Otford, and thought it sounded perfect. Far enough away from everyone she knew, but close to a busy little village so she need not be entirely solitary. She'd so wanted it, just weeks ago. The idea of the cottage, her independence, and a new life had filled her with excitement and anticipation. At the time, it had been beyond her meagre savings, and she'd put it from her mind with regret, but now—with Mr Richardson's help—she could take on the lease and settle into the life she'd always believed she longed for.

Alone.

It was earlier than her plan had allowed for, but she'd returned to see Mr Richardson who had given her a generous advance on the deal they had made for three further stories. He would publish each of them in the form of a novel, once the magazine had run the story in its entirety. Mr Richardson was confident they would be hugely successful.

He'd been sceptical at the change in tone to *The Dark History of a Damned Duke*, but after reading it he had smiled at her and nodded his approval. She'd even seen an almost fond expression in his eyes as he read the rather surprising ending.

Mr Richardson had been especially taken with the outline for her next story, about a young girl who nearly ruined her own life and those of the people she cared for by being too ready to listen to gossip.

When he'd praised the idea, Prue had returned a rueful smile and said there was nothing better than writing from experience. Except that she would deliver her misguided heroine from a lonely fate as an old maid, alone and unloved, and give her the gilded happy ever after that she longed for, even if the spiteful creature didn't deserve it. She had no illusions about her own fate, though; that was one she could not rewrite to her satisfaction.

Prue jumped as a soft voice spoke close to her ear. Turning, she braced herself for another icy set down as she found Minerva staring at her, a thoughtful expression on her face.

"What's in the next chapter?" she asked, a rather brittle tone to the question, which Prue could hardly blame her for.

"Redemption," Prue said, smiling a little. "Mine, not his," she added in a hurry. "He never needed it, only… only understanding."

Minerva nodded, a small frown pleating her smooth forehead. "I'm sorry," she said, rather abruptly, as if she'd forced the words out before she could change her mind.

"What for?" Prue asked, a little taken aback. Minerva had never apologised to her before, not ever.

She watched the girl take a deep breath. "I never liked you," she admitted, wrapping her arms about her waist, a rather defensive glint to her eyes as her chin went up. "You always made me feel stupid, as though I ought not care about my clothes or my hair, even though that's all I've got to work with."

Prue opened her mouth to object, but realised she couldn't. For a long time she'd thought Minerva a rather vapid creature, too frivolous for good sense, and too ready to spend her mother's meagre savings on finery. Of late, Prue had come to realise there was more to Minerva than this, but she knew there had been times in the past when she'd treated her cousin unfairly.

"I'm not clever like you, Prue," she said, looking annoyed but also frustrated. "You're brave enough to change things, to do something reckless like writing a story in secret and getting the world to read it. I could never do that," she said, her eyes a little too bright. "But I *am* pretty," she said with defiance. "And I know how to listen to a gentleman, how to make him feel wanted and appreciated, and that's something I can use to get us out of this half-life. We're stuck on the fringes, Prue, always wondering if we'll have enough to make it to the end of the month and I'm sick of it, but...."

She paused and, to Prue's astonishment, reached out and took her hand.

"But I ought never have showed your writing to Bedwin. It was cruel of me, both to him and to you, especially... especially as you're so obviously in love with him. I'm sorry, Prue. I know that doesn't mean much now, but I am."

Prue felt her face crumple and bit her lip, fighting for composure. Giving up on it, she pulled Minerva into a hug and held her tight.

"You're wrong," she said, sobbing a little. "It means a great deal, more than you'll ever know, and I must apologise too, Minerva. If I have ever made you feel stupid or silly, then that was unforgiveable of me. Idiotic, too, when you are quite obviously neither. It was foolish of me, when we could have been friends all this time if I'd only stopped and given you the chance."

To her relief, Minerva gave a little huff of laughter and returned the hug before letting her go. "Don't feel too bad," she said with a remorseful smile. "I really am rather silly."

Prue shook her head and took Minerva's hands. "No. Never say that or think it. We must all make our choices and take our chances for happiness. We are none of us free to live how we might like to, but we do the best we can in the circumstances, yes?"

"Yes," Minerva said, smiling now. "Yes, we do, and… and I will take a leaf out of your book, Prue," she added, chuckling at the pun. "Well, not directly, perhaps, but I will be braver. From now on I will do things I want to do; not what Mama would have me do. I'm tired of trying to catch a title. It's not what I want, not really. I just want to be happy."

Prue squeezed her cousin's hands, torn between pleasure at finding a friend in one of her only relations, and feeling a deal of regret for having not seen what was right in front of her. For someone who fancied themselves a writer, she really was terribly unobservant, and too ready to make assumptions. That she would have to change. She'd hoped the change had already begun.

They looked around as a murmur rippled over the room, and Prue's stomach did an unpleasant little flip as Minerva turned back to her wide-eyed.

"It's Bedwin," Minerva whispered.

"Oh, no."

Prue withdrew her hands from Minerva's hold and shrank back into the corner.

"Perhaps you should speak to him, try to explain?" Minerva suggested, her voice gentle.

Panic erupted in Prue's stomach, like a thousand butterflies with wings of steel. She shook her head, hardly daring to breathe in case he looked in their direction.

"There's nothing I can say," she said, feeling hot tears prick at her eyes. "I can't pretend I didn't write all those dreadful things, can I?"

"No," Minerva agreed, glancing back at the room to where the hostess was greeting the duke. "But you could tell him you're sorry, and that you love him."

Prue wiped her cheeks with a gloved hand, unable to stop the first tears from spilling over.

"You do love him, don't you?" Minerva pressed, staring at her.

"Yes," Prue said, laughing, though she didn't know why. She'd never felt more like crying in her life. Perhaps she would cry *for* the rest of her life. It felt entirely possible. "Yes, I rather think I do."

Minerva smiled at her and nodded. "Wait here," she said, a decisive look in her eyes, and Prue watched as she headed out into the throng.

Chapter 18

Oh, my word, did you read today's chapter? I can't believe it. I never saw it coming!

—Excerpt of a letter from Miss Bonnie Campbell to Miss Alice Dowding.

***

May 4th Mrs Charlton's musical Soiree. Berkeley Square. London. 1814

Robert stiffened as he saw Minerva Butler moving towards him. His instinct was to cut her, to move away and concentrate on finding Prue among the hordes, but he wasn't that cruel. Besides, Minerva might lead him to Prue, if her blasted mother wasn't nearby.

"Good evening, your grace," Minerva said, dipping an elegant curtsey.

"Miss Butler," he said, his tone cautious. "Are you here with your family tonight?"

The young woman's lips twitched a little. "My mother is deep in conversation with some old friends, as she didn't know to expect you this evening. You are safe for the time being," she said, making him smile at her honesty. "Prue isn't with me, but... she is here, and I can take you to her."

Robert let out a breath. "I would appreciate that."

Minerva nodded and then hesitated, surprising him by reaching out and laying a hand on his arm. He forced himself not to snatch it away, realising at the last moment it was not a flirtatious move, but rather one of sympathy.

"I'm sorry for what I did. It was unfair of me to do that to you, and to Prue. I ought to have given her the chance to explain it herself but... I was angry."

He shrugged, returning a twisted smile. "So was I."

"She got it wrong," she said, squeezing his arm. "She knows it, and she's sorry. Sorrier than you perhaps realise. Did you know she's...."

Robert's breath seemed to catch as she hesitated, wishing she'd say the words he hoped for, but she shook her head and smiled.

"I think I'd better let her tell you. After all, she's better with words than I am."

"Very well," he said, a drum beating in his chest, harder and faster than it should, sounding in his ears.

"You will give her a chance?" Minerva pressed, searching his face. "You'll not... you'll not be unkind to her?"

Robert shook his head, wondering if he was being a fool all over again. He'd let a woman destroy his life once before, forgiven her, and given her the chance to repeat her destruction, over and again. Was he about to fall into the same trap, to forgive a woman for rubbing his name into the dirt, and lay his heart on the line for her to trample in the same fashion?

There was no way to be certain. No guarantee. He could only follow his heart, even though he was no longer sure he could trust it, and even though he was scared to death.

"I just want to speak to her," he said, surprised that his voice was steady when he was certain his hands were shaking. "I want to understand, but I'll not make a scene, you have my word."

Minerva nodded, and led him through the crowds. Everyone was staring and whispering, too many eyes full of condemnation. People parted before him as though a tiger prowled in their midst, liable to strike out at any moment. She'd done this, he reminded himself, only to deny it again. She had not. Lavinia had begun it; he'd made it worse. Prue had only raked over the coals of his dark past. She'd not caused it, only encouraged the flames to burn hot again.

He didn't care about that. Not now. The only thing he cared about was the future, and if there was the possibility he had one. With her.

They crossed from the entrance hall into a room as crowded as all the others: too full, too much chatter, the entire house stuffy and too hot. It was claustrophobic and he longed to escape, longed to get away from all these bloody people and their judgement. Perhaps, if the conversation with Prue went the way he hoped….

Perhaps she'd escape with him?

To his amusement, Minerva hesitated beside a potted palm.

"Wait here a moment," she said, and ducked behind it. A second later she reappeared, looking a little perplexed. "She was here a moment ago."

Robert's heart sank. "Did she know you were coming to speak to me?"

Minerva nodded, her hands clasped tightly together. "Please, don't think she didn't want to see you, but…."

"But?" Robert repeated, willing her to speak before his nerves gave his heart cause to stop from exhaustion.

"She's drowning in guilt," Minerva said with a little shrug. "I think I underestimated how badly. She might be too afraid to face you." He watched as she scanned the crowds of people crammed about them with a sigh. "We must split up if we're to have a chance of finding her."

Robert nodded, and then reached out, delaying her before she could move away. "If you find her first, tell her I'm… I can't say I'm not angry," he said, shaking his head in frustration. "I'm bloody furious, but… but I can understand if… *damn it*," he cursed, low and savage. "Tell her I want to understand, to talk, not to berate her or cause a scene. I'm *not* a monster. I won't act like one."

Minerva smiled and nodded, and they headed into the throng.

***

May 4th. Upper Walpole Street. London.

With a stroke of luck she ill deserved, Prue found a hackney on Hill Street, just moments after escaping Mrs Charlton's soiree. Giving her aunt's address on Upper Walpole Street, she stared, unseeing, out at the shadowy streets of the city.

Robert was back there. She could have stayed, tried to explain, but she couldn't bear it. She wanted to remember the look in his eyes when he'd asked if she wanted to marry him; not if she *would*, but if she wanted to. There had been such hope, such longing. When she'd told him yes, his expression had been joyous, that boyish smile dawning over his mouth for the briefest moment, until he understood that it changed nothing.

That moment was engraved on her heart and she'd not give it up. She didn't want to see accusation in those green eyes, to see the hurt and contempt at having been so wrong about her. That he would regret her in the same way he regretted his first wife was a pain in her chest so severe she could hardly breathe.

Prue pressed the heel of her hand against her heart, rubbing slow circles and trying to draw breath, but her lungs refused to co-operate. Tears pricked at her eyes and the urge to let go and sob until she was empty and limp as wet paper was hard to resist. She had to, though. Just a little longer. Once she was gone, once she closed the door on the cottage she had rented, she would be alone. Then she could cry. She could cry and wail for as long as she liked, for there would be no one to comfort her. No one would know where she was.

She'd tell them eventually, of course. It wasn't fair to disappear when her friends would worry for her. A maid would have to be engaged, too, for practical reasons as much as to give a nod to propriety. So, then she would not be so utterly alone.

The thought did not reassure her.

Once at Upper Walpole Street, she bade the driver wait and hurried inside. As silently as she could, so as not to wake Sally, who was a light sleeper, she crept up to her room. Prue knelt beside her bed and reached underneath, snagging the handle of the bag she'd packed and dragging it out. With one last look about the room to check there was nothing of importance she would miss, she reached inside the bag and removed the letter she had written earlier. Ignoring that her hand trembled, she placed it on her pillow and left the room.

With as much stealth as she'd entered, she padded down the stairs… and then screamed loud enough to wake the dead as a figure broke free of the shadows.

"It's only me, miss," Sally said with an impatient tut. "You jumped like you thought the devil had come for his kin. That's a guilty conscience you're carrying, if I'm not mistook."

"Holy God!" Prue said, leaning against the wall for support and covering her heart with one hand in case it tried to escape her ribcage. It felt like it was making a significant effort to do just that.

"Now, now, Miss," Sally scolded, shaking her head. "I don't mind if you curse like a sailor, but blasphemy I won't stand for."

"Forgive me, Sally," Prue wheezed, still turning hot and cold in quick succession. "But you scared me half to death."

"That's what you get for creeping about like a blasted burglar and trying to run away in the dead of night without so much as a word of goodbye."

There was an indignant and rather unsteady sniff, and Prue took a better look at Sally now her heart had decided she wasn't about to be murdered after all.

Sally was dressed, including hat, coat and gloves, and with a capacious bag not unlike Prue's waiting at her feet.

"What...?" Prue began, a tight sensation closing about her throat.

"I don't know what you done, nor where you're off to at this time o' night, but I'd not sleep sound again if I let you go alone," Sally said, her voice firm, though her eyes were shining a little too bright. "You can't so much as boil an egg, you'll forget to eat at all once you get a pen in your hand, and heaven alone knows what will become of your gloves. You can't go on without me, so don't go supposing you can. I'm coming. I made me mind up."

"B-But Sally...." she protested, so touched she could hardly speak at all. "Aunt Phyllis—"

"I knew something was up and, when I saw some of your stuff missing this morning, I looked about and found that bag. So, I arranged for a friend of mine to come in first thing to take over my duties. She's a good girl and needs a job. They'll hardly notice I'm gone. You, though...."

Sally wrestled a large handkerchief out from her sleeve and blew her nose.

"Sally," Prue began, her voice soft, but Sally held up her hand.

"You can explain later, if you want to, but I don't need no explanation. I'm as fond of you as if you were my own girl and I'll not let you go out into the night alone. I'm with you, miss, so you may as well get used to the idea."

Too emotional, and too grateful, to consider arguing, Prue gave up and threw her arms about Sally, hugging her tightly.

"Thank you," she whispered, fighting the urge to break down as Sally hugged her back. "We'd best go, then. There's a chance they'll come looking for me if they discover I'm missing."

With a nod, Sally let her go and reached down and hefted her bag. Prue did the same, and they hurried out to the waiting carriage.

***

Robert waited outside the address on Upper Walpole Street, trying and failing not to pace. Surely Prue would speak to him, once Minerva explained the situation? His pacing halted as the front door opened and Minerva appeared once more. Her expression did not bode well, and his heart sank. Then he saw the letter in her hand.

It transported him back to that moment, just a few days ago, when she'd put a handwritten sheet of *The Dark History of a Damned Duke* into his hand, and when his heart had broken as he'd realised the truth.

"She's gone," Minerva said, blinking back tears.

"Where?" he demanded, his voice rough with panic, with the fear he might never see her again, might never have the chance to tell her he didn't bloody care.

At that moment, he realised it was true. He didn't care about the bloody story. Unless she believed that was who he was, but she didn't. He knew that. Robert remembered the first time they'd met, remembered the panic in her eyes, and knew then it hadn't just been his reputation that frightened her... it had been the fear of discovery.

"It doesn't say," Minerva said, her expression full of sorrow and regret. "I'm so sorry."

Robert's jaw tightened against the desire to curse as frustration burned within him. "Where would she go?"

He looked back at the girl, wanting to shake her as she shrugged. "I've no idea."

"Damnation," he muttered under his breath, wanting to say far more, wanting to climb back onto his carriage, take the reins from the driver and race at breakneck speed until he found her.

He couldn't just drive off into the night, however, when he hadn't the slightest idea of what direction she'd taken. He'd find her, though. Somehow, he would find her.

"She's not alone," Minerva said, breaking into his thoughts.

For a moment he believed his heart stopped beating as the words sank in. *No.* That couldn't be true. Prue wouldn't …

"Oh, no!" Minerva said, appalled as he grew still and likely turned the colour of ash as he felt the colour drain from his face. "I mean our maid, Sally. She's gone too. I meant to reassure you she wasn't all by herself."

Robert let out an unsteady breath.

"She says she'll be in touch, once she's settled," Minerva added, giving him a hesitant smile. "I'll let you know the moment I hear anything, or if I think of anywhere she might have gone. You have my word."

He nodded, frowning, knowing he couldn't just go home and go to bed. "Is there the chance she would return to Otford? Perhaps to collect her belongings?"

Minerva thought about that. "Perhaps," she said. "She has hundreds of books, and Mama would only let her bring a few to London. It's possible she'd fetch them."

Robert didn't wait a moment longer. He had a destination in mind, something to do.

It was better than nothing.

***

It was mid-morning by the time he returned to Beverwyck, tired and dispirited, and sick at heart. If Prue had returned to the cottage in Otford, she had beaten him to it, and she hadn't lingered.

He'd waited there for several hours, just to be certain she wasn't coming. At least it gave the horses a break after pushing them too hard on moonlit roads over the three-hour journey.

It had been a slower return journey, as he'd allowed the driver to take the reins and had ridden inside. Taking pity on the fellow, he'd told him to take his time. It wasn't as if there was anything to hurry home for. He'd scared the poor fellow out of his wits, driving like a man possessed. Robert had seen the desire to tell him to get a grip on his sanity on the man's face, but you didn't tell a duke he was a bloody fool and to stop this madness, even if he was liable to get you both killed.

He trudged inside the doors of the great house, giving over his hat, gloves, and coat in silence and then stood in the entrance hall, not knowing quite what to do next.

"Lady Helena is in the breakfast parlour, your grace," the butler ventured, as if this instruction might snap his master out of whatever strange trance had caught him.

It worked well enough and Robert gave a nod, forcing his feet forwards. It was only when he reached the door and opened it a crack that he realised he didn't want to see anyone... least of all Helena, as she would want explanations.

He backed up, moving as quietly as possible so she wouldn't notice him, and then paused as he saw his sister wipe a tear from her cheek. Helena was a stoic creature, despite her fragile looks. He'd rarely seen her cry, even when their mother had died. She'd kept the worst of her grief to herself, though he knew she had wept in private.

That tear was enough to have him moving forwards again, forcing his own troubles aside. "What is it?" he asked, hurrying to stand beside her, laying his hand on her slender shoulder. "Helena, what's wrong?"

She looked up at him, her green eyes lovelier than ever as they sparkled with tears.

"Nothing," she said, her voice a little unsteady. "Only, it was so lovely I… I couldn't help myself."

Robert frowned, perplexed, and then looked down to see what it was she'd been concentrating on when that tear had slid down her face.

That morning's copy of *The Lady's Weekly Review* was open before her, at the latest chapter of Prue's story.

"Here," she said, picking it up and offering it to him. "See for yourself."

He took several paces back, shaking his head as if she had offered him a venomous snake.

"No," he said, feeling his heart contract. He couldn't read any more of Prue's words, describing him as a wicked, heartless monster. He couldn't bear it.

"Read it," Helena said softly, her expression full of affection for him. "You need to read what she's written. She's made it right, Robert. She's shown the world who you really are. The hero, not the villain."

His breath caught and he stared back at her for a moment longer, still unable to reach for the magazine she held out to him. He watched as she stood and moved closer, reaching for his hand and closing his fingers about the paper.

"Read it," she said again, before lifting on tiptoes to kiss his cheek and leaving him alone.

Chapter 19

Dear Alice,

I hope you can forgive me for disappearing in such a scandalous manner and for still not giving you my address, even now. I know it's odd but it's for the best, for the moment at least. I can assure you I am quite well, however. I just needed to get away. There is also something I must confess, to you and to all the Peculiar Ladies.

I am Miss Terry. Please forgive me, dearest Alice and tell the others how sorry I am for not confiding in you sooner.

—Excerpt of a letter from Miss Prunella Chuffington-Smythe to Miss Alice Dowding.

***

May 27th. A cottage in the country. Location undisclosed. 1814

Prue looked up from over the pages of her writing and smiled as Sally gave a happy little sigh of pleasure.

"Oh, Miss, that was just… lovely," Sally said, clutching her arms around herself. "And to think you thought it up yourself!" The maid made a soft clucking sound, shaking her head in wonder. "I always puzzled over what it was you spent so long writing, when you didn't send that many letters."

"Well, now you know," Prue said, tucking the sheets back into the folder she kept them in.

"Thank you for reading it. It was the highlight of my week, listening to Miss Minerva read out the new chapter."

And hadn't that been a surprise, Prue thought ruefully. It had never occurred to her that Minerva would do such a thing as take the time to read to Sally, who had never learned herself. It had never occurred to *her* to do such a thing. She allowed the guilt of that to settle alongside all the rest. Not just what had happened with Robert, but having so misjudged her cousin, and made her feel less than she was. What a wretched creature she had been.

"At the end of the last chapter I was so sure the duke had chased the heroine to her death. It was such a shock to discover she didn't die in the fall, and that he was protecting her from the hero, who was the *real* villain! I was never more surprised, nor happier neither," Sally added, hugging herself a little tighter. "I always liked the duke, despite his wicked ways. It's good to know he had a heart all along and was just... misunderstood."

She gave Prue a shrewd look. "Reckon that duke of yourn is misunderstood too, don't you?"

Prue swallowed hard and got to her feet, turning away from Sally and picking up the notebook where she'd made lists of things they needed to buy. "He's not my duke," she said crisply. "But yes, I think he was."

"I think he is your duke," Sally continued, a matter-of-fact tone to the words. "I think he's yours for the taking, but you're too scared to chance it."

"Sally!" Prue said, telling herself she was simply appalled that the woman should be so bold as to speak to her in such a fashion. "That's not... not true," she managed, her voice quavering.

Sally stood and walked towards her, folding her arms. "Why then? Why, when he wants to marry you so badly?"

"He doesn't!" Prue exclaimed, feeling the inevitable tears clog her throat and make her eyes burn. "Not any more, not after what I did."

"And you know that how, exactly?" Sally demanded, reaching out to grasp Prue's arm when she would have turned away. "You must face him, Prue. Tell him you're sorry and listen to him tell you how he feels. You owe him that much."

Prue shook her head, fighting to keep her composure even as her tears spilled. "I can't," she said, struggling to get the words out. "I can't bear it…. He must hate me, and I can't bear it."

Sally pulled her into a hug and rubbed slow circles on her back, as if she was soothing a child and not a grown woman. "There, now. You listen to me. You're stronger than you know, my girl. I promise you that. Whatever happens, you'll survive, and you'll live, and you'll laugh again. You've made amends, you've given back that which you took from him. You shouldn't have done it, of course you shouldn't, but we all of us make mistakes. Yon duke isn't perfect, I reckon. He's had his share of wicked deeds, I don't doubt. There's no smoke without fire, and I don't think he's an angel by any means, so don't go acting like he is one."

Prue drew in a shuddering breath and wiped her cheeks, forcing herself to calm as Sally let her go. "I know I should face him," she said, relieved to discover her voice a little unsteady but more like herself now. "I should be brave enough to own up to what I've done and apologise, but… but I don't think I am brave enough, Sally. At least, not yet. If I see him and he's angry, I… I'm afraid that I'll just cry and make a fool of myself and I can't—"

Sally nodded and took both of her hands.

"All right, my lamb. Don't get into such a taking over it. Perhaps you need time to feel strong again. I'll not keep on at you, but I hate to think you might lose an opportunity to be with the man you love."

Prue flushed and stammered, but Sally rolled her eyes.

"Oh, stop it," she said with a huff. "I'm half in love with him myself after what you've told me, and a woman of my age should know better. Now, run along and write something, and stop cluttering up my kitchen. I have work to do."

Prue did as Sally bade her, too unsettled by her words to stay. Heaven alone knew what she'd say next. Writing seemed unlikely, though. Her mind couldn't settle, too full of shame and guilt, and a healthy dose of self-pity.

Instead, she wandered about the cottage, which didn't take long as it was tiny. It was also charming and everything she'd dreamed of, and yet she could take no pleasure in it.

She was self-sufficient, an independent woman who earned her own keep, and lived her own life, despite the restrictions of society, and she could find no satisfaction in that... because of a man.

The irony did not escape her.

Damn it, Prue, pull yourself together, she scolded, staring out of the window to a pretty patch of garden, currently lashed by a heavy downpour of rain. She shivered and got to her knees by the fireplace, intending to light it and chase the gloom away. A blazing fire would be cheerful company and make her feel better. Besides, she reasoned, she wasn't miserable *because of a man*, she was miserable because she had mistreated and abused a man who did not deserve it, and that was a different thing entirely.

A little mollified, she concentrated on coaxing a fire to light, and did her best to put Robert out of her mind.

***

29th May. Otford. Kent. 1814

"Anything?" Charles asked, a hopeful glint in his eyes as Robert strode into his study.

"If there was any sign of her, I'd hardly be back here alone, would I?" Robert snapped, and immediately regretted it. His uncle had been marvellous, doing everything he could to help him track down Prue, but they were getting nowhere. "Forgive me," he said, closing his eyes and rubbing the back of his neck. "I didn't mean to—"

Charles tutted and got to his feet, waving the apology away. "Never mind, never mind. I can see you're out of your wits worrying about her, and I feel the same way. I feel so bloody useless. If I were a younger man—"

"You've done everything you can, Uncle. More than I would ever have expected. We must simply hope she gets in touch with her friends soon, and that one of them lets me know where she is."

"But if she's run away, they will think she's hiding from you, that she doesn't want to see you."

Robert snorted. "Well, that rather seems to be the case."

Charles sighed and shook his head. "I had a thought. That magazine she works for—"

"I already tried," he said, a darker look entering his eyes. "I spoke to Mr Richardson, the proprietor. He swore he didn't know her new address and then told me he'd not give it if he had it. *A lady's address is her own to give out*," he mimicked, capturing the man's London accent.

"Well, I can't say I can fault him," Charles said, shrugging.

"No," Robert agreed, rubbing a weary hand over his face. "I wouldn't, if the circumstances were different."

"Anyway," Charles continued, picking up where he'd left off. "That wasn't what I meant. I thought perhaps a private advert in the paper."

Robert snorted. "What? Like, 'duke seeks young woman, blonde hair, hazel eyes, slender....' My god, I'd be inundated."

His uncle returned a reproachful expression and shrugged. "It was just an idea," he said, sighing.

Robert smiled a little, knowing he was trying his best. He opened his mouth to apologise, and then closed it again as an idea occurred to him.

"What?" Charles sat forward in his seat. "What is it? You've had an idea, haven't you?"

"I...." Robert began, and then smiled, the first proper, genuine smile he'd given since before Prue had disappeared from his life, since before he'd discovered what she'd done. "I have," he said, laughing a little. "Yes, I really think I have."

***

30th May. Premises of *The Lady's Weekly Review*. Drury Lane. London. 1814

Robert felt foolish, and rather like he was standing before one of his old schoolmasters for some misdemeanour or other as a boy. Sitting a little straighter, he reminded himself he was a bloody duke and refused to allow the blush that was threatening to crawl up his neck at any moment.

Mr Richardson glanced up from the papers before him, a look of mild surprise glinting in his eyes, nothing more.

"So, you don't mean her any harm? You'll not retaliate for the story she wrote?"

Robert quirked one eyebrow, trying to hold on to his usual arrogant persona, the trace of a sneer at his lips. It had been a damn sight easier when everyone believed him a villain. "Considering half the *ton* is now in love with me, I don't see why I should be the least bit dismayed by her story, but as you can see... my intentions are honourable. Otherwise, I'd hardly write something like...." He waved a hand at the papers on the table by way of illustration, fighting the urge to wince with embarrassment.

His fame had ratcheted up another notch since *The Damned Duke* had gained his happily ever after. Women fluttered and batted their eyelids in full view, sighing and flirting if he gave them half a chance, which he hadn't. He'd avoided society unless it was to do with gaining information on Prue's whereabouts, but the blasted woman had disappeared off the face of the earth. He'd always longed to be a hero instead of a villain, but at this precise moment he couldn't fathom why. Perversely, he rather longed for the good old days.

"Well, your grace. I hope that a declaration of marriage is what I hold in my hand, for if not, you'd best rewrite it."

Robert felt the flush prickle a touch more insistently at the base of his throat but held Richardson's gaze, unblinking. "It is," he said, rather pleased that he sounded bored and ready to be done with this interview when his heart was jolting about like a March hare.

"*An Apology from a Hero to a Villainess,*" Richardson read aloud, quirking one eyebrow. "You sure about that title?"

"Quite sure," Robert replied, biting off the words with impatience. Damn the man, he would agree to publish the piece if Robert had to buy the bloody magazine to make him do so.

Mr Richardson sat back in his chair, lacing his fingers over a generous stomach that spoke of too much time sitting on his arse. He also bore a ruddy countenance that pointed the finger at a half empty decanter on the bureau to the left of his desk. Robert forced himself to keep still and not rise to pour out a generous measure.

"I don't let just anyone publish in the magazine, your grace," Mr Richardson said, a shrewd glint in his eyes.

"I'm the Duke of Bedwin," Robert replied with icy civility. "Not *just* anyone." He wasn't certain if behaving like an arrogant bastard was the best course of action towards getting what he wanted, but he was too close to losing his bloody mind for anything subtler. He needed to find Prue, find her and tell her he didn't give a tinker's curse about the bloody story so long as she knew the truth of him now. That truth being he wanted her, wanted to know her, and love her, and do his damnedest to make her happy if he could.

"Normally there is a selection process to go through," Richardson carried on, with a faintly paternal air. "However, seeing as it is yourself, your grace, I suppose it might be possible to persuade me to… er, circumnavigate the usual procedures."

"How much?" Robert barked, drumming his fingers on the arm of his chair to stop himself from reaching over the desk and giving the blasted man a hard shake.

Mr Richardson smiled.

***

9th June. Beverwyck. London. 1814

Robert had to kick his heels for a further ten days before the story made its appearance.

"It's here!" Helena squealed, after rifling through the magazine to find the article and almost upsetting her teacup over it. They were sitting at the breakfast table, though Robert hadn't eaten a bite while they awaited delivery of the magazine.

He let out a breath, torn between gut wrenching relief and utter mortification. Everyone would know it was him who'd written it, he felt sure, even though it was anonymous. He'd put a few details in that Prue would recognise, just enough for her to be certain and, if it worked, he wouldn't give a damn if the whole world thought him a hopeless sap. If it didn't, however, and people guessed it was him, he'd be humiliated before the *ton*. He shuddered at the idea and snatched the magazine away from Helena as she bent her head to read.

"That's private," he muttered, setting it down on the table beside him and out of her reach.

Helena stared at him incredulously, and then lifted one elegant eyebrow just a touch.

Robert sighed. "I don't care if it's being read by thousands of people, it's still—"

His sister got to her feet, leaned over the table and snatched the magazine back again. Robert glowered at her, but there was really no point in arguing. She'd only buy another copy. He folded his arms and assumed a mutinous expression, refusing to meet her eyes when she looked up a few moments later.

"Oh, Robert," she said, laughing and teary all at once, her voice choked. "She'll come running back. She'll have to after reading that. It's… it's perfect."

He allowed his gaze to flick to hers, frowning a little. "You think so?"

She reached out and squeezed his hand. "The only problem is she must hurry. I've never been so popular as these past weeks, but I know all too well every woman of my acquaintance is just angling to meet you. Now they know how you've been wronged, there are bleeding hearts all over town. They'll trample me in the rush, given half a chance. Now this is out, it will be even worse." Helena gave a dramatic sigh. "For heaven's sake, Robert, marry her as fast as you can, or I'll never have a moment's peace."

"I'll do my best," he said, smiling at her. "I can promise you that."

***

12ᵗʰ June. A cottage in the country. Location undisclosed. 1814

"Come and sit down will you? Your tea's getting cold." Sally said, for the third time as Prue waved her quill in acknowledgement. "There's a new story in *The Lady's Review*," her maid added, unable to restrain her excitement.

"I know," Prue muttered, frowning as she tried to recapture the phrase she'd been working on. "You've told me five times today."

"Yes, and I told you yesterday and the day before, and you've still not read it to me."

Prue gave a soft laugh and looked up. "I'm sorry, Sally. I'm a dreadful trial to you, I know I am. It's just I haven't been able to write for weeks and suddenly I can. I have deadlines to meet. If I don't, then I won't be paid, and...."

Sally rolled her eyes and waved the excuses away. "You still need to eat and rest. Driving yourself so hard is just as bad as moping about the house, sobbing your heart out when you think I can't see you. You're still punishing yourself and I don't like it. Something has to give, miss."

"I never moped," Prue replied indignantly.

Sally looked back at her, expressionless.

Prue huffed and set down her quill. "Well, all right. I may have moped, but with good reason."

"Well, I'm going to mope if you don't come and read me this blasted story," Sally retorted, taking a slice of plum cake for herself.

In the past weeks, Prue had been so lonely that the line between maid and friend had blurred rather more than it ever had before, and Sally often came and took tea with her in the afternoon. Society would no doubt think it scandalous and another sign of her obvious eccentricity, but Prue didn't care. Sally had been a good friend, and she'd not forget that.

"You could always read it yourself," Prue said, getting to her feet, knowing she'd not get a moment's peace now until she came and had tea and read the blasted story.

Sally pulled a face. "That's hard work, miss. I just want to listen and enjoy it."

Prue smiled. One thing she'd done, to make amends for never having read to Sally—and for her loyalty in coming with her to the middle of nowhere—was to teach Sally to read. She was doing nicely, too, but it was still a chore, even though Prue had promised she'd enjoy stories much more once she could read them by herself.

"Well," she said, accepting a steaming cup and slice of cake. "At least read the title for me, while I drink my tea."

"Right you are," Sally said, reaching for the magazine and flicking through to find the story. "*An Ap ...o..lo..gy,*" Sally read, sounding out the letters. She looked up at Prue, who nodded.

"An apology."

"*An Apology Fr ...om ... From a Hero to a Vill ... ain ...*"

Prue frowned, listening to Sally struggling over the sounds. "An apology from a hero to a villain?"

Sally shook her head, not looking up. "No, miss. A villain ...ess."

Prue's heart gave an unsteady thump in her chest. A villainess was exactly how she'd seen herself of late, a cruel woman who'd tormented a good man when he'd already suffered too much at the hands of gossips and tattletales.

"Give me that," she said, taking the magazine from Sally's hand.

"Oh, now you want it," she said, throwing up her hands.

"*An Apology From a Hero to a Villainess*, by Anon," she read aloud. "What a strange title."

"Sounds like one you ought to read, miss, if you don't mind me remarking it."

Prue stiffened. Never had Sally reproached her for what she'd done, though she had to think worse of her for it. That was inevitable, but the comment was hurtful, even though she deserved it.

"You think me a villainess, then," Prue said, forcing the words out, though she didn't wish to hear the answer, but Sally only rolled her eyes.

"Of course not!" she said, impatient now. "Honestly, that's a guilty conscience that is, assuming I think bad of you, when I don't."

Prue let out a breath and gave Sally an awkward smile. "Sorry. I'm afraid that's quite true."

Sally snorted and lifted the teapot to refill their cups. "I know that," she replied, unperturbed. "I only meant that you see yourself that way, which is just as hare-brained as thinking the duke was a villain when you had nothing to go on but gossip."

"But this isn't gossip, I *know* what I did," Prue protested, refusing to allow the comparison. "I can judge the evidence because I know all the details."

"Oh, for heaven's sake!" Sally muttered. "And you're a blasted hanging judge, you are. What about the fact your father was a brute, what about the fact you thought the duke was the same, that he'd humiliated and bullied his wife? You sought to make an example of a man who abused a position of power, to stand up for those who couldn't do it themselves. Only thing is you went about it all back to front, and you chose the wrong man. As soon as you realised, you changed things, and once you face him and own up to your mistake, you'll feel a good deal better."

Prue's nerves surfaced at the idea. She swallowed and set down her cup and saucer as they clattered together. "I know you're right," she said, wringing her hands. "I'm being a coward by staying away. I must face him, sooner or later. I should just get on and do it."

"You should," Sally said, giving a decisive nod before pouring a little more tea into her saucer and sipping it.

Prue smiled, feeling a rush of affection for Sally's steadfast friendship. "Very well, Sally," she said, gathering her nerves and ignoring the fact that she felt dizzy with misgiving. "There's no time like the present. If we leave now, we can be in London by mid-afternoon. I know one of my friends would put me up for the night. Ruth, perhaps, though it's a dreadful imposition to turn up unannounced." Prue chewed her lip for a moment, thoughtful as she turned the plan over in her mind. "I suppose, while I'm about it, I may as well face Aunt Phyllis, too. I don't think she'd turn me away. Yes, better if we return and spend the night with her, if she'll have us."

"Now?" Sally exclaimed, wide-eyed.

"Yes." Prue got to her feet. "Come along, Sally. We must pack, just enough for overnight. I will get this ordeal over with, and then I really can start again. A fresh start," she said, forcing a smile, even though her throat was tight with anxiety and sorrow.

Sally gave a huff and put down her own cup and saucer. "But what about the story?"

"It will still be there tomorrow, Sally, or you can read it yourself in the carriage if you're that desperate," Prue said, a little impatient now as she ran up the stairs. "Now do hurry or we'll not be there before dark."

Chapter 20

Dear Prue,

I am writing this, hoping that you will send me your direction soon so I will know where to send it. Oh, Prue, Bedwin was here, asking for you. He's obviously desperate, darling and I don't think he's the least bit angry. If you'd only come back. I pray you will.

—Excerpt of a letter from Miss Matilda Hunt to Miss Prunella Chuffington-Smythe … awaiting direction.

***

12th June, Beverwyck. London. 1814

"There's always the possibility she hasn't seen it yet."

Helena's face was too full of sympathy and Robert avoided looking at her, staring instead into the fire. The weather was wet and dismal, the previous sunny spring weather snuffed out and sodden under the weight of grey clouds and puddle strewn streets. It seemed fitting somehow.

Three days. Three days since the bloody article had appeared, and not a word. No letter, no contact, and certainly no sign of Prue throwing herself into his arms and telling him, *yes!* Yes, she loved him too, yes, she would marry him, yes, they could put this whole ridiculous mess behind them.

He'd kept telling himself the same thing, that she might not have seen it yet, but surely, she would have? She usually read the magazine, and having written for it herself, and so successfully, surely she'd be curious about other contributors?

So, perhaps she'd read it and... and she wasn't interested. Perhaps she hadn't run because she felt bad, perhaps she hadn't left that day to do something to stop the story appearing, but... she had given him an ending fit for a hero. She'd redeemed him in the eyes of the *ton*. If she didn't care, why would she do that? It made no sense.

Questions and possibilities circled his head, making less and less sense the more he tried to think things through. He needed to see her, that was all. If only he knew where she was, then he could put things straight.

"It is possible," Helena said again.

Robert frowned, having forgotten his sister was there for a moment.

"Oh, yes," he said, distracted by thinking of what he would say if Prue was here right now. How he would tell her how he felt, or that he wanted them to start over, if that was what she wanted too?

He was so deep in thought he hardly noticed the butler, nor his information—delivered to Helena as she was the only one paying attention—that there was a Miss Chuffington-Smythe here to see his grace.

"Robert!" Helena exclaimed, giving his arm a hard shake as he jolted back to the here and now at the mention of her name. "She's here!"

"S-She's here," he stammered, frozen for a moment as he wondered if he was still daydreaming.

"For heaven's sake, Robert," Helena said, pulling at his hand as he hurried to his feet. "Run to her, tell her you love her, just... just don't let her go until she knows that!"

"No, right," he said, his heart leaping to his throat. Where in god's name had his wits gone? "Do I look all right?" He tugged at his cravat, which felt like it was about to throttle him, when it had been perfectly comfortable before.

"Very handsome, now *go!*" Helena said, pushing him towards the door.

He dug his heels in for a moment, panic a living thing beneath his skin. "What… what if she doesn't want me?"

Helena's voice was low and soft and full of reassurance. "You'll never know unless you speak to her, Robert. You'll figure it out, but I don't think you've got anything to worry about."

Robert nodded, squared his shoulders, and followed the butler down the hall to the woman he loved.

She was facing away from him, staring out of a window at the gardens. The weather was still foul, rain lashing at the glass, the wind howling like a tormented soul as it funnelled around the great house. Robert rather thought he might do the same if the next few minutes didn't go as he hoped.

"Prue?" he said, his voice soft as the butler closed the door on them.

She almost jumped out of her skin at the sound of his voice and then turned and gave an awkward curtsey. "Your grace," she said, head bowed, not meeting his eyes.

Robert's heart sank. That was not an auspicious beginning.

"Thank you for seeing me," she said in a rush.

Her posture was rigid, her gloved hands gripping the handle of a small reticule, her complexion pale. She looked tired, he thought, as if she'd slept little of late, and badly at that.

He knew how she felt.

"I won't take up much of your time," she hurried on, still avoiding his eye. "I just wanted to come and face you and tell you

I was sorry, so… *so* sorry, for what I did. I believed everything that was said about you. I listened to gossip, and I believed you were a villain and that you deserved all the wicked things I wrote about you, but then I met you and… and I realised, almost at once, that it wasn't true."

She stopped, swallowing hard and staring down at her toes. Robert waited, sensing she needed to say this, that she had been waiting to say the words that poured from her now. He watched as she drew in a deep breath and stood a little straighter.

"I tried to stop the worst, the most damning chapter from publication. You must understand, I did not know the circumstances of your wife's death. If I had… but in any case, I should have tried to stop it sooner… but it was so hard to believe… to believe in you. I wanted to believe in you so badly, you see."

She looked up then, meeting his eyes and flushing hard, the colour vivid against her pallor until she turned away, turning her back on him. As she spoke, she stared out at the storm, which grew ever fiercer, the skies darkening further by the moment.

"My father was a charismatic man. Charming and funny, so very likable, and such a liar. My mother believed in him, over and over she believed in his lies, but they were always lies. He always smiled and promised her the world, that she'd be safe, that she could trust him, that they would be happy. The world thought him a good man, they thought my mother a lucky woman, and as he ground her into the dirt, everyone felt sorry for him for having married such a faded, listless creature,"

Robert's heart clenched at the sorrow in her voice, his chest aching as he heard her voice tremble, heard her strength as she continued.

"But he did it. He broke her heart and her spirit. She was clever and bright and loving, and he took that from her. He took her from me. I swore no man would ever do that again, not to me. I would never marry, never believe the lies men tell. I would live my own life, alone and stronger for it. Except… all men are not the same, and I forgot that. I forgot that everyone deserves a chance, everyone deserves a second chance, too, and I didn't give you one."

Robert waited, but she didn't speak again, and he dared to move a step closer.

"Yes, you did," he said, wishing she would turn around so he could see her face. She gave a humourless huff of laughter.

"Too late," she said, the words heavy. He could see the weight of them crushing her.

"No," Robert replied, taking another step, longing to just pull her into his arms and kiss her, but aware that she was fragile, and too full of pain and guilt to allow him that. "Not too late."

She nodded, and he saw her raise a hand and wipe her cheeks with a brisk, no nonsense movement. "Good," she said, the word decisive. She turned then, shoulders square, chin up. "I'm glad the ending put things right, how they ought to be. You're a good man and… and I hope that people will see that now."

To his astonishment, she held out her hand to him, as if he might shake it. Robert frowned down at it.

"Well, that's all I came to say. I'll… I'll not take up any more of your time."

She stood there, pale and trembling, expecting him to shake her hand and dismiss her. As he made no move to take it, her hand dropped and she flushed, dipping into a curtsey instead.

"Good afternoon, your grace."

His heart gave an uncomfortable thud in his chest, kicking at his ribs at the idea she might walk out of the door again, jolting him out of his shock.

"Don't go."

She paused, daring to look up at him.

"Didn't you see it?" he asked, his voice gentle, smiling at her now. "I thought I'd been so clever in telling you how I felt, but… but you didn't see it, did you?"

"S-See what?" she stammered, her colour rising, one hand moving to press against her heart.

"I…." Robert began, just as an almighty commotion arose just beyond the closed door. They both looked around as voices grew nearer. His butler sounded on the verge of an apoplexy.

"*Madam*! His grace is speaking to a visitor, you cannot simply—"

"His grace is speaking to my mistress and she needs to know—"

The door burst open, and Robert's eyebrows flew up as he recognised Prue's maid, the one who'd stood up to him when he'd gone to propose to her the first time around.

"Oh, miss!" the woman cried, hurrying forward, waving a rather battered copy of *The Lady's Weekly Review*. "Miss, you ought to have read that story afore you saw him. It's his story, miss, yours and his, but just like a fairy tale. I just finished it now, and…." She clutched the magazine to her chest and sighed. "It's so romantic. He wants to marry you."

Prue gaped, her gaze swinging between her maid and Robert.

"What? I… I don't understand."

"He's proposing to you!" the woman said, throwing up her hands in frustration.

"Well," Robert said, torn between amusement and frustration. "I would give it another try, but I seem to have been interrupted. I suppose I ought not be surprised. My proposals are never met with a great deal of enthusiasm."

"Oh, this 'un will be," the woman assured him, folding her arms and nodding.

"Sally!" Prue exclaimed. Robert beamed at her.

"Don't you let her leave this room till she's said yes," her maid continued, wagging a scolding finger at him. "She loves you and these past weeks she's been broken hearted. I can't stand to see two people who ought to be together tearing themselves apart. So, I figured I'd best step in and damn the consequences, your grace." All at once the woman fell silent, as if she'd just then realised she was addressing a duke as though she was scolding a small boy.

Robert watched, fascinated, as her colour rose, and all her fire and indignation seemed to curl up and die. She looked mortified. He reached out his hand and took hers, raising it to his lips and kissing her fingers in an old fashioned, courtly gesture.

"I thank you, Miss...?"

"Sally, your grace," she mumbled.

"Sally, I thank you, from the bottom of my heart. You've saved me a deal of anxiety, but perhaps you might leave us alone now, so I can try that proposal again."

"Oh!" Sally exclaimed, flushing harder still and beaming at him. "Yes, indeed!"

"Jenkins," Robert said, addressing the butler who had witnessed the scene without showing a hint of surprise or interest, as his lofty station demanded. "Please, have rooms prepared for our guests."

He turned back to Prue, who had gasped at his words. "You will stay, won't you, love? Please. Don't run away from me again."

His heart calmed the rapid-fire clattering in his chest as she gave a tremulous smile and nodded. He waited until they were alone once more, still breathing a little fast as he turned back to her. The room was still, save for the sound of their breathing, and his own pulse rushing in his ears.

"Hello," he said softly, moving closer, and then reaching out and touching her cheek with the back of one finger.

"Hello." She blinked up at him, eyes filled with wonder. God, he wanted to see her look at him like that forever. "You... you wrote me a story?"

He pulled a face, feeling awkward. "I did," he confessed. "It's awful," he added, smiling as she gave an unsteady laugh.

"How lovely," she said, smiling now. "No one ever wrote me a story before. Am I the villainess?"

"No," Robert said, daring to put his hand on her waist and pull her a little closer. "You only think you are, to begin with."

Silence filled the room, heavy with words unspoken, with emotions that battered him on all sides, but it was a hopeful silence.

"I asked you once if you wanted to marry me, and you said yes."

She nodded, her eyes sparkling as her throat worked.

"Is that still true?"

"Yes," she whispered, her lovely face flushed.

How had he ever thought her plain, he wondered? Honestly not understanding it. She was the most precious, beautiful thing he'd ever seen in his life. He'd once thought such things of Lavinia, but that had been shallow in comparison, a superficial desire for something he'd thought perfect without ever troubling himself to understand her. That dreadful mess had been as much his fault as hers, and he felt regret for her unhappiness.

"So," he said, drawing it out, speaking slowly, even though his blood was racing in his veins, his heart aching for the moment she would allow him to hold her, to kiss her. "If I were to propose again…?"

"Yes!" she said, before he could say another word. She dropped her reticule, allowing it to hit the rug beneath them with a soft thud, and threw her arms around his neck, pressing closer. "Yes, with all my heart. If you can be brave enough to forgive me for everything I did, then I can be brave enough to trust you with my heart, with… with my future."

Robert held her face between both his hands, stroking the soft skin with his thumbs. He longed to kiss her, but this needed to be said, this vow made.

"You will never be my property," he said, his voice firm. "I cannot change the law, but I give you my solemn vow, I will never hurt you. I will always seek your opinion, and not make decisions that affect your life without your consent. We will be together, you and I, in all things, and I will never be your master." He watched the tears gathering in her eyes and felt his heart swell, longing for everything he hoped for them both, for a future where they could be happy. He laughed, then. "In truth, you're master here, love. Whether you like it or not. Good god, Prue, don't you know? I'd do anything for you. Command me as you wish, my heart is yours. Ask what you will of me."

Her breath caught and she shook her head. "I would never command you, but… I will love you, if you'll let me."

She pressed closer and lifted her mouth towards him and Robert closed the distance, touching his lips to hers. A breath left him, ragged and uneven as his fears rushed away with that soft touch.

He drew back, staring at her in wonder as she smiled at him, a little shyly.

"I love you," he said, relieved to say it aloud at last. "Do you mind?"

She laughed, a sound that lifted him, that made his heart as light as a soap bubble. "As long as you don't mind if I feel the same," she said, one hand smoothing over his lapel. The pallor had gone from her face and she looked rosy and happy, her eyes sparkling.

"Say it," he said, hardly daring to believe he'd understood. "Say it aloud."

"I love you, Robert," she said with conviction, her lovely face alight with the truth of those words.

He couldn't stop smiling. He doubted he'd stop for some considerable time yet. Well, perhaps if he kissed her….

Robert bent his head, pleased when she reached for him again, though they both leapt apart as the door flew open.

"Oh, Robert! I'm so happy for you!"

He blinked as his sister whirled into the room, flinging the door open to show that Sally, several housemaids, a sheepish looking butler and his uncle, were all gathered outside the door.

"I-I," stammered the butler, looking uncharacteristically discomposed.

Robert waved a hand, too full of joy to bar his household from sharing in his excitement.

"Well done, my boy, well done!" Charles said, shaking his hand with enough vigour to dislocate his shoulder. Though, soon that wasn't enough, and he was pulled into a hug. "I couldn't be happier," the old man added, sniffing and reaching for a large handkerchief when he finally let Robert go.

He blew his nose with some force and then turned to Prue. "Welcome to the family, Prue, my dear. I feel you've been here for some time," he said, with warmth. "But I'm very happy that we'll make it official."

Prue beamed and made him blush as she reached and kissed his cheek.

"Well, then, Robbie?" he said, using a pet name that Robert hadn't heard since he'd become duke. "When's the wedding?"

Robert cleared his throat and reached for his inside pocket. "Well, if you approve, Prue... tomorrow?" He showed her the special licence which had been burning a hole in his pocket for days now. "Unless... if you prefer, we can wait and do the whole thing properly with hundreds of guests and—"

"*No!*" she said, turning a deathly shade at the idea. She gave a vigorous shake of her head and pointed at the licence. "Does that mean we can marry here?"

He nodded, relieved that she was in as much a hurry as he was.

"And... may I invite some of my friends?"

Robert laughed and pulled her close, ignoring the happy sighs from their audience. "You can invite anyone you want, so long as you're there."

"I'll be there," she said, clutching at his lapels. "I'm not going anywhere, I promise."

Chapter 21

My dear friends,

I'm so sorry for my disappearance, and for worrying you all so. Please, be assured that I am well, and very, very happy. To that end, I would like to invite you all to Beverwyck, tomorrow at 2pm.

We are to be married!

—Excerpt of a letter to The Peculiar Ladies, care of Miss Ruth Stone, from Miss Prunella Chuffington-Smythe.

***

Midnight. 12thJune. Beverwyck. London. 1814

Prue sat at the elegant dressing table in the most beautiful bedroom she'd ever seen. The walls were covered in patterned silk damask, in shades of blue and green. Birds and butterflies flitted through flowers and curling vines and gave the sensation of wandering in a sunny garden. A large four-poster bed dominated the room, hung with more luxurious swathes of silky green, and the polished wood floor was thick with heavy rugs. Prue had never seen such extravagance.

Happily, the room had belonged to Robert's mother. His last wife and the previous Duchess of Bedwin had preferred a room that overlooked the front of the house, which was a relief to Prue. That the title was soon to apply to her seemed at once ludicrous and magical. She'd never desired such a thing, never even daydreamed of it, and was ridiculously unprepared. She had no intention of giving up her writing, and she knew Robert would never ask it of her, but still, she would have a deal of responsibilities she'd never bargained for or wanted.

Yet the title came with Robert, and she'd dreamed of and wanted him with all her heart. So, the rest would follow. He would help her, and she would help him, and together they would muddle through to find their places in this new and unexpected life.

She caught Sally's eye in the looking glass as the maid stood behind her, brushing out her hair. The woman was humming softly to herself and smiling.

Prue grasped her hand, holding it against her cheek.

"Dearest Sally. Thank you for everything. You've been such a friend. I don't know what I would have done without you."

Sally blinked hard and shook her head. "Now, stop that, miss, or you'll have us both watery-headed. I couldn't be happier, that's the truth." She hesitated, brush in hand as a doubtful look crept into her eyes.

"What is it?" Prue demanded, alarmed.

"Nothing, miss," Sally said at once. "Only, you'll be needing a proper lady's maid now, and a fancy dresser too, I don't doubt. I'm just a maid of all work as you well know, though I have a fair hand for dressing hair and I'm not too bad with a needle, but—"

"Oh, Sally!" Prue exclaimed, wide eyed with dismay. "You cannot believe I would cast you aside?"

"Oh, no," Sally said at once, clearly appalled at the idea. "That's just it, miss. You never would. You're too tender-hearted and I didn't want to give you any difficulties, now you will be a duchess, it's only right that—"

"Not another word, Sally," Prue said, raising a hand to deflect any further objections. "We both have a deal to learn about my new position, but we are both intelligent women, and neither of us are hen hearted enough to run from a challenge. *Are we?*"

"No, miss," Sally replied stoutly, looking a little indignant.

"Well then," Prue said with a sniff worthy of a future duchess. "I'll hear no more about it."

Impulsively, Sally leaned down and gave Prue a fierce hug. "Thank you, miss," she whispered, before letting go and bidding her mistress a fond goodnight.

Prue sat at the dressing table for a long time after, daydreaming and watching the candlelight flicker against the silken walls, the shadows fluttering as though the painted birds had come to life. She jumped at the sound of a soft knock, and felt her heart beat harder still as she realised it had come from the door that linked the duchess' room to that of the duke.

She padded across the plush rugs and stood on the polished wood floor before the connecting door. With a breath to steady the pounding in her chest, she opened the door to find Robert awaiting her. Her breath caught as she looked at him, dressed only in a loose shirt and trousers, his feet bare. She'd never seen him this way before and it seemed intimate and wonderful, and just a little wicked. Especially when she caught the rather mischievous look in his eyes.

"I know I ought not, but... I couldn't sleep without a goodnight kiss, at least," he said, sounding adorably sheepish.

Prue grinned at him and opened the door wide. "Come in," she said, wondering if she ought to feel more bashful at facing him in only her night-rail, but finding she'd didn't feel the least bit shy, only happy, almost giddy with it.

Robert hesitated. "I don't know if that's a good idea," he said, rubbing the back of his neck. "I honestly did only mean a kiss, but... but if I come in...."

Prue moved towards him and slid her arms about his neck. "We're to be married tomorrow."

He nodded, solemn now. "I know, but I want to do the thing right, Prue. I want it to be perfect this time, for… for both of us."

She smiled and gave a dramatic sigh, laying her head on his shoulder and looking up at him. "Why on earth did I have to fall for such an honourable fellow? I ought to have chosen someone wicked and villainous."

"Oh, ho!" he said, chuckling. "That's how it is, is it?" He swung her up into his arms, eliciting a squeal of protest as he carried her to the bed. "And what kind of depravity would this despicable fellow have in mind?"

Prue pursed her lips and gave a shrug. "How should I know? I am nought but an innocent maid," she said dramatically in breathless tones. "More than a goodnight kiss, though," she added, much more herself as she folded her arms and pouted.

Robert snorted and laid her on the bed, keeping his arms about her. "How about this?" he asked, leaning down and kissing her.

Prue sighed, sliding her arms about his neck once more as he pressed his mouth to her lips, teasing and coaxing and caressing, his tongue sliding against hers in slow sweeps that made her shiver with longing and impatience.

He drew back and she tightened her hold on his neck. "Tomorrow is too long to wait," she grumbled, pulling him back.

"I know," he said, sitting on the edge of the mattress beside her. His hand slid up from her waist in a slow, teasing glide. "Far, far too long."

Prue gasped as his large hand cupped her breast, his thumb rubbing casual circles around the peak which grew taut, aching for more under his touch.

"You like that?" he murmured against her ear, and she could hear the smile in his voice.

"Yes," she replied, sounding breathless for real now, no acting required.

Prue felt his chuckle rumble through her and watched as he lifted his head, gazing down at the place where his thumb tormented the tender flesh through the fine gauzy cotton. She mentally spared a moment to thank his sister for the loan of it, as her own rather more serviceable version wouldn't have been half so erotic. As it was, she could see the darker outline of her nipple, feel the touch of his fingers on her almost as if there was nothing between them. When he ducked his head and suckled her through the cloth, the heat of his mouth enveloped her, and she arched off the bed with a cry of surprise.

Robert sat back, surveying her with a look of deep satisfaction. He was a little flushed, his hair mussed, his shirt gaping open to his navel, giving a tantalising glimpse of a hard chest. Prue sat up, reaching for him and Robert jerked, stumbling away from her, getting to his feet.

"Oh, no," he said, sounding just as breathless as she was. "No, I can't. Stop trying to tempt me. I mustn't. I—I have to go or all my good intentions…." He trailed off, staring down at her, his chest rising and falling as though he'd just run for miles.

"Are you quite sure?" Prue said, understanding and not disagreeing with the sentiment, but feeling rather bereft all the same.

"No!" he said emphatically, and then turned on his heel and stalked from the room, closing the door behind him.

Prue fell back against the pillows and gave a huff of disappointment but could not stop the slow smile that curved over her mouth and remained there until she fell asleep.

***

13th June. Beverwyck. London. 1814

They were married the next afternoon in an intimate ceremony in a hastily arranged room at Beverwyck. The staff, thrown into crisis, moved heaven and earth, and somehow the room was filled with flowers, a wedding breakfast supplied fit, if not for a king, then most certainly for a duke *and* his new duchess.

That morning, Prue was introduced to Helena's dresser, Mrs Marigold, who was as impressive as Sally feared, but far kinder and more welcoming than either of them expected. One of Helena's dresses was expertly fitted to Prue's slenderer, shorter figure, whilst Sally took pains over dressing her hair.

"Oh, you look lovely," Helena said, gesturing for Prue to turn in a circle.

She did as Helena asked her, returning to her own reflection in the full-length mirror a moment later with as much surprise as she had the first time. She looked rather fine, she thought with a grin.

The dress was a pale green satin, trimmed with Mechlin lace and tiny glass beads that caught the light. It was simple, cut a little off the shoulder with short, capped sleeves and without too many frills and fancy touches, for which Prue was grateful.

Prue was still admiring herself—a rather novel experience— when there came a soft knock at the door. Sally hurried to open it and Prue turned to find Minerva at the threshold.

"Minerva!" she exclaimed, holding her hands out towards her cousin.

"I just wanted to say congratulations, before you came downstairs," Minerva said, looking a little awkward as she took Prue's hands. "I'm so pleased it worked out. Poor Bedwin was bereft when you disappeared. I'm happy for you, Prue, I really am."

Prue looked into her pretty blue eyes and smiled, seeing the truth of her words there. "You really never wanted to marry him, did you?" she said, realising she was right as Minerva returned a rather rueful expression.

"Not really. I mean, the idea of it was tantalising, I suppose, like a daydream of being a princess, but I just played along as I knew how much Mama wanted it. It's not what I want, though, not really."

"What *do* you want?" Prue asked her, curious now.

Minerva shrugged, laughing a little. "I've no idea." She grew serious for a moment and then added. "Someone kind." She looked back at Prue and then blushed like fury. "Oh! Not that his grace... I didn't mean...."

Prue chuckled and shook her head. "I know what you meant, and I will speak to Robert about getting you some introductions to some nice young men, but far more importantly, after the wedding I will introduce you to some friends of mine. I think it's time you joined my book club."

***

After the ceremony, Prue looked around at the ladies clustered about her and felt a swell of happiness. She had never felt so content, and such a sense of belonging. Glancing across the room, she saw Robert deep in conversation with the Earl of St Clair. The Earl's younger brother, Jerome, stood with them, laughing at something Robert had said. He looked up then, her husband, pausing in his conversation to smile at her, and blow her a kiss.

"It's so romantic," Bonnie said with a sigh, drawing Prue's attention back to see the young woman covering her heart with her hand. "Oh, if only I could have such a love story. I swear, Prue, I could hate you, I'm so green with envy."

"You'll be green if you eat any more of those lobster patties," Matilda remarked with a smirk, nodding towards Bonnie's overflowing plate.

"They're my favourite," Bonnie said. "And you clearly underestimate my capacity for lobster patties." She stuck her tongue out at Matilda, who laughed and shook her head.

"Well, there's always Gordon Anderson," Matilda said casually, knowing full well it would elicit a groan of despair from

Bonnie at the reminder of her ward's threats of marriage to her despised cousin.

"Over my dead body," she muttered, folding her arms. "The man has knock knees, breath that could kill a highland cow, and," she added darkly, "an attitude."

Everyone chuckled and admitted to a longing to see this dreadful creature, who grew ever more revolting every time Bonnie mentioned him.

Prue spoke to everyone, receiving hugs and kisses and exclamations from Ruth and Lucia, Jemima, Kitty, and Harriet in turn.

"I'm so happy for you, Prue," Alice said, reaching out and taking her hand. "No one ever deserved such a happy ever after as you."

"Nonsense," Prue retorted. "All of us do, every single one."

"Yes," Matilda agreed, her face serious. "Yes, we do, and we'll get them, too. Not by sitting about and waiting at the side lines either. We'll go out and get them. What say you, Alice?"

There was a note of challenge behind the words, and Alice flushed a little but nodded. "I say yes," she replied.

Chapter 22

Dear Alice,

I can't believe it's real. I'm so happy I keep thinking it must be a dream, or perhaps I fell into the pages of one of my own stories. Oh, dearest Alice, I hope with all my heart that we can find a match to bring you the same joy. Tell me, did you ever complete your dare?

—Excerpt of a letter to Miss Alice Dowding from Her Grace, Prunella Adolphus, Duchess of Bedwin.

***

13ᵗʰ June, Beverwyck. London. 1814

"Are you sure they're gone?" Robert demanded, hours later. "There's no one hiding behind a vase or waiting to leap out at us from the curtains?"

"Quite sure," Prue replied, leaning into her husband, her head on his shoulder. "Does that mean we can go to bed now?"

Robert's eyes widened with an expression of mock outrage. "But it's only seven o'clock," he said, making a show of checking his time piece. "Why ever would you want to retire at this early hour?"

"Stop teasing or I'll stamp on your toes."

"You did that already, when we danced in the garden at midnight."

Prue gasped. "You take that back! I never did. That evening was perfect, the most romantic of my life. I won't have you spoil it by accusing me of being clumsy enough to tread on your toes, you dreadful man."

She gave a squeal of protest as he swung her up into his arms with a swish of silken skirts.

"The most romantic night of your life?" he repeated in disdain. "Oh, dear me, no. I must do something about that."

"Must you?" Prue asked, brightening and putting her arms about his neck.

"Yes," he said, lowering his mouth to press it against hers. "I must."

"Oh, well, go on then," she said, with a dreamy sigh as he released her mouth. "If you must. Though I still deny that I trod on your toes when we danced in the garden."

"You're right," he admitted, turning sideways to manoeuvre them through the door, heading for the stairs. "That was at the Cavendish Ball. You accused me of being a randy stoat and I offered to show you how right you were."

Prue gave a delighted snort of amusement and buried her face in his cravat. She looked up a moment later. "You never did, though," she said, trying to sound forlorn.

"Don't worry, love," Robert said, huffing a little with effort as he turned to lean against the bedroom door, forcing the handle down with his elbow and barging inside. "I'm going to right now… or at least, once I get my breath back."

She squealed as he flung her so hard onto the bed she bounced, and then clambered over her, staring down and grinning like a lunatic.

"Well, duchess, how do you like married life so far?"

"I like it fine," she said, smiling up at him.

"Fine?" he exclaimed, leaning down to nip at her earlobe and nuzzle against her neck. "Are you certain that's the correct word?"

Prue arched her neck to allow him better access as he kissed a trail down to her collarbone.

"Very fine," she offered, hearing a snort of indignation. "Well, try harder," she suggested.

Robert lifted his head, a glint of challenge in the green. "Right you are, your grace," he murmured, smirking a little as he gave her dress a sharp tug, pulling it completely from her shoulders and exposing her breasts.

"Ah, there you are," he said with a happy sigh. "No more hiding behind night dresses." He trailed one finger, round and round her left nipple, never touching, just circling slowly as her skin prickled with anticipation and the soft bud tightened to a peak.

Prue felt her breathing speed up, holding her tongue against the urge to demand he hurry and kiss her as he had last night. She stared at him, willing him to do it and frustrated when he didn't.

"Tell me," he said, his voice low and sinful in the dim light of the room. "Tell me what you want, how to please you."

"I can't!" she exclaimed, horrified by the idea.

He chuckled, amused, and moved to lie beside her, his head braced on his arm. "You must learn, darling."

Prue frowned at him. "Why?"

His face grew serious and he reached for her hand, drawing it to his lips and kissing her fingers. "Because I never want to do something you don't want, or don't enjoy, and if you don't tell me, or tell me instead what you think I want to hear...."

He shrugged as she studied his expression.

"I won't be a villain again, Prue. Never on purpose, but not from ignorance either. I'd do nothing to hurt or offend you, but you must help with that. You must be honest, especially here," he added, leaning down to press another kiss to her lips.

"Very well," Prue said, understanding what he was saying. "Though, I don't yet know—"

He grinned at her and kissed her again. "I know, but we can enjoy finding that out, can't we? Just never worry about telling me no, or stop, or not yet. I won't be offended or annoyed, you have my word."

Prue reached up and traced his jaw with a fingertip, smiling as he shivered under her touch. "I love you," she said. "And… and I would very much like for you to kiss me like…." She swallowed, blushing a little but determined. "Like you did last night."

The smile that brought to his lips was broad and smug. "Your wish, duchess, is my command," he murmured, ducking his head.

Prue gasped as the wet heat of his mouth covered her and he sucked and teased at her delicate flesh. Her hands went to his head, stroking his hair and his neck as she held him close, not wanting him to stop. Each gentle pull at her breast seemed to tug at something deeper inside her, hot and liquid as her breathing grew erratic.

Lifting his head, Robert blew a stream of cool air over her skin, making her shiver with desire. He stared down at her, a questioning look in his eyes.

"Yes," she said, struggling to sound grave when she only wanted to laugh with delight. "I liked that."

With a snort of amusement, Robert plucked at the fabric of her dress and pulled a face. "There are too many clothes involved in the proceedings."

"Well, take them off, then!" Prue said, impatient now for what came next.

The next few minutes were full of laughter and frustration as they wrestled with buttons and ties, eager fingers fumbling the delicate fastenings and tugging and yanking at boots and chemises, stockings and shirts.

At last, an untidy heap of clothing lay beside the bed, and Prue could finally look at her husband in all his glory. He lay back on the bed, perfectly at ease, one arm crooked behind his head as he allowed her to look her fill.

"Do I pass muster?" he asked, green eyes alight with amusement.

"Hush, I'm investigating," she scolded him, lips quirking. "May I touch you?"

He laughed at that. "It will be a very long and painful night if you don't."

Tentatively she ran her fingers over the dark hair on his chest, finding it wiry and coarse. Trailing her hand downwards, she followed the path it led her on. His sex lay heavy and proud, twitching as her hand grew nearer. Hardly daring to breathe, and wondering at her own boldness, she touched the blunt head with a fingertip, and then dared to slide it down the length of him.

"I think your skin is softer than mine," she marvelled as she turned to smile at him.

His eyes were dark now, his gaze intent and her breath caught, excitement simmering beneath her skin.

"Lay back," he said, his voice rough and gentle at the same time.

She did, wondering at the look in his eyes, at the desire blazing there. Prue had never expected to see that, never expected that she could elicit such a response from a man. It was a powerful feeling, more so when she knew she could trust him. She'd given her heart, her soul, and her body to this man, and he would never misuse or abuse them. It was more than she'd ever believed possible.

They kissed, his hands roaming, caressing, gentle and warm, soothing any remaining nerves away. He toyed with the soft triangle of curls, dipping his fingers between her legs and seeking the little bud of her sex. With tenderness he stroked and teased the silken nub and Prue could do nothing but breathe, captivated by the eyes that stared down at her, the green full of heat and longing. His clever fingers parted her delicate folds, exploring gently and finding her wet and aching for his touch.

Prue fought back a surge of shyness at his discovery, but he just smiled and kissed her, one finger moving inside her.

"You're so beautiful, so soft. I can't wait to be inside you. It's all I've thought of since that day in the carriage. You and me together, like this."

There was no way to hide in the face of such honesty and she didn't try, arching as his finger moved deeper, sliding and caressing her, stretching her intimate flesh.

"I've thought of it too," she whispered. "At night, when I'm alone. I've dreamed of you."

Robert gave a soft moan and moved over her, kissing her lips, her jaw, her neck, hot, tantalising kisses and nips as he moved lower. His mouth tickled over her stomach, making her laugh with nerves and delight. The trail was fire and ice, the damp little path cooling as he moved on, moved lower. He nuzzled the delicate skin that formed the crease between thigh and torso and her breath caught in her throat at his proximity to the part of her that ached for him.

"I want to kiss you here," he said, pressing his mouth to the inside of her thigh and then looking up at her. He wasn't speaking about her thigh, she realised, and her cheeks blazed with the knowledge.

"Is… is that… n-normal?" she queried, shocked, though mostly by the discovery that she very much hoped the answer was yes.

"Yes, love," he said, smiling at her.

"Oh." *Good heavens.* "Do you want to?" she added, finding that a more pertinent question.

"God, yes," he murmured on the back of a heavy sigh. The warmth of his breath fanned over her most private skin and Prue gave up on any possibility of keeping her dignity intact. She suspected that dignity was something that needed setting aside in the bedroom, where honesty was far more rewarding.

His lips moved just a little closer to their goal, soft and warm and so inviting. "Well?" he asked, his expression curious but not insistent.

"Yes," she said in a rush. "Yes, please."

To her consternation he didn't hurry, and she shivered as his tongue licked a barely there path along the crease of her thigh. Settling more comfortably between her legs, he parted the fragile folds and then teased her further with delicate strokes that were never quite firm enough, never quite where she wanted them. It was torment of the most delicious kind as her blood coursed through her, her breath catching as she closed her eyes and simply… submitted. There seemed little point or value in being coy or embarrassed, Robert certainly wasn't. Indeed, from the approving growls and murmurs he made, he seemed as pleased by her as she was by him and his devilish tongue.

Soon she was clutching at the sheet beneath her, writhing as he held her in place, chuckling when she tried to arch towards that infuriating, delicious tongue.

"Patience." He chuckled, his hot breath adding to the torment. "I'll give you what you want, but waiting is a part of the pleasure," he said, illustrating his words with a brief swipe of his tongue that had her crying out. "The anticipation of what's coming will make everything far more rewarding."

Prue opened her mouth to tell him that anything more intense would probably kill her, when he gave in and closed his mouth over her, suckling and tugging gently.

She arched beneath him, words and explanations no longer required as pleasure pulsed through her in fierce, heated waves. Robert stayed where he was, the touch of his tongue softer now, gentling her through the pulses of her climax when the intensity became almost unbearable.

Prue lay back against the mattress, wondering if she might dissolve into the fabric. She felt boneless, sated and replete, like a cat lazing in the sun.

A sigh escaped her as she returned to herself, dimly aware of Robert moving over her until she opened her eyes to find him staring down at her, equal parts smug male pride and concern. A rueful smile curved over her lips as she blinked up at him, hazy and happy.

"I liked that," she said helpfully.

The smug expression grew, all traces of concern gone in an instant, as he leant down to nip at her earlobe. "You don't say," he murmured.

"Oh, but I do say," Prue replied, adamant now. "I'll keep saying it if you want me to."

A rumble of laughter moved through him as he settled between her thighs and Prue gasped at the sensation of his aroused body, silken and hot, sliding against her still throbbing flesh.

"Tell me you want me," he whispered, braced on his arms above her, his eyes dark with need.

"I want you," she said, wrapping her arms around him, pulling him closer, raising her hips to meet his as he ducked his head and shivered, a low groan torn from him as he nudged inside her a little.

Prue's breath caught at the sensation, far different from the delicate slide of one finger.

"All right?" he asked, the words ragged as he looked back at her.

"Yes," she said, smiling up at him, meaning it. "A little nervous," she added, remembering her vow to be honest. "But yes, don't stop."

"If you want me to, I will," he said, and she smiled, stroking her hands over his broad back, thrilling in the feel of his muscles bunching and shifting beneath her touch. With exquisite gentleness he moved, easing deeper in shallow thrusts, letting her body grow used to him, ducking his head to seek her mouth before moving again.

Prue clutched at his shoulders as the feeling shifted between pleasure and discomfort, a sense of fullness that was not altogether pleasant until he paused again, caressing her and relaxing her until the pain receded.

"Better?" he asked, anxiety in his expression as he stared down.

"Much," she agreed, gasping as he moved again, but this time finding the awkwardness gone, the tension still with her but of a different kind, the anticipation he'd spoken of gathering in slow waves as he moved deeper. It was an astonishing intimacy, not just because of the way they were joined, but because of everything it meant, everything that had brought them here, to this place. Prue savoured every moment: the closeness, the tenderness he showed, the simple fact of being here with him as she relaxed and moved with him, finding the rhythm with him.

Robert murmured in her ear, soft words that made her smile and blush a little as he told her how good she felt, how soft, how lovely. She felt the tension gathering in him now, felt the tautness of his muscles, the rapid heat of his breath over her skin as his movement became faster and more erratic.

The knowledge had excitement and desire chasing her once again, knowing she'd done that, she was the one he was calling for as he lost control. He gathered her closer, as she clung to him, moving faster as she sought her own pleasure.

He shuddered, a harsh cry torn from his lips as his hands tightened on her skin and she gasped, almost laughing with joy as his guttural moans came in a rush of damp heat against her neck.

Prue stroked his back as his breathing steadied, her hands sliding down and daring to enjoy the curve of his buttocks. How fascinating to explore him like this, to know that they were joined now, in so many ways.

Robert let out an unsteady breath and she turned her head, finding his bright green gaze upon her.

"Are you all right? I didn't—"

Prue put a finger to his lips and shook her head. "It was wonderful. Every moment. I loved it; I love you."

He sighed and let his head fall back to the pillow. "I'm never leaving this bed again," he said, his voice sleepy and sated.

She moved with him as he turned onto his back, his arm still around her, holding her close as she laid her head on his shoulder. They were quiet for a while, enjoying the closeness, the exquisite novelty of being together in such a way.

"Tell me about your new story," he said, one hand toying lazily with her hair.

"Who says I have one?" Prue replied, lifting her head to look at him.

Robert snorted and shook his head. "Of course you have one."

She smiled and rested her chin on his chest, one hand tugging gently at the hair on his chest. "Very well, I do."

"Is it about me?"

"No!"

"How disappointing. I've become rather used to such notoriety. I'm not sure I'm ready to slip into obscurity."

Prue made a dismissive sound. "I somehow doubt you'll ever do that. Anyway, this one is more about me, or at least, a girl like me who makes the mistake of listening to gossip."

His hold on her tightened and she smiled, knowing she'd long been forgiven for that. "Anyway," she added, watching his expression. "I want to hear your story again."

"Oh, no," he groaned, flinching at the idea. "No, not again."

"Yes, again. It's my story and it's bedtime. I insist you tell me it again."

"Darling, anything but that," he pleaded as she shook her head, unrelenting now. "You've read it ten times at least. I was never more embarrassed than when you read it with your friends, and you know it off by heart already."

"Yes, I know that," she said, grinning and wriggling against him. "But I want you to tell it to me and, when we've got children, you can tell it them."

"Oh, my god," he muttered. "I will never live it down."

"No," Prue said happily. "You won't."

Robert raised his head to glower at her and then gave a defeated sigh.

"Oh, very well," he muttered, tugging the covers up around her shoulders. "Are you quite comfortable?"

Prue leaned over and kissed him, nuzzling against him for a moment before replying, "I am."

"Then," he said, smiling at her. "I'll begin. Once upon a time, there was an ogre...."

Prue sighed as her husband's voice washed over her, reciting the words of the silly story he'd written for her, to show her that fairy stories did, occasionally, come true.

The story she'd written him had been harder, crueller, especially for one who had lived through parts, but even that story had ended as it should. Perhaps the hero was not quite as perfect as the readers had expected him to be, but with his not-quite-perfect heroine, he still made it in the end, and arrived at his perfectly happy ever after.

For the first time in her life, Prue had high hopes of doing the same.

Girls Who Dare– The exciting new series from Emma V Leech, the multi-award-winning, Amazon Top 10 romance writer behind the Rogues & Gentlemen series.

Inside every wallflower is the beating heart of a lioness, a passionate individual willing to risk all for their dream, if only they can find the courage to begin. When these overlooked girls make a pact to change their lives, anything can happen.

Ten girls – Ten dares in a hat. Who will dare to risk it all?

Next in Girls Who Dare.....

To Steal A Kiss

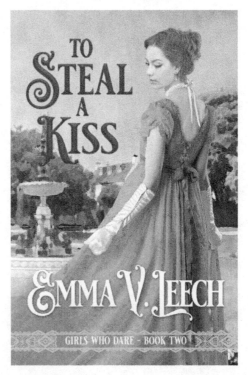

The desire to take a chance and snatch at happiness

Being dared to kiss a man in the moonlight is all well and good, but men and moonlight do not fall from the skies at will.

Until they do.

Under instruction from a friend, drab Alice Dowding lingers alone on a moonlit balcony. Not the most sensible course of action for a usually sensible girl. Yet being sensible has gained Alice a seat among the wallflowers and her only likely chance of marriage to a man she finds nigh on repulsive.

Something must be done.

A guilty conscience and a bad man.

When Nathanial Hunt's sister begs him for a favour, he can hardly refuse. Nathanial, part owner of one of the most scandalous gambling dens in London is responsible for Matilda's tattered reputation, and she knows he is no position to deny her anything.

When she begs him to kiss her mousy friend on a moonlit night, however, a chain of events is set in motion that none of them could have predicted.

When a little favour ignites an inferno.

Ignited by one soul-stealing kiss, mousy, sensible, dull Alice, is setting off sparks wherever her feet touch the ground, and all Nathanial can do is pray he doesn't get burned.

Chapter 1

My dear Prue,

I'm so happy for you. You and Bedwin are a perfect match. I shall miss you while you are away. Do write, if you can tear yourself away from your handsome husband for long enough! No, by the way, I never did complete my dare. At least… not yet.

—Excerpt of a letter from Miss Alice Dowding to Prunella Adolphus, Duchess of Bedwin.

13th June 1814, London.

"They looked terribly happy, didn't they?" Alice said with a wistful sigh as the carriage rumbled through London.

Alice was returning home with Matilda after the marriage of their dear friend Prunella to the Duke of Bedwin. That Prue was now a duchess was extraordinary and so at odds with her friend's character she could not help but smile. What a bold young woman she was. She would not be your everyday duchess, that was for sure.

Alice turned to look across the carriage to her friend, who was staring out the window with a frown creasing her brow.

"What?" Matilda looked around and then sat up a bit straighter, as if tearing her thoughts from a dream. "Oh! Yes," she said, smiling now. "Yes, indeed. They did. I think that marriage will be a great success. Lucky Prue."

Alice nodded and gave a wistful sigh. She wasn't jealous. Not really. That would be unworthy of her. Prue deserved her happiness and Alice was completely, wholeheartedly delighted for her.

Dash it.

Well, maybe a tad envious, then.

"Chin up, Alice. Your time will come." Matilda's voice was soft, her expression warm. She would make a good mother, Alice thought. The young woman had certainly taken to mothering the Peculiar Ladies, taking everyone under her wing. Alice especially.

With a disparaging sound, Alice indicated her thoughts on the likelihood of that prediction.

"Oh, it will indeed," she said, surprising herself a little with the bitterness of her words. "In the form of the Honourable Mr Edgar Bindley."

Alice didn't bother hiding her dejection over the idea. Matilda had become one of her closest friends over the past weeks, and an ally in the war to thwart her parents' plans. They were social climbers of the most ferocious kind and saw their daughter as fair game for their own advancement, no matter her ideas on the subject.

The *honourable* Edgar Bindley, youngest son of the Earl of Ulceby had shown an interest in Alice, and they were keen for her to make an advantageous marriage. That Alice not only found him physically repugnant, but could find nothing good to say about him, seemed of no importance. There was something cold, something lacking in Edgar Bindley, and Alice had no wish to discover what it was.

Matilda grimaced and shook her head.

"No, no. We're not giving up yet, Alice. They gave you to the end of the season."

263

Alice gave a snort and shook her head. "It's the middle of June, Tilda." A fact which was driven home to her each evening as she crossed another day from the calendar. "Time is running out. I can't even get up the nerve to speak to a man in public, let alone tempt him into completing my dare. What chance do I have of getting one to propose?"

"Faint heart," Matilda scolded, wagging a finger at Alice.

As a member of The Peculiar Ladies' Book Club, an establishment for wallflowers, oddities, and the unmarriageable— Alice had been one of the first to take part in a series of rather outrageous dares. Not that she had yet completed her dare, only taken one from the hat in a rare display of courage, or perhaps insanity.

Her actions had shocked her as much as the other ladies of their number. Alice was shy. So shy she had trouble speaking to people outside of her immediate family or friends without stuttering, blushing, and making a fool of herself. That she had been the second to pipe up and take a dare from the hat was still something she was a little perplexed by. Yet, she was desperate: desperate to change her life, to change herself, to *live.*

Prue's dare—to dance in a garden at midnight—had culminated in marriage to the Duke of Bedwin, the man with whom she'd danced. Silly as it might have seemed, Alice clung to the hope that such a romantic fate might await her.

Alice's dare was to kiss a man in the moonlight. A lovely idea, if there were a single man of her acquaintance, outside of the revolting Mr Bindley, willing to do the honours. As she could hardly accost a man in the middle of a ballroom and ask him to help her complete a dare—even if she had an ounce of the nerve required for such a feat—she was rather stuck.

"Did you mean what you said?" Matilda asked, drawing Alice's attention away from such gloomy musings.

"What was that?" Alice frowned, trying to recall, and then felt a jolt of apprehension as she remembered her rather spur-of-the-moment comment earlier at Prue's wedding.

"You said you weren't going to sit on the sidelines any longer, but that you would go out and get your happy ever after."

Anxiety stirred in Alice's chest at the thought of doing anything other than sitting about and waiting for her fate to change, but she had so little time left. Her parents had determined she would have Mr Bindley if no better offers were forthcoming, and she had until the beginning of September. Little more than six weeks. She had to do something.

"I-I," she stammered, before taking a deep breath. "Yes," she said, wondering if she ought to stop the carriage. She felt rather ill.

"Excellent," Matilda said, beaming at her. There was a look in her friend's eyes she couldn't quite like. A glint of determination. "And you're ready to complete your dare?"

Alice swallowed hard. She felt ready to run away and hide, but she kept that to herself for fear Matilda would think her a wet blanket. She *was* a wet blanket. If she were totally honest, wet blankets had a deal more weight to their characters.

"Well?"

Do it. Do it. Do it, a little voice in her head repeated, the words in time to the desperate thudding of her heart.

Matilda had offered to help her with her dare weeks ago, but Alice had been too afraid to agree. The idea that Matilda would arrange for a man to kiss her... a complete stranger....

Alice shivered with apprehension.

It was not that she didn't trust Matilda, she did. She knew the beautiful young woman had a good and kind heart and would never set her up with an unpleasant fellow, or someone who would compromise her or take advantage, but... but Matilda was *ruined.*

She was wealthy and beautiful and from a distinguished family, but her father's fall from grace, her brother's notoriety, and her own reputation rendered her unmarriageable to any decent gentleman. The family had fallen on hard times due to their father's excesses, and her brother had established a notorious gambling club to recover their fortune. Recover it he had, too, in grand style. It was not a respectable occupation for a gentleman, however, and then… there was the matter of Matilda being caught alone with a man.

It had happened through no fault of her own, it was true, but still, was she really the person Alice ought to trust with this particular dare?

"Kitty has only given you this final full moon to complete your dare, Alice," Matilda warned. "You've already had two months. You were only supposed to have two weeks."

"I know, I know!" Alice wailed, wringing her hands together. "I wish…."

I wish I'd never taken the stupid dare.

No.

For heaven's sake, Alice, grow a backbone.

Do something.

Anything.

For if she didn't, she might as well resign herself to being Mrs Edgar Bindley.

Alice shuddered.

"Yes!" She squeaked more than spoke the word, forcing it out before good sense could remind her of all the reasons this was a ridiculous, terrible, and dangerous idea. Yet, Prue had been brave, and she'd gained everything she ever dreamed of. Surely Alice could do the same?

Matilda beamed at her and shuffled along the carriage bench to take Alice's hand.

"Wonderful. Well done you, Alice. Now, are you going to the Ransoms' ball?"

Alice nodded. She felt light-headed; her skin clammy. Perhaps she was going down with something. Something that would consign her to her bed until after the full moon, with a bit of luck. Then she'd be out of time, and unable to complete her dare through no fault of her own. No shame in that.

Nonetheless, shame overwhelmed her. Alice was no fool. She knew kissing a stranger in the moonlight would not change her fortune. Yet it had become somehow symbolic. If Alice could do this one reckless, daring thing, surely there was more to her? A painfully shy wallflower would never do such a dreadful thing, so if *she* did it… she'd no longer be a painfully shy wallflower. Would she?

It made sense to her, at any rate.

"That's the perfect time, then," Matilda said, giving Alice's hand a squeeze. "A full moon, and the Ransoms' place is vast, full of balconies and romantic gardens. Now, don't you worry about it. I shall arrange everything."

Alice felt her stomach twist and wanted to laugh or possibly sob at the idea she could stop herself worrying. She'd be able to think of nothing else between now and then. She'd make herself ill with it, not get a wink of sleep, and be red-eyed and blotchy by the night of the ball. A delightful prospect for any young man. She swallowed a groan of misery and, as Matilda let go of her hand, she pressed it to her stomach, which was threatening retribution.

"W-Who?"

She couldn't ask more than that, too afraid she'd cry or vomit or do something equally repulsive if she tried to speak further.

Matilda gave her a reassuring smile and reached out a hand to tug at one of Alice's red curls. "Someone I trust, darling. Someone who will be sweet and kind and respectful. You have my word."

Alice nodded. She couldn't have done anything more if she tried, and she was too concerned with keeping the contents of her stomach in place to make the attempt.

"Look at you," Matilda said, frowning and shaking her head. "Why has no gentleman snatched you up? You're perfectly lovely."

Alice glanced up at Matilda to see sincerity in her eyes.

"You're like a lovely porcelain doll, fragile and perfect."

Alice grimaced. Her father had often described her thus, thinking it a grand compliment, as Matilda obviously did. Alice didn't want to be fragile and breakable, though. The idea that she needed protecting and shielding from the harsh realities of life was something she came across from every quarter. If a gentleman ever approached her, it was this that drew them. She was petite and slender, waiflike, a description she'd heard all too often. Yet her inability to speak to people she didn't know, let alone men, and her annoyance at being treated like a child, soon had them giving up and moving on to more convivial company.

No one realised there was a fire burning in her heart, fuelled by frustration and the desire for more, even when her wretched nerves would not allow her to speak her mind. She'd inherited her red hair from her grandmother, a woman of grand passions and determination. Why hadn't Alice inherited more than just her fiery locks? Why couldn't she have had inherited the spark that had driven the woman on and made her rather a scandalous creature, known for her sparkling wit and a string of much younger lovers? Alice wished she'd known her, but she'd died when Alice was a baby.

She snorted at the idea that such a description could ever be levelled at her. No doubt she'd end up like her great aunt, Agatha.

A faded little creature who spoke in a whisper, smelled strongly of peppermint, and was forever searching for her handkerchief.

Please, God, no.

Alice's mother always refused to speak about her outrageous parent, her lips thinning and a look of deep displeasure in her eyes when the subject arose. Mrs Dowding was a stickler for propriety and had instilled her daughter with an unhealthy terror of doing anything she ought not. Yet her grandmother's portrait hung in one of the lesser used guest rooms, gathering dust, and Alice often went to look at it… perhaps in the hope the woman would lend her courage.

"Come home with me," Matilda said, giving Alice a conspiratorial grin. "We'll discuss what you're to wear for the ball. I have an idea how you should wear your hair. Those tiny little curls make you look about twelve. I'll have my maid try it and you can see what you think."

With a soft laugh, Alice agreed. It would make little difference. No amount of primping ever gave her the nerve to speak up and make herself heard, but there was little point in trying to thwart Matilda once her mind was made up. She was a force of nature. So, with a nod of agreement, she allowed her friend to redirect the carriage and they headed off to Matilda's home.

Chapter 2

My dear Lucia,

Do you think Alice has the nerve to go through with it? I do hope so. If ever a girl needed an admirer to boost her confidence….

My wretched brother had better do the job.

—Excerpt of a letter from Miss Matilda Hunt to Senorita Lucia de Feria.

The evening of the 13th June 1814. Half Moon Street, Mayfair, London.

Once Alice had departed, Matilda stared into the empty hearth and rather wished there was a fire burning there. It was so much easier to think when there was a merry fire to focus one's attention on. Midsummer was not the time to be heating the already stuffy room, however. Her brother's home was an elegant space, the entire house decorated with taste and in the height of fashion, no expense spared. Matilda had seen to that.

The walls of the room were a delicate robin's egg blue, and heavy silken grey-blue curtains fell in lavish drapes at the large windows that looked out onto an elegant and fashionable street. A richly patterned rug in golden tones covered the polished wood floor, the warm colours bringing a softer feel to the cool blues and accentuating the many gilt frames of the artworks that festooned the walls. All the most modern furniture designs by the most sought-after makers were arranged about the stylish room.

Above the fireplace was an impressive gilded bronze and black marble French clock with a large *putto* holding a bird. The clock struck both the hour and the half hour, and Matilda had come to resent it more every day. She felt the sweet-faced *putto* was measuring out her life chime by chime. Perhaps she would replace it. Nate wouldn't care, despite the fact the thing had cost an unholy fortune.

Her brother was always on at her to spend his money, encouraging her to buy new dresses, jewellery, whatever she desired. They both knew why that was, but Matilda let it go without comment. She didn't take advantage of his generosity, but neither did she feel any compunction about spending when she wanted to. He owed her that much.

He owed her a great deal.

She moved to the window, turning the latches and pushing the sash to let a welcome breeze flutter into the room. Movement farther along the road caught her eye, and she noticed the glossy carriage belonging to her brother coming along the street.

Thank goodness.

As the owner of one of the city's most exclusive and notorious gaming clubs, Nathaniel Hunt kept rather unsociable hours. Usually he was away all night and slept most of the day. He had said he'd be home early this evening, but what Nate said and what Nate did were not always compatible.

She had plans for her brother, however, and she would ensure he played along. No matter what he said. If a bit of blackmail was required to achieve her ends… so be it.

Poor, sweet Alice. Such a little mouse of a girl. If she wasn't very careful, she'd find herself married to the odious Mr Bindley. Alice had pointed the man out to Matilda a few weeks back and Matilda's heart had clenched. She had a sixth sense about men, and her instincts told her Bindley was a snivelling little rat, the kind to bully those over whom he had power.

Little Alice wouldn't stand a chance.

Well, her own future might be in ruins, but Matilda was damned if she'd let Alice make a bad marriage. The girl just needed confidence, that was all. The kind of confidence she might gain from hearing a handsome man tell her she was lovely, desirable, that he was inflamed by her. A man like Matilda's brother, for example. For Alice *was* lovely, and she did not understand the power that could give her, if she could only believe in herself.

Matilda had no illusions. Nate would refuse. He'd rage about the idea, and become utterly furious, and then Matilda would remind him of what he owed, and he would capitulate. His guilt weighed heavy, and it was for this reason she never used it against him.

To do so now was underhanded, she knew, but she had never played the card before, nor would she do so now if it wasn't something she felt so strongly about. Why, she didn't know. Only that Alice's happiness had become important to her. All her friends' happiness. The Peculiar Ladies had become a refuge, a focus in her life which seemed already so full of regrets. Matilda would not see her friends regret as she did. They deserved better. They'd get better, if she had anything to do with it. She would guide and nurture and advise them the best she could. She would see them all married and happy, and then perhaps her life would feel less empty.

Besides which, Nate needed a wife.

A smile curved over her mouth at the idea of Nate and Alice. Nate wouldn't see it. Not at first. She might be quite mistaken, of course, but....

Something told Matilda that Alice had hidden depths. Now and then she saw a spark of something in the girl's eyes, something hot and fierce like that red hair she always scraped back in such an unbecoming and childish style. Alice just needed the courage to let that spark flame like her fiery locks.

A handsome fellow like Matilda's brother, well... maybe he could provide the tinder? Though Nate would die before he admitted it, his current lifestyle was never one he'd longed for. Before their world had crumbled, Matilda had known that Nate would marry a nice girl and settle down and have a family. He was suited for it and, unlike many of his friends, had never made a show of trying to evade his fate. He'd welcomed it.

Then their father had squandered their fortune and their futures, and everything had changed. Nate had changed. He'd become harder, colder, his feelings forced down into some dark place where they'd not trouble him. Not obviously, at least. He'd become the epitome of the handsome young scoundrel, and many young men tried their best to emulate his nonchalant grace and devil may care attitude. Yet, Matilda felt certain the Nate she'd once known was still there, still longing for a home, for a wife and family. If only he'd acknowledge it.

Such a life would be a deal better for him than his present lifestyle, that was for certain. Besides, she'd never tried her hand at match making before and, if she was to ensure her friends were all suitably settled, she may as well begin with her brother. Her own life would hold no such romance, after all, so the least she could do was indulge herself in manoeuvring others into their happy ever afters.

Matilda looked up as the man himself entered the room.

"Evening, Tilda." He greeted her with a flash of a crooked grin before he took himself off to the decanter that had been left ready for him.

"For heaven's sake, Nate," she said with a sigh of reproach. "Can't you get in the door before pouring a drink?"

"I'm in!" he exclaimed, gesturing to the room about him. "Or am I mistaken, is this the garden? It is a bit chilly."

He nodded at the open window and Matilda rolled her eyes at him.

"It's stifling in here, as well you know. The whole city is stifling," she added with a sigh, waving a delicate hand-painted fan back and forth with more vigour than her usual understated style would allow. It was only her brother, after all. Matilda stared about the fashionable room—with not a thing out of place, no sign of wear or age—and a pang of longing for their childhood home in the country stabbed at her heart. She forced it down. No point in crying about that. The place had long been sold to cover their father's debts.

"Ah, well, that explains my raging thirst," her brother replied, raising the glass to her and taking a large swallow. With a sigh of satisfaction, he crossed the room to stand beside her at the window and dutifully kissed her cheek. "What's ailing you, sis?" he asked, casting a knowing eye over her. He knew her too well.

Matilda gave a huff of annoyance she wasn't really feeling. That was the trouble with Nate. It was so hard to be cross with him. Tall and broad and blond, with twinkling blue eyes, he cut a dashing figure. Add to that an abundance of charm and a devilish smile, and he could have most women eating out of his hand in no time. Matilda was immune to charm of that nature, being his sister and knowing all his worst traits, but still, it was never easy to scold him when he was such a lamb.

"You drink too much, you don't sleep enough, and you keep bad company," she said, folding her arms and feeling like the worst sort of nag, but someone had to say it.

"Ah, the life of a gaming club proprietor," he replied with a nonchalant shrug.

Matilda sighed and shook her head. There was no point in remonstrating. It made no difference, and he had a point. How else was he supposed to live, under the circumstances? That meant circumstances needed to change before he could, which brought her back to the point in hand.

"Nate, I want you to do something for me."

It was always best to attack Nate head on. He was too straightforward for subtlety and despised subterfuge.

"Of course, Tilda. Name it," he said, sitting himself down by the empty hearth. He frowned at the fireplace. "It never feels the same with no fire burning, does it? Not half so welcoming."

Matilda rolled her eyes. "It's the middle of June," she pointed out, despite having observed the same thing herself.

"What do you need then?" he asked, returning to the conversation. "A new frock? Hats? Or is it decorating? Surely you've done every room in the house by now? Twice, in fact."

Matilda felt a twinge of guilt over that debacle but retreated into irritation, knowing he was baiting her. "You know very well I only did one room twice, and that was because the colour of those curtains was not what I ordered. I had to redecorate the entire room to match. It was most aggravating."

Nate made a mild sound which might have been amusement, or possibly incredulity. Matilda ignored it.

"Very well. Not frocks or jewels or decorating. A horse?" he suggested.

"Oh, stop it, Nate. I'm serious; I want to talk to you." She settled herself down in the chair opposite him as he pursed his lips.

"Horses *are* serious business, Tilda," he said, a touch reprovingly. "Don't you even think about buying one before I've looked it over. Can't have someone selling you a miserable rip. I've got a reputation to think of."

"The less said about your reputation, the better," Matilda said, immediately regretting the tartness of her voice as guilt flashed in his expression. She sighed. "I don't want you to buy me anything, Nate. I just need you to do something for me. It will only take a moment of your time, but it would mean a great deal to me."

Nate's eyes narrowed and he studied her, turning the glass in his hands back and forth.

"A favour, then," he said, and she could hear the suspicion behind the observation.

Well, there was no point in prevaricating.

"Yes, a favour. You remember I told you about my friends and the dares they'd accepted?"

Nate snorted and shook his head. Matilda scowled at him.

"Well, you remember I told you about Alice? She's a sweet girl, pretty as a little doll, but terribly shy. Her time is running out, Nate and…. Oh, I just want her to accomplish the dare. I know it's silly, but I think it would give her some much needed confidence, put a bit of fire in her blood."

Her brother's gaze darkened, and Matilda could see then the figure that others spoke of, the one she rarely saw. Nathaniel Hunt was a ruthless businessman, cutting off credit to dukes and earls alike if he had the slightest inkling they couldn't pay. He didn't suffer fools and was not one to be taken advantage of… by none but his sister, at least.

"What in blue blazes has that got to do with me?" he demanded.

"You're going to help her," Matilda said, putting up her chin and holding his gaze. His blue eyes were crystalline, glittering with indignation.

"The devil I will!" he exclaimed, surging to his feet. "A fine way to get myself trapped into marriage."

Matilda sighed, well aware of Nate's thoughts on that particular subject. They were akin to his thoughts about rising before midday, hangovers, and tripe. At least that was the impression he put about, like any self-respecting libertine. As his sister, however, she felt certain she knew better. She hoped she did.

"She has no ideas of marrying you. I can assure you of that. She's all but engaged to Mr Bindley, much against her wishes, but he's a repulsive creature and… oh, damn it, Nate. I won't condemn her to the likes of Bindley without, at the very least, completing her dare. And what's it to you? It's just a little kiss."

Nate snorted and returned a dark look. "It's never *just* a little kiss."

"I wouldn't know," Matilda retorted, hating the acerbic tone that escaped before she could check it.

Her brother flinched and a stilted silence followed.

"Bindley?" he said, frowning a little.

"You know him?" Matilda asked, brightening. Nate had become a very powerful man, not simply because of the debts he held over many of the most illustrious names of the *ton*, but because of the gossip and information that filtered through the club. If he had something on Bindley, something that would make him less of an inviting proposition to Alice's parents....

Nate shook his head. "No. Name rings a bell, that's all."

"He's the youngest son of the Earl of Ulceby."

"Ulceby?" he repeated, wrinkling his nose. "By God, if he's anything like his father, I pity the girl."

"So do I!" Matilda exclaimed, frustrated. "Which is why you will escort me to the Ransoms' ball tomorrow night. You'll meet Alice on a moonlit terrace, say a few pretty words, and kiss her."

"Damned if I will!" Nate exploded, heading to pour himself another drink. "You've got rocks in your head if you think I'd ever agree to that."

"Oh, for heaven's sake," Matilda shouted back, exasperated. "I'm not asking you to stick pins in your eyes. It's not as if she's unattractive. In fact, she's quite lovely. You should thoroughly enjoy it, or have you completely given up on the fairer sex? Your reputation would suggest otherwise."

Nate glowered at her.

"I don't go around kissing little innocents on balconies, Tilda. I don't know what kind of man you think I am—"

"Oh, yes," Matilda said, interrupting him and sneering a little. "What little affection remains is reserved for opera singers, or was it a dancer this week? I forget."

"Matilda," Nate said, with a warning in the way he spoke that she could not ignore.

"No, *Nathaniel.* I rarely ask you for anything, as you well know, but I am asking you for this." A thread of anger laced the words, pulling them tight. "I appreciate you think it silly, but nonetheless, it is important to me. I want Alice to be happy, or at least to… to have as few regrets as possible."

Nate stilled, and she knew she had him.

Unlike me, she didn't say. She didn't need to.

Matilda sighed. "Please, Nate," she said softly, moving closer to him and laying her hand on his arm. "It's only for a few moments. Just be your charming self, make her feel beautiful, desired, make it romantic. One little kiss, that's all. I shall stand guard and make sure no one interrupts you, so there's no danger."

She felt the muscles in his arm grow rigid with tension. He hated this, was furious that he felt he couldn't refuse her. Perhaps she ought to feel guilt at manipulating him so, but she'd changed too over the years. Her heart was harder too.

"And what if she recognises me?" he asked, his displeasure obvious. "Won't she feel foolish when she discovers it's your brother you forced into meeting her?"

Matilda shook her head. "She's never met you, and it will be dark but for the moonlight. With the hours you keep, it's unlikely you'll meet her again anytime soon. Besides," she added, smiling, "if she ever discovers it, I'll tell her you needed no persuading. In fact, you leapt at the chance. It wouldn't be hard to believe, would it?"

"Naturally," Nate said. There was a flash of something in his eyes, something raw and hurt. He moved away from her.

Belatedly, a pang of guilt struck at her heart for using her brother so, but there was no one else she could ask.

"I just want her to be happy, Nate. That's all."

There was more emotion in the words than she'd meant to show. For all her thoughts of blackmailing him, she didn't mean to burden him with her unhappiness. Indeed, she took great efforts in appearing happy and vivacious, everything she'd always been before... before her father, her brother, and the Marquess of Montagu had stolen her future from her.

"I know, Tilda," Nate said, turning to look at her, his mouth quirking a little in a crooked smile. "Fine," he said with a sigh, clearly unhappy, but resigned at least. "Your Alice will have her kiss in the moonlight, you have my word, but you'd better keep a sharp eye out, for I'll not get leg shackled. Not even for you."

Matilda held her tongue, knowing he'd never ruin Alice like she'd been ruined, no matter how he despised the idea. Instead she let out a breath of laughter and nodded her agreement.

"Fair enough." She went to him and kissed his cheek. "Very best of brothers."

Nate gave a bark of laughter at that.

"Too much?" she asked, smirking a little.

"Far, *far* too much," he agreed.

Available on Amazon and Free to read on Kindle Unlimited

To Steal A Kiss

Want more Emma?

If you enjoyed this book, please support this indie author and take a moment to leave a few words in a review. *Thank you!*

To be kept informed of special offers and free deals (which I do regularly) follow me on *https://www.bookbub.com/authors/emma-v-leech*

To find out more and to get news and sneak peeks of the first chapter of upcoming works, go to my website and sign up for the newsletter.

http://www.emmavleech.com/

Come and join the fans in my Facebook group for news, info and exciting discussion...

Emmas Book Club

Or Follow me here......

http://viewauthor.at/EmmaVLeechAmazon

Emma's Twitter page

About Me!

I started this incredible journey way back in 2010 with The Key to Erebus but didn't summon the courage to hit publish until October 2012. For anyone who's done it, you'll know publishing your first title is a terribly scary thing! I still get butterflies on the morning a new title releases but the terror has subsided at least. Now I just live in dread of the day my daughters are old enough to read them.

The horror! (On both sides I suspect.)

2017 marked the year that I made my first foray into Historical Romance and the world of the Regency Romance, and my word what a year! I was delighted by the response to this series and can't wait to add more titles. Paranormal Romance readers need not despair however as there is much more to come there too. Writing has become an addiction and as soon as one book is over I'm hugely excited to start the next so you can expect plenty more in the future.

As many of my works reflect I am greatly influenced by the beautiful French countryside in which I live. I've been here in the South West for the past twenty years though I was born and raised in England. My three gorgeous girls are all bilingual and the youngest who is only six, is showing signs of following in my footsteps after producing *The Lonely Princess* all by herself.

I'm told book two is coming soon ...

She's keeping me on my toes, so I'd better get cracking!

KEEP READING TO DISCOVER MY OTHER BOOKS!

Other Works by Emma V. Leech

(For those of you who have read The French Fae Legend series, please remember that chronologically The Heart of Arima precedes The Dark Prince)

Girls Who Dare

To Dare a Duke

To Steal A Kiss

To Break the Rules

To Follow her Heart

To Wager with Love (coming soon)

To Dance with a Devil (coming soon)

Rogues & Gentlemen

The Rogue

The Earl's Temptation

The Regency Romance Mysteries

The Rum and the Fox

The French Vampire Legend

The Key to Erebus

The Heart of Arima

The Fires of Tartarus

The Boxset (The Key to Erebus, The Heart of Arima)

The Son of Darkness (TBA)

The French Fae Legend

The Dark Prince

The Dark Heart

The Dark Deceit

The Darkest Night

Short Stories: A Dark Collection.

Stand Alone

The Book Lover (a paranormal novella)

Audio Books!

Don't have time to read but still need your romance fix? The wait is over…

By popular demand, get your favourite Emma V Leech Regency Romance books on audio at Audible as performed by the incomparable Philip Battley and Gerard Marzilli. Several titles available and more added each month!

Click the links to choose your favourite and start listening now.

Rogues & Gentlemen

The Rogue

The Earl's Tempation

Scandal's Daughter

The Devil May Care

Nearly Ruining Mr Russell

One Wicked Winter

To Tame a Savage Heart

Also check out Emma's regency romance series, Rogues & Gentlemen. Available now!

The Rogue

Rogues & Gentlemen Book 1

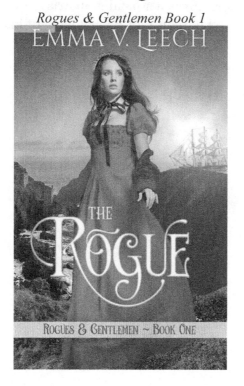

1815

Along the wild and untamed coast of Cornwall, smuggling is not only a way of life, but a means of survival.

Henrietta Morton knows well to look the other way when the free trading 'gentlemen' are at work. Yet when a notorious pirate, known as The Rogue, bursts in on her in the village shop, she takes things one step further.

Bewitched by a pair of wicked blue eyes, in a moment of insanity she hides the handsome fugitive from the local Militia. Her reward is a kiss that she just cannot forget. But in his haste to escape with his life, her pirate drops a letter, inadvertently giving Henri incriminating information about the man she just helped free.

When her father gives her hand in marriage to a wealthy and villainous nobleman in return for the payment of his debts, Henri becomes desperate.

Blackmailing a pirate may be her only hope for freedom.

Read for free on Kindle Unlimited

The Rogue

Interested in a Regency Romance with a twist?

Dying for a Duke

The Regency Romance Mysteries Book 1

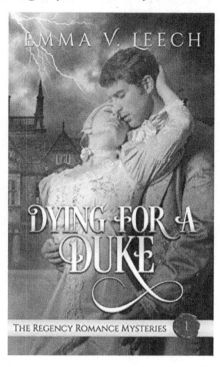

Straight-laced, imperious and morally rigid, Benedict Rutland - the darkly handsome Earl of Rothay - gained his title too young. Responsible for a large family of younger siblings that his frivolous parents have brought to bankruptcy, his youth was spent clawing back the family fortunes.

Now a man in his prime and financially secure he is betrothed to a strict, sensible and cool-headed woman who will never upset the balance of his life or disturb his emotions ...

But then Miss Skeffington-Fox arrives.

Brought up solely by her rake of a step-father, Benedict is scandalised by everything about the dashing Miss.

But as family members in line for the dukedom begin to die at an alarming rate, all fingers point at Benedict, and Miss Skeffington-Fox may be the only one who can save him.

FREE to read on Amazon Kindle Unlimited.. Dying for a Duke

Lose yourself in Emma's paranormal world with The French Vampire Legend series.

The Key to Erebus

The French Vampire Legend Book 1

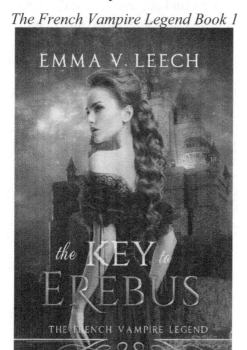

The truth can kill you.

Taken away as a small child, from a life where vampires, the Fae, and other mythical creatures are real and treacherous, the beautiful young witch, Jéhenne Corbeaux is totally unprepared when she returns to rural France to live with her eccentric Grandmother.

Thrown headlong into a world she knows nothing about she seeks to learn the truth about herself, uncovering secrets more shocking than anything she could ever have imagined and finding that she is by no means powerless to protect the ones she loves.

Despite her Gran's dire warnings, she is inexorably drawn to the dark and terrifying figure of Corvus, an ancient vampire and master of the vast Albinus family.

Jéhenne is about to find her answers and discover that, not only is Corvus far more dangerous than she could ever imagine, but that he holds much more than the key to her heart …

Free to read on Kindle Unlimited

The Key to Erebus

Check out Emma's exciting fantasy series with hailed by Kirkus Reviews as "An enchanting fantasy with a likable heroine, romantic intrigue, and clever narrative flourishes."

The Dark Prince

The French Fae Legend Book 1

Two Fae Princes
One Human Woman
And a world ready to tear them all apart

Laen Braed is Prince of the Dark fae, with a temper and reputation to match his black eyes, and a heart that despises the human race. When he is sent back through the forbidden gates between realms to retrieve an ancient fae artifact, he returns home with far more than he bargained for.

Corin Albrecht, the most powerful Elven Prince ever born. His golden eyes are rumoured to be a gift from the gods, and destiny is calling him. With a love for the human world that runs deep, his friendship with Laen is being torn apart by his prejudices.

Océane DeBeauvoir is an artist and bookbinder who has always relied on her lively imagination to get her through an unhappy and uneventful life. A jewelled dagger put on display at a nearby museum hits the headlines with speculation of another race, the Fae. But the discovery also inspires Océane to create an extraordinary piece of art that cannot be confined to the pages of a book.

With two powerful men vying for her attention and their friendship stretched to the breaking point, the only question that remains...who is truly The Dark Prince.

The man of your dreams is coming...or is it your nightmares he visits? Find out in Book One of The French Fae Legend.

Available now to read for FREE on Kindle Unlimited.

The Dark Prince

Acknowledgements

Thanks, of course, to my wonderful editor Kezia Cole.

To Victoria Cooper for all your hard work, amazing artwork and above all your unending patience!!! Thank you so much. You are amazing!

To my BFF, PA, personal cheerleader and bringer of chocolate, Varsi Appel, for moral support, confidence boosting and for reading my work more times than I have. I love you loads!

A huge thank you to all of Emma's Book Club members! You guys are the best!

 I'm always so happy to hear from you so do email or message me :)

emmavleech@orange.fr

To my husband Pat and my family ... For always being proud of me.

Made in the USA
Monee, IL
02 November 2024

69165604R00177